THE GODDESS GAMES

THE ATLANTIS CROWN
BOOK 1

ERICA RUE

Starwoven Books

For Rachel Caudill

Without you, this book would not exist for many reasons. Thank you for helping me embrace the romance genre as both a reader and writer. I never would have had the courage to write this book without you, and in doing so, accept this part of myself.

Ex animo, tibi maximas gratias ago!

THE
GODDESS
GAMES

ONE

THE TINY, GREEN APPLE in my hand felt more like an insult than a reward, but I was still excited to share it with my best friend Flora. After enduring extended shifts for two weeks to prepare for the ridiculous contest tomorrow, an apple and the afternoon off from work didn't prompt the gratitude my manager had expected. I struggled not to hate my warehouse job now that I had no hope of leaving it. I'd been so close to that weather analyst apprenticeship. Stupid Brett. He'd ruined everything.

Lost in pleasant thoughts of revenge, I nearly walked past Flora.

"Chloe!"

My name snapped me out of my brooding, and I stretched out next to Flora in the shade of an oak tree. The ground was still a little damp and strewn with debris from a brutal spring storm earlier in the week. I studied the poster she held in her hands and took another bite of apple before passing the fruit over to her.

"I wish these posters had pictures of the prince," she said. She crunched into the apple and lowered the poster.

"Maybe he's ugly." I shrugged. "That would explain why there are no pictures of him on any of the posters around the city."

"That wouldn't be fair, though," she urged. "He's a *prince*." She took one more bite and returned the apple to my outstretched hand.

"An *alien* prince." I took the last bite, ignoring Flora's frown. My friend wasn't mad about the apple. Tomorrow was a special day, after all. Or so Flora and the entire city kept reminding me. She was mad that I wasn't going to enter the competition.

"They're not aliens!"

"I know, I know." I glanced around for a place to toss the apple core, but the park was packed. It seemed like everyone had gotten off work early and decided to come here. I set the spent core on the ground, and a few seeds fell out. "They're humans taken from earth long ago, and now they're back to save us." *Allegedly.*

I read the poster to myself once more: *The Goddess Games. Prince Agathon seeks a bride to unite two worlds, Atlantis and Earth. Be ready to compete.* The fine print went on to provide the specifics. Any contestant had to be unmarried, childless, and between the ages of eighteen and twenty-two. The Goddess Games were trials of skill, beauty, and wit that would reveal who would make a suitable princess and future queen of Atlantis.

Flora had been ranting about the lack of a picture ever since the signs had gone up a month ago, but considering the uncommon attractiveness of the Atlantean rulers, King Darius and Queen Theodora, I assumed the prince was the exact opposite of a hideous mutant.

"I can't believe I'm going to miss the age cutoff by a month," Flora moaned.

"I know, Flora. I'm sorry." I appraised my friend. Even in her dirty work clothes, her beauty was untarnished. Her long hair was braided down her back, so black it was nearly blue. Her eyes were dark brown and warm, and her skin was fair and flawless. "I really mean it. But I won't compete just because you're not old enough."

Months ago, when the contest had been announced, I'd had my heart set on a completely different set of dreams: a weather analyst job and a relationship with Brett. Now, I didn't know what I wanted. I was already nineteen. Doors were closing all around me, and I was probably doomed to my warehouse job for the rest of my time on Earth. Maybe even on Atlantis, too, once I was evacuated.

A commotion a little farther down the path pulled me out of my spiraling thoughts. A young man was yelling, and I recognized the voice.

"Is that Brett?" Flora asked.

"Yes," I growled, already on my feet.

"Who's that poor kid? He's on the verge of tears." A boy cowered in front of my ex-study partner. Calling him an ex-boyfriend, even in my head, didn't feel right.

"Brett has that effect on people."

I darted off before Flora could talk any sense into me. I'd been dreaming of a chance to get back at Brett, and while I didn't know if this was it, I sure as hell wasn't going to let him terrorize some twelve-year-old. He'd gotten away with too much cruelty already.

"Brett!" I shouted, slowing down as I got closer. "Brett Vasquez!" His blue eyes turned their focus on me.

"Chloe Woods." He rolled his eyes. "What are you doing out here? Lose your inventory job too? How dumb do you have to be to get fired from moving boxes?"

His words stung. When it came to Brett, I'd been a complete idiot. Unlike Brett, however, I had learned from my mistakes. Now, I trusted no one.

"Nope, just released early for tomorrow's holiday. What can I do to convince you to stop harassing this poor kid?"

"He's the one harassing me. He stole my spot here in the shade."

Brett certainly knew a thing or two about stealing other people's spots. "Oh, please." I made a show of folding my arms across my chest for the three people who had gathered to watch the budding drama. "I *know* you. Pretty much every interaction with you is harassment."

"Funny. You didn't used to mind."

Every clever comeback I'd thought of in the months since I'd last seen him evaporated from my thoughts. I wanted to hurt him, but I had nothing. I settled for the first lame insult that popped into my mind. "You're a worthless cheater."

Brett smirked. "That's not how I recall things going down. The apprenticeship is great by the way. We got the whole day off." The boy he'd been bothering tried to break free of his grip, but Brett held firm. "Now if you'll mind your own business, I was teaching this child his place." Brett pushed the slim boy to the ground in a disgusting abuse of his physical power. The boy stayed down and covered his head and neck, bracing for the next attack.

I positioned myself between Brett and the boy. "Oh, so you don't want this back?" I reached into my pocket and pulled out a gold pocket watch. My plans to sell it to a coworker had fallen through thanks to the festivities. It had belonged to Brett's great-great-grandfather, assuming that story was true. The watch was ancient and didn't even work half the time, but Brett had carried it with him everywhere.

He stepped toward me. "Where did you find it?" The weight of his focus settled on me, and I took a step back. I paused a moment, holding his gaze while the boy slipped away in Flora's general direction. His brown hair looked dull in the shade of the trees, and his mouth was a grim line. How had I ever found those features handsome?

"You left it at the library. I never had a chance to return it. But since you're not interested, I'd better get going." I shrugged and turned, hurrying down the path in the opposite direction of Flora. Truthfully, I *had* intended to return it. Throw it in his face, really, but I'd just gotten a better idea.

Brett pursued me, but I ignored him calling my name. He'd catch up soon, and I was almost in place. The footpath crossed a small stream, and the compacted earth turned to wooden planks beneath my feet. I stopped in the middle of the bridge. The water gurgled cheerfully, oblivious to the anger that radiated off me and Brett, who had finally caught up.

"Give it back, and I won't report you for stealing."

"Gladly." I extended my hand, then pretended to stumble. The watch flew over the railing and into the middle of the stream. "Oh my! What a terrible accident." The water flowed deeper and faster than usual thanks to the recent storm, but a fallen branch in the water caught the heirloom, keeping it in place. He'd be able to recover it, but he'd have to get wet to do it. Pathetic revenge was still revenge.

Darkness flashed across Brett's face, and for a second, I thought he might hit me. Then he got himself under control. His voice was low but firm. "You ruined my watch, Chloe, but I ruined you. You'll never amount to more than you are now."

He stepped away, took off his shoes, and prepared to wade into the stream to retrieve his memento. I turned my back and retraced my steps, trying to ignore Brett's words, but they clung to me like cold, wet clothes. As much as I hated to admit it, he was right.

Two

AFTER MY ENCOUNTER WITH Brett, the prospect of staying in the park had lost its charm. Time to find Flora and go home. I was an only child, but Flora might as well have been my sister. Our families lived in the same building, and we looked out for each other. Flora and I worked different jobs, so this afternoon off together had been a rare treat. Then I'd ruined it in some lame attempt at revenge. I returned to our shady spot. She was still there, though a hungry squirrel must have swiped my apple core.

"Chloe! Are you all right?"

I forced a laugh. "Of course I am. A little sweaty, though. Want to head home? I heard a rumor that we all get extra water allotments so we Earthlings will look clean at tomorrow's celebration and won't embarrass the whole planet."

"You're lying!" The gleam in her eye made me laugh. She'd had to rinse the shampoo out of her hair in the kitchen sink more than once after taking too long.

"Just a rumor I heard at work."

"I wish I worked with you."

"Me too." My job in inventory offered me some variety, but not much in the way of mental stimulation. Sometimes I moved boxes; other times I counted and repacked individual items, checking for any obvious quality issues. One perk was that I had first dibs on buying any slightly damaged goods at a discount.

The major downside was that work was mind-numbing and mean-ingless. That was why I'd applied for a weather analyst apprenticeship in the first place, but that had ended in disaster. With my heart and dreams crushed, I had little motivation to study and apply for a new job. Despite having recently turned nineteen, I still lived with my parents. Most people in my situation did. I was lucky that they didn't depend on my income, so we put any extra into emergency savings or used it to help Flora's family. Flora was not so lucky. Her family would need her income for a few more years, until the twins were old enough to work. Her factory job was even more boring than mine with the added misery of longer hours.

"I think you're right about wanting Earth to look its best," Flora said. "Look at the streets. And look over at that bus stop. Has that bus stop ever not been covered in food wrappers?"

I examined my surroundings. Outside the park's green refuge, buildings loomed. There was an increased flow of people, many of whom had been enjoying a rare half day off, shopping and celebrating. In the pristine street, a black car yielded to a young family of three. A pair of girls giggled at a Goddess Games poster.

Was this what it looked like in the old days, before the collapse? A convergence of crises had destroyed the United States of America, all set off by the domino of climate change: droughts, fires, floods, famine, power failures, and plagues. One disaster rolled into the next until the dark times set in. What emerged—and my history books had been quite vague on the how—were three major districts—High-mont, Lightbridge, and my own Belvale—that formed an alliance, becoming the American Federation. Slowly, and with much smaller, more sustainable numbers, we had rebuilt.

We had books, movies, and just enough food, but nothing to reach for. The daily reminders of the dark times and the threat of their return were enough to keep most people in line in spite of the frequent blackouts, food shortages, and raging floods. I often thought that dark times were ahead of us, too, but there was nothing I, a lowly warehouse girl, could do. As a weather analyst, I could have at least helped people and saved crops, livestock, and lives.

We'd been enjoying our walk home in silence when suddenly Flora asked, "You don't *really* think they're aliens, do you? Like from the books?"

"Depends on whether you mean scary monster aliens or the purple guys with abs from your roof books." I called them "roof books" because that's where she had to read them most of the time. Her parents were history buffs and didn't understand the appeal of romance novels, alien-themed or otherwise. She rolled her eyes at me, but I kept going. "I'm going no on all counts. Not monsters, not purple, and if the prince had abs, they would have put them on the poster."

Flora laughed at that. "I believe them when they say they're from ancient Earth."

So did I, but yielding on that point might have sparked a renewal of her attempts to get me to join the contest to marry the prince. I still struggled to believe that the Atlanteans were real and were going to help us. Supposedly, the Atlanteans had been taken from Earth millennia ago by a crew of benevolent aliens who called themselves "Olympians," at least here on Earth. They'd taken a selection of humans to another planet and given them technology, education, and laws, then left them to develop on their own. According to the king and queen, the Olympians had been aliens, but the Atlanteans were merely long-lost humans.

One year ago, nearly to the day, an Atlantean scouting party had come to Earth. They'd expected to meet with an alternate version of their own civilization: metropolises bursting with art and music, fields abundant with the crops of *their* ancient myths, and new technologies.

Instead, they found a husk of a world. Long-range communication across the globe had ceased altogether during the decade of the plagues, and it had never picked back up. Infrastructure crumbled. The Atlanteans had shared some of the first news from overseas we'd gotten in a while; what remained of humanity was surviving in pockets like our districts.

The Atlantean expedition had come down to Earth, unannounced, and sought refuge in city after city, first in Europe, then Africa. They were turned away time after time, and the Atlanteans despaired of finding any sign of hospitality or, in their eyes, true civilization, on Earth. At last, they came to the coast of North America to the Lightbridge District and were received by a family of artisans. This was why, of all the cities and countries left in the world, the women of the American Federation had been granted the opportunity to qualify for the Goddess Games. Hospitality seemed especially important to the Atlanteans.

Several months ago, the formal Atlantean delegation had arrived. News clips had played the same footage of half a dozen massive ships in orbit, white and gleaming as if they had traveled to Earth in marble palaces. Each had a squat cylinder at the center with six arms extending out, like identical snowflakes. One ship, according to reports, could transport over ten thousand refugees.

And that was what we Gaians, as the Atlanteans called humans from Earth, would be.

I looked around once again. The streets were packed. Instead of sprawling suburbs, there were tiny apartments within Belvale City proper and then the farmland beyond. There was no in between. Most of our food was preserved in some way before it reached us. I tried to imagine what it would have been like to have a backyard garden and chicken coop, enjoying fresh eggs and vegetables all year long, but it was as out of reach for most of us as owning a car. The few cars in the streets, like the black one idling a block ahead, were luxuries.

Despite the water rationing and extreme weather, I'd been surprised to learn the Earth was beyond salvation. Reports had been optimistic until the Atlanteans arrived. Once there was a plan to save us, I supposed the government figured we could handle the truth about how bleak Earth's future looked. With the help of the Atlanteans, we would leave Earth, and despite the decimation of our population at the hands of plagues and natural disaster, the relocation would take a very long time. Lucky for me, the American Federation had priority. It would take decades to move the four million or so citizens of the American Federation, though they promised they were building more ships to speed up the process.

"Do you hear that?" Flora's brow creased as she looked around.

Chanting. Angry chanting. I stopped and peered down the cross street and got the answer I'd been looking for. "Protestors." Brett had talked to them once or twice when they'd gathered outside the library, but he'd always seemed to agree their theories were crazy. With the Goddess Games set for tomorrow, they were out in full force, and I was glad our path home wouldn't cross theirs. A black car rolled by, obscuring the view, so I started walking again.

The protests had surprised me more than the grim predictions about Earth's future. The resistance was a vocal minority, but vocal was the key word. Soon after the Atlantean delegation arrived, the conspiracy theories popped up and multiplied: the Atlanteans were gruesome aliens in disguise; they were cannibals; they planned to take us to Atlantis and make us slaves. I understood the skepticism of the Atlanteans' motives. I might wonder about the Atlanteans' true reasons for saving us, but these theories were ridiculous.

I sighed and glanced over at Flora, whose pace had slowed. "I don't buy into all those conspiracy theories, but just because they're not alien cannibal slave-traders doesn't mean that I trust them. Or want to marry their prince."

"I want to believe they're good."

I thought about quipping how well that had gone when it came to believing Brett, but I was too tired to get worked up again. I couldn't stop my thoughts from echoing back his parting words: *You ruined my watch, Chloe, but I ruined you.*

The walk home from the park was long. In poor weather, we would have crammed onto a bus, but in the warm glow of spring with good air, the walk was more of a treat than a chore.

"Can we rest a sec? My feet are killing me," Flora said. I glanced down, feeling guilty. Of course they hurt. My shoes were relatively new. Hers were old. She'd been saving up to buy a new pair, and she kept refusing my help. Her factory work didn't involve nearly as much walking as my job, but she was on her feet most of the day.

We sat down on a nearby bench that offered a miserable view of my favorite library in the city.

Brett and I had spent a lot of evenings studying side-by-side, and we'd waited together for the overdue bus back to our neighborhood, talking away. The once-tedious delay became a highlight of my day. In hindsight, I wondered if any of it had been real, or if he'd always planned to use me and screw me over.

Flora's melodic voice interrupted my sulking. "I'm ready to—hey, are you okay?"

"Huh? Yeah, let's go. It's just the library and seeing Brett today."

"I'm sorry! I didn't realize how close we were. I also hate that you now associate the library with him."

"It'll pass, I'm sure." I hadn't stepped foot in the library since the day before the test in February, and it was now April.

We stood to continue our trek, and a sleek, black car crept along behind us. A familiar black car. *This car has been following us.*

"We should go back to the bus stop," I muttered to Flora. "I'll cover your fare." The car pulled over ahead of us and rolled down the back window. I didn't have a good angle, so the car's occupant remained a mystery.

"The bus? But it's such a nice day," Flora said.

I was about to explain that we were being followed, but we were close enough to be heard through the open window.

"Please get in, Ms. Woods." The firm, female voice was familiar, but I couldn't place it.

I moved closer. The car's occupant was leaning forward now, revealing her easily recognizable features. There were crow's feet at the corners of her green eyes, even though she didn't offer more than a perfunctory smile. Her blonde hair was streaked with gray, and her lipstick was deep red. I knew her at once from her weekly broadcasts as Edwina Russo, the mayor of Belvale City.

I swallowed, though my mouth felt unnaturally dry. My mind raced. There was a good chance I was in trouble for what had just happened with Brett. What else could the mayor want with a nobody like me?

Three

The mayor of Belvale City, the capital of the district, had ordered me *by name* to get into her car. There was no choice, no excuse I could make. I obliged, walking around to the far side of the car and opening the door.

"You, too, Ms. Simmons, if you'd like. You both live in the same building, right?"

It disturbed me how much the mayor knew about me, but with her connections, I couldn't be too surprised.

"Yes, ma'am. Thank you," Flora said, sliding into the front seat at the behest of the mayor's driver.

I swallowed again, but the lump in my throat didn't budge. "Hello, Mayor Russo. Uh, how can I help you?"

"I thought a ride home might be appropriate payment for the service you rendered my nephew just now."

"What service?"

"Distracting the bully who was harassing him."

My stomach unclenched. "That boy was your nephew?"

"Yes."

"Oh, is he okay?"

"Yes."

She studied me, and I became painfully aware of my patched jeans and worn T-shirt. I gulped again. This was going to be an awkward ride, but at least I wasn't in trouble. Probably.

"Are you excited for tomorrow's contest, Ms. Woods?"

Not particularly, but I didn't know how the mayor would react to that much honesty. "Not as excited as Flora, but I'm curious to watch the contestants get selected. No one quite knows how they'll do it."

"Watch? But Ms. Woods, you just turned nineteen. Aren't you planning to compete for a spot?" Her stern expression reminded me of my second-grade teacher. How did she know so much about me? My age, where I lived—it was creepy considering I'd come onto her radar less than an hour ago.

"I'm not sure I'm princess material," I replied cautiously.

That got a smile out of her. "There are more prizes than just the prince," she said. "Medical treatment, first-wave departure, and, if you make it to the finals, a title of nobility on our new home."

A ladyship. It sounded as ancient and absurd as our Atlantean saviors.

I'd considered those perks. Though my mom recently broke her arm, it had healed well. "My family drew a lot for the tenth wave, which is the same as Flora's, so we're lucky in that we won't have to miss each other. We're in good health too. I'm not sure if the benefits of nobility are worth it."

The mayor clasped her hands in her lap. "I'll be blunt with you because your response has already told me a great deal about you. I know you were passed over for a weather analyst apprenticeship. Your warehouse job won't exactly put you at the top of talent lists on our new home. If you are among the nobility, you'll have your pick of careers, assuming you even want one at that point. You have the chance to rise above your current mediocrity."

The suggestion killed the protest on my lips. "Why are you telling me this?" I asked.

"Because there are people who don't want our move to Atlantis to go smoothly, people who would see this opportunity quashed and have humanity wither away on this dusty rock. We've carved out a small bubble of peace, but the storms will only get worse. You've seen the projections. The city districts were built in some of the most stable places left from the Mid-Atlantic to the Midwest, but we only bought ourselves time. The Atlanteans are offering a fresh start, and the prince will need defenders." Mayor Russo leveled a stare at me. "From what I've learned about you today, Ms. Woods, I believe you would stand up for what's right."

I broke eye contact and stared out the window. We were approaching my apartment building. I considered explaining that I'd been targeting Brett and saving her nephew had been an added bonus, but there was no time. The car stopped. Flora, who'd been listening in silence the entire ride, unbuckled her seat belt, and I did the same.

Flora turned and bowed her head slightly toward the mayor. "Thank you for the ride, Mayor Russo," she said. Her door opened with a click and closed with a bang as I reached for my own door handle.

"Yes, thank you." I smiled.

"I'm not finished, Ms. Woods. I'm not telling you this out of the kindness of my heart. While I am grateful you helped my nephew, I've got a task for you. The prince is in danger. The rebels believe some egregious lies about the Atlantean royal family."

"Like that they're cannibals?"

Mayor Russo sighed. "Yes, among others I won't do the disservice of repeating. The rebels are organized and determined to ruin our budding alliance. Every eligible rebel woman will be competing tomorrow for a spot in the games. I've recruited a few women of my own, much like I'm doing now with you, but the competition will be intense. I looked into you. I know why you wanted to become a weather analyst. Joining this competition and keeping the prince safe is another way to help people. If the rebels are successful, there will be no second or third waves, let alone a tenth. Everyone else, including you and your friend Flora, will be trapped on Earth."

I rubbed my neck, but the tension remained. "I'll think about it."

Once I was outside the car, she beckoned me back to her open window.

"If you change your mind, here's my recommendation. Wear something comfortable—what you're wearing right now would do nicely. And don't forget sturdy shoes."

"This?" I glanced down at my new sneakers crowned by the fraying hems of my jeans. A large stripe of dust sliced down the side of my black shirt. "This is my warehouse outfit."

Mayor Russo was already rolling up the tinted barrier, blocking her face from view.

Russo thought she knew what made me tick, but the girl who had applied to become a weather analyst was gone now. I had wanted to help, and that was what got me into trouble. Like how I'd tried to help Brett. Big mistake. I wasn't sure I would ever be in a helping mood again. Plus, how impossible was it that I could save humanity by entering a prince-marrying contest? Russo's entire proposal was completely absurd. I would not be entering the Goddess Games, and that was final.

FOUR

AT FIRST GLANCE, THE building before me looked like every other one in this section of the city. The fifteen-story building was tall, gray, and dreary, but a second look revealed its touches of home. The ever-present herb garden in the second window over on the third floor was growing greener and taller in early spring. Even in winter, a few of the hardier herbs added that reassuring flash of green. The fifth-floor window halfway across displayed a new piece of artwork. I wondered how old the artist was by now. Six? Seven? I'd never met the family that lived in that unit, as far as I knew, but I'd watched this child grow through the progression of their art. My gaze moved quickly up the building, accounting for each piece of personalization, each sign of home, before entering.

Flora fidgeted inside the lobby. Her raised eyebrows invited me to explain what had just happened, but I shook my head. *Not now.*

The mayor had made it clear she was hedging her bets. There was nothing special about me except that she thought I had some sort of hero complex she could exploit. I suppressed a smile. If only she knew that I was more of an avenger than a protector. Anger and revenge had been my true motivations this afternoon, but at least I had come out looking good.

"So, does this mean you're going to enter the contest tomorrow?" Flora asked tentatively as we huffed up the stairs.

"I don't know. I'd only be competing for a spot in the real contest. It's like a qualifier that's designed to weed out ninety-nine percent of contestants."

"Marsha thinks it's a beauty contest. They'll choose the prettiest women to move ahead."

"Then it's a shame you're just shy of eighteen. You'd be selected for sure."

She blushed. "I think you'd do well too."

I shrugged and laughed. "The sun and the moon both shine." It was something my mom used to say when Flora and I were younger. Flora was always the pretty one. I went through a bit of an awkward phase, but now that I'd grown up, I'd come into my own. "Pretty enough to be interesting but not in danger" was how I liked to think of it.

"Did your mom ever explain that phrase to you?"

"I always assumed she meant I'd find someone once you were out of the way, Miss Sun." I nudged her gently with my elbow, realizing we were on the landing for her floor.

"That's not it at all!"

"I'm teasing! There's more to life than beauty contests. Maybe one day I'll find the satisfaction in shuffling around boxes that my parents do."

Flora smiled at me. "I don't think the warehouse is what makes them happy, Chloe. They really love each other."

I grinned. "Yeah, they do. But who knows? Atlantis may have warehouses spectacular enough to satisfy my restless mind. See you at dinner."

She gave me a slight wave, then opened the door onto her floor. I continued up several more flights of stairs until I reached my family's unit. My parents weren't back yet. They'd probably gone for a stroll through the city, fingers and hearts intertwined as always. Or maybe they'd gone up to the rooftop gardens, though it would be packed on a day like this.

I took the opportunity to tidy up. Our unit was small and had no windows, but it was full of life and light. As an only child, I got my own room. Flora had to share the second bedroom of her family's apartment with her twin sisters. Once things were a little neater, I remembered that rumor I'd heard at work about the extra shower rations. I went to the bathroom to check and did a little happy dance when I discovered I'd been given five extra minutes. After today, I needed it.

By the time my parents came home, laughing at some shared joke, I'd already started dinner.

"Need any help?" Dad asked, peering over my shoulder as I opened a tin of corn.

"No, I already put the rice on, and these won't take long to cook," I replied.

He kissed the top of my head. "All right. Mom and I will set the table."

I looked up from my can-opening long enough to see my parents setting the table as if it were a dance they'd practiced to perfection. The moves—the folding of napkins, the placement of plates, and arrangement of silverware—were second nature, joyful products of muscle memory. I smiled and returned to dinner prep. I doubted whoever married the Atlantean prince would ever get to dance around the dinner table like that.

Twenty minutes later, when I had nearly finished cooking, the Simmons family arrived. Flora's parents, Miguel and Christina, had been blessed—or cursed, as the government saw it—with three children: Flora and a set of twins, Charlotte and Daisy. Though the government subsidized two children, the Simmonses had to pay an extra tax for their third on top of the added expense of another child. Fortunately,

Flora was seven years older than her little sisters and had been able to contribute her income once she was old enough to work. This, combined with the assistance my parents gave, had reduced their hardship.

Dinner was fortified rice and vegetables, with a little bit of fresh fruit for dessert. I watched Flora sneak her portion of the fruit to Charlotte and Daisy, and I was glad we'd shared that apple earlier. After the meal was over, the twins offered to do the dishes as usual.

"Flora said Mayor Russo drove you home today," Mrs. Simmons said, "as a thank-you for helping her nephew. What happened exactly?"

I shot Flora a look, but she ignored me. "I told you," she said. "Chloe rescued him from Brett Vasquez."

My parents exchanged a quick glance, but Mom didn't pry. "That was very nice of you, darling."

Flora had more to report. "The mayor also encouraged her to enter the contest tomorrow," Flora said. "Don't you think Chloe would make the best princess?"

Dad agreed with a chuckle and was mercifully about to move on to a new topic of conversation when Mr. Simmons piped up. "It's not too late to change your mind. What do you have to lose now that you won't be starting a new job any time soon?"

I shrugged and tried to hide how much those words stung. Mr. Simmons, who probably wished his daughter could enter the games, had only meant to encourage me. Flora, realizing her mistake, mouthed an apology across the table. The flow of conversation swept by, leaving me to drown in my own thoughts. I'd already lost my chance at the weather analyst apprenticeship, and my relationship with Brett, if I could even call it that, had been a disaster. Failure sucked. Losing sucked. I wasn't ready to deal with the public humiliation that would come from trying and failing the qualifiers for the Goddess Games in front of everyone.

"Chloe?" Charlotte said, coming out of the kitchen. The twins had finished the dishes and wanted to play cards. "Will you be my partner?"

"Sure thing, Char. I'll grab the good deck."

"Oh, no, you don't!" Flora chided me. "I swear you've marked the cards on that one."

"Fine, you pick the deck."

We played a few rounds of pinochle. Charlotte and I handily beat Flora and Daisy, which made me feel better than it should have. Winning? Winning felt nice.

"Tomorrow we're playing something else," Daisy said grumpily.

"You'll pick," I replied. That seemed to appease her.

After the Simmons family had left, Dad sat down next to me. "Pumpkin," he said, "you know we don't care whether you decide to compete tomorrow or not. But I'm worried this Brett fellow has gotten into your head. You never explained what happened." He paused, offering me a chance to speak. I looked down, suddenly interested in a chipped fingernail. "And you don't have to explain. Not to us."

Mom, who was far more curious than Dad about what had happened, called from the kitchen, "But if you want to tell us, we'd be happy to listen." She brought in a tray with three mugs of fragrant mint tea. "Don't sip it too slowly. Lights out is in fifteen minutes."

The clock by the sink confirmed her warning. It was best to be in bed rather than fumbling around with a solar lantern. "It's not Brett. Not like that. We were only ever study partners for the apprenticeship test." It was technically true. We'd never been on an official date.

"And when only one of you qualified, the partnership ended?" Mom asked.

"Something like that," I replied. I didn't want to tell them the truth. Only Flora knew the whole story, and telling her had been like reliving the humiliation all over again. I finished my tea, said goodnight to my parents, and was in bed with two minutes to spare.

I lay awake that night. My parents clearly thought my feelings for Brett were preventing me from joining the contest tomorrow. But that wasn't it. Or was it? Why hadn't I seen it before?

He'd been the one to talk about how stupid the contest was. I'd agreed with him, though. The concept of competing against a bunch of other women to marry a stranger was absurd. But what if I was competing for something else?

Mr. Simmons was right. I had nothing to lose by trying. I doubted I would actually win, but Mayor Russo had made a good point. If I managed to qualify, my family wouldn't have to wait for the tenth wave. We could leave in the first. They would get medical checkups. I might even make it far enough to gain an Atlantean ladyship, and then I could access any job training I wanted. Once we made it to Atlantis, I didn't want to trade one meaningless job for another.

I almost laughed away my lofty dreams, but why? It was possible. Improbable but possible. I might lose, but if I didn't try, I would never win. With so many others competing tomorrow, losing might not feel so bad. It wouldn't be anything like failing to get the apprenticeship. Brett had already taken one opportunity from me. I wouldn't let my insecurity and the ghost of what might have been take another. I wasn't ruined. I was going to compete tomorrow, and I was going to give it everything I had.

FIVE

DespITE the early hour, the Simmons household was bustling when I arrived unannounced. Flora and the twins were finishing their breakfasts.

"Porridge?" Charlotte asked, offering me her own bowl.

I shook my head. "I already ate, thanks."

"I'll take some," Daisy said, trying to sneak her spoon into her twin's bowl.

"I didn't offer it to *you*," Charlotte shot back.

Flora rolled her eyes. "Come with me," she said, leading me back to the tiny bedroom she shared with her sisters. She closed the door and sat in front of it to prevent any unwanted interruptions. "Okay. What's up?"

I took a deep breath, then exhaled. "Flora, make me beautiful."

Her reaction was instantaneous. "Really? Does this mean you're going to compete?"

I nodded, feeling a bit ridiculous, but last night's decision had become real the moment I told Flora.

"This is going to be fun!" She pulled a small stack of hairpins and a couple of ribbons out of an old tea tin.

About twenty minutes into styling my hair, I began to regret my decision. My scalp ached from all of the pulling and twisting.

"A little eyeliner and mascara, and you'll be all set. I used up all of the eye shadow, and this lipstick isn't right for the occasion."

I'd given her the makeup for her birthday last year, but we both ended up using it.

"What are you wearing?"

"Uh, this?" I gestured down to my gray blouse, dark blue jeans, and white work shoes with their thick laces.

"You can't wear that. You can't!" She shook her head. "You have at least two dresses that would be a great look."

"There's something I didn't have a chance to tell you yesterday. Something the mayor said."

"I knew it. Spill."

"Russo suggested that what I was wearing would be a good outfit for the trial."

"Your work clothes?"

"My shoes in particular."

"So it's not a beauty contest. Then why did you have me fix your hair?"

"Flora, I have no idea what this contest is, but I'm going to look good while doing it."

She giggled. "You will. I get the pants and shoes, but why the gray? Wear the green one with the ruffles. You love that top."

"Nope. That one's bad luck."

My words puzzled Flora for a few seconds before it clicked. "You wore it on test day. For luck."

"Yep. Wrong kind of luck. Can't wear it."

"False. Every article of clothing gets a second chance before you can deem it bad luck. Plus, it looks great on you. Maybe the good luck was realizing what a jerk Brett was before it was too late."

"I don't—"

"Trust me on this one. Have you looked outside? It's spring. Green is in."

The top was pretty, and it felt wrong to blame the disaster of test day on a shirt.

"Fine, I'll go change."

Flora was right. The green did look better, and my hair was incredible. Normally a wild, frizzy mess, my medium brown curls had been braided and wrapped around my head in a style that reminded me of an ancient Greek goddess. I couldn't be sure whether Flora knew I would change my mind or just liked the look that had become more popular since the Atlanteans' arrival.

When I exited the bathroom, my parents, who had slept in, were caught off guard.

"I've changed my mind. I need to go register before it's too late." I waved and ran out the door, not wanting to discuss it further.

I arrived at the city's stadium, which was where all the posters had advertised, in big, blaring letters, that the qualifiers for the Goddess Games would begin. Registration and check-in were easy to spot, thanks to the long lines of young women that wrapped around a cluster of tables.

There were a dozen or so people registering and checking in contestants, and I had the luck of getting called up by the surliest one.

"Name?"

"Chloe Woods."

"You're not on my list."

"I need to register."

The woman pursed her lips and entered my name and citizen ID. "Hold out your left arm." She gave me a wristband with my name and a contestant number on it.

"Use the stadium entrance and wait with the others."

"How much time do I have? I'd like to say goodbye to my family."

"Proceed directly into the stadium. I'm sure you'll have plenty of time to spend with them after the competition is over." The woman rolled her eyes and called out, "Next."

Rude. With a final glance at the crowd behind me, hoping and failing to catch sight of a familiar face, I headed toward the indicated entrance.

A man and a woman in their fifties, each wearing an orange vest, let me through after I showed them my wristband. Another man, this one younger but also in an orange vest, directed me to an open door. I'd expected to go out into the arena itself, but instead found myself in a large room with high ceilings and cinder block walls. Inside, a mass of dressed-up young women chatted excitedly. Some wore simple cotton dresses with flats. Others wore glamorous fitted skirts. Some wore everyday clothes, and a few were even in athletic gear. No matter the outfit, everyone looked clean and put together. Most had come with a friend or group of friends, and they were engaged in bubbly conversation and laughter. Not wanting to stand alone, I stationed myself awkwardly near one group, but no one let me in. Then, a little bolder, I integrated myself into a group of four women who, as it turned out, knew each other already. They gave me a mix of confused and disdainful looks.

"Can we help you?" the tall blonde asked.

If I were smoother, I would have introduced myself and complimented their dresses. Instead, I asked if they knew where the restroom was. The blonde shook her head, and the other three mimicked her. One of them even murmured an apology as I stepped away and hurried out of sight.

This will be fun.

I resigned myself to staring at one of the Goddess Games posters on the wall, trying to imagine what the prince looked like. The king appeared in newsclips, as did the queen, even though she was still on

Atlantis. The prince was a mystery, and despite my ulterior motives for competing, I found myself hoping he was handsome.

Lost in my thoughts and functionally invisible to those around me, I overheard two contestants whispering in a nearby alcove.

"What's so secret you dragged me over here?"

"My uncle said to make sure I get put on a van, not a bus. Supposedly, some paths are easier than others."

"So it's rigged?"

"Isn't everything around here? Earth was never going to leave the contestant pool completely to chance."

Oh, wonderful. An unfair test. At least now I knew the secret, too, though I had no clue what she had meant by path.

I considered looking for the restroom in earnest when I caught sight of someone I knew. Lily Vasquez, Brett's sister, was a few feet ahead of me. Her profile was unmistakable. Her aquiline nose and pointed chin vaguely reminded me of a witch, but I was willing to admit that my personal feelings gave that thought more steam that it deserved. Her sleek, auburn hair was half up, half down. Most people would find her beautiful. I groaned and tried to slip back through the mass of bodies before she noticed me, but I was saved instead by a woman's voice over the speakers.

"Contestants, please proceed to the garage level. Volunteers in orange vests are stationed at intervals to direct and assist you. Please follow their instructions. Failure to do so will result in disqualification."

We moved along, energy humming through the crowd like an electric current. Some of these women had been dreaming of this moment for months, and even I, as a brand-new contestant, felt jittery. Moving helped calm my nerves, even though we were going slowly. In the flow of bodies, I had lost sight of Lily. I hoped she was farther ahead, as I didn't like the idea of having her at my back.

Eventually I reached the top of the wide ramp that led to the garage. From my vantage point, I had a clear view of women being loaded into buses and vans by the dozen. A few volunteers were directing women down different paths. To most observers, it would look random, but thanks to the snippet of conversation I'd overheard, I knew otherwise. I watched a contestant exchange a friendly smile with the volunteer, and she was promptly waved to the right where the vans were waiting. The ones directed to the right were on average prettier with nicer clothes, whether dresses or athletic gear.

Well, it can't hurt to try.

I slowly made my way to the right-hand side of the ramp, hoping that I would be directed to the right out of convenience. When I reached the volunteers, I flashed the woman my best smile. She studied me a moment, then waved me over to the right. Another man directed me into a van. I'd made it.

The van's three rows of seats had the capacity to hold ten contestants. The front was already full, so I took the window seat in the second row. The three young women in the front were quiet, probably separated from their friends.

"Hey," I said. "Do you know where they're taking us?"

"Outside the city," replied the brunette with a red bow in her hair.

Two more women came in and sat beside me as I processed Red Bow's revelation. Outside the city? What could we possibly be doing out there? How far were they taking us? There were fields outside for athletics, but the stadium would have worked too. Except there were a lot of young women competing. We wouldn't all fit on the stadium's field.

Before I could ask Red Bow for more details, a head of auburn hair ducked through the door. Lily. She would be riding with us. I turned and devoted my attention to the window, resolved not to draw her notice by speaking. She took the seat directly behind me. I caught my green blouse in the reflection, doubting my decision to give the shirt a second chance. What if it *was* unlucky? I heard Lily introduce herself to the woman who entered after her and gritted my teeth.

Out of the corner of my eye, I saw the last three spots get filled. One of them was a woman in tight leggings and a sports bra, an outfit that revealed her toned abs. Her black hair was pulled back into something practical yet elegant. Her arms were toned as well.

Lily, who had worn a skirt, scoffed. "I'm pretty sure this isn't a fight to the death."

The other women laughed. I risked turning a bit now that Lily's attention was elsewhere. Fit Girl ignored them.

"I doubt the prince likes buff girls, but maybe you can put in an application to become a royal guard," Lily continued in mock sympathy.

"That doesn't sound so bad," Fit Girl replied, shrugging. I was on the verge of saying something, but Fit Girl didn't seem bothered, so I let it go. Plus, the longer I kept my mouth shut, the longer we could all enjoy a peaceful van ride.

Lily, having failed to get a rise out of Fit Girl, started chatting with Red Bow about what the contest would be. The two were still deluding themselves into thinking that it was a simple beauty contest and that the prince would be there and choose the prettiest women to join the contest. After the mayor's advice to wear comfortable shoes, I knew it wouldn't be that simple.

I kept my eyes glued out the window and watched the buildings blur by. Soon we passed the city walls, and the buildings were replaced by farms and meadows. I hadn't been outside the city in years, and I'd forgotten how open the country was. Colorful fields of spring flowers alive with butterflies and bees popped up between the farms. Monoculture farms had been replaced by permaculture food forests, but even that wasn't always enough to keep us fed.

Twenty minutes later, we reached a brightly colored tent with people milling about. The other vans and buses were arriving. I tried to get a better look and, in the process, forgot to avoid Lily's gaze.

Unfortunately, she saw me. "Chloe! What on earth are you doing here?" she crowed as if we were old friends. "If my brother didn't want you, Prince Agathon certainly won't."

Don't smack her. Don't.

I put on my best fake smile. "I'm surprised to see you here too! I would have thought you'd be busy luring children into your cottage in the woods."

Fit Girl chuckled.

"I'm taking the day off," Lily snapped back, getting her own laughs. Then squaring herself back up to her audience, as I now thought of them, she said, "Chloe practically begged my brother to date her. He took her on a pity date or two, but the poor thing couldn't take a hint, so he had to spell it out for her."

Her words had enough truth in them to sting, and I sensed a mix of disdain and pity from the other women. "Like you said, here I am now. Guess I figured it out eventually. And I've gotta say," I continued, "at least you, unlike your brother, never pretended to be anything other than a witch. With any luck, you'll be back to eating babies by dinnertime, and I'll be on my way to Atlantis."

Lily probably would have found a way to pull out my intricate hairdo if we hadn't arrived at our destination. The van doors opened and Fit Girl was first out of her seat.

"By the way," she said, as she hopped out of the van, "it's a race. Nice shoes." She patted Lily on the shoulder and jogged off like a modern-day Amazon warrior, leaving the rest of us to scramble out into the bright, midday sun. From the look on Lily's face, this had come as a true surprise. Most of the other women looked shocked and confused too. Even Red Bow. However, one woman from our van who had worn leggings under her dress pulled tennis shoes from her bag. *Smart move*, I thought. *Prepared in either event.*

An orange-vested volunteer with a clipboard herded our group toward the starting line. Again, I noticed a disparity between the directions in which the bus women and van women were being directed. This time we were being steered to the left-hand side of the course.

"See those two marks on the ground?" the volunteer asked, pointing to long, white marks on either side of our group. "They indicate your starting zone. Do not leave this zone. The race begins at noon. Directions will be given right before we start."

I was still trapped in close quarters with Lily, but at least I could keep out of hair-pulling range. Fit Girl was stretching, so I joined her.

"I'm Chloe, by the way."

"Anna," she replied.

"So you knew?" I asked, trying to keep the jealousy out of my voice.

"I work in the mayor's office, and I may have overheard a few discussions I wasn't supposed to. Either way, I figured this outfit would work for beauty or brawn." She laughed.

I cracked a smile. "I'm a bit overdressed," I said, glancing down at my fancy blouse and sneakers, "but it could have been worse." I nodded my head toward Red Bow, who was blinking back tears. I felt a little bad for her.

"Your friend doesn't look like she's going to let it stop her," Anna replied.

On the other side of our zone, Lily was jogging in place. She had removed her shoes and had pulled on a pair of modesty shorts, offered by the orange-vested volunteers to young women in skirts or dresses. Her tenacity extended beyond terrorizing me and into marrying for money.

"I can't say I'm surprised," I replied. "Why didn't they tell us how to dress? Maybe the prince likes the optics of women duking it out in a muddy arena."

"The prince didn't set this challenge. Mayor Russo did. Earth was in charge of organizing its own qualifiers. Maybe Russo wanted to make sure that only the people who really want to win will compete. Looks like her plan's working too." Anna nodded toward Red Bow, who was leaving our assigned zone. She wasn't alone either. Dozens of women were leaving their starting areas, no longer interested after learning it was a race, not a pageant.

We continued stretching in silence, and I took the opportunity to survey my surroundings. The course itself was wide to accommodate the large number of competitors, but its length was relatively short. In the distance, I could see a string of pennants that stretched above the finish line. Beyond the starting line were a mud pit and a wall that obstructed my view of the rest of the course. I was certain there would be more obstacles but doubted my ability to scale the wall and ever see them. Camera drones flew above us, which I assumed belonged to the Atlanteans. I could also see a few cameras attached to obstacles within the course. The competition would be recorded and displayed on screens in the stadium back in the city. Noon was fast approaching. The race would start soon.

A few large screens were set up at intervals behind us at the starting line, and their standby image was replaced by a handsome man. Wavy brown hair framed his face, and his deep brown eyes looked straight at the camera. The prince had finally revealed himself, and I couldn't tear my eyes away.

"I am Prince Leonidas Agathon, and I am honored that so many of you have agreed to compete for a spot in the Goddess Games. It is an old tradition on Atlantis, meant to ensure that the royal line never forgets its duty to the people. It is a way for every Atlantean to see themselves represented in government. We want the refugees from Earth to feel this same way, which is why I have decided to choose a bride from Earth. My hope is that we can unite our two civilizations. Atlantis is eager to meet you, as am I." He smiled a dazzling smile, and then his image disappeared.

I gauged the other contestants' reactions. There was some blushing, eager whispers, and even a little swooning. If Mayor Russo had put in the mud pit to deter us, she should have blurred the prince's handsome face too.

A new face appeared on the screen. This time King Darius of Atlantis addressed us.

"The Goddess Games are a competition. In order to rule, you must be strong, wise, and generous. The Olympians, whom you know as the gods and goddesses of ancient Greece, were the aliens that took us from Earth and settled us on Atlantis. They each embodied various traits and skills, and each trial of the games will test you in a new way. Today, we open the Goddess Games' qualifying round with the Artemis Trial.

"In Earth mythology, Artemis was a huntress and protector of maidens. As an Olympian, she was a skilled pilot, one who tracked down and eliminated any threats to their ships. She was also fond of competition, which is why on ancient Earth, unmarried women were allowed to compete in footraces in her honor. In this iteration of the Goddess Games, considering that you are still on Earth, the Artemis Trial will take the form of a footrace. The first thirty-five women in each of your three districts will be taken to our flagship, where the rest of the games will take place over the course of the journey to Atlantis. I wish you all luck. Let the Goddess Games begin!"

Six

ON THE SCREEN WHERE the king's face had been moments earlier, there was now a countdown: thirty seconds until the race began. Women pushed one another as they clambered back toward the starting line.

"Follow my lead," Anna muttered. "I'll boost you over that wall if you give me a hand up."

"What makes you trust I'll help you?" I asked.

"If you betray me, I'll have one more reason to get over that wall. I find revenge to be an excellent motivator."

I grinned. "A girl after my own heart."

Anna winked. "Try to keep up."

Ten seconds left. Farther down the starting line a couple of fights had broken out as women jockeyed for good starting positions. Volunteers dragged the offending women away, and the gaps were instantly filled in. I hardly had time to feel nervous. It hadn't even been twenty-four hours since I decided to compete, and now the moment was seconds away.

I had finally shut out the noise of the other women and gotten into a mental zone when Lily's voice pulled me out of it. She slipped in close. "The prince wouldn't marry you if you were the last woman on Earth. You might as well quit now," she whispered.

I would have turned and smacked her, probably earning myself a disqualification, but a loud buzzer sounded. Anna bolted for the mud pit, and there was no question. *Follow Anna.*

She set a lightning pace, but plenty of the women were just as fast. I managed to keep up, but this course had better be as short as it looked or I wouldn't finish at all, let alone in the top thirty-five. My legs were tiring, but a hint of auburn hair in my peripheral vision renewed my energy as we reached the mud pit. Anna was right. Revenge *was* an excellent motivator. I put on an extra burst of speed and plunged into the ankle-high, muddy water. It was freezing, but I kept my eyes on Anna's back as she forged ahead. There were far more women behind us than in front of us. I heard splashing and shrieking from my right but ignored it. I wanted to get out of this icy water as soon as possible. What then? Anna had offered to boost me over the wall, but what if I didn't help her up? That meant one less competitor, and any delay could cost me a spot in the top thirty-five. But I didn't want to be on Anna's bad side. Plus, we could need each other again depending what was on the other side.

Anna reached the wall first. She turned, saw I was close, and got into position. Her back was to the wall, her knees bent, and her hands cupped into a makeshift step for me. My shoes were wet and muddy, but she knew they would be after the pit. I kept running toward her, using my momentum and her boost to grab the top of the wall and pull myself up. I straddled the wall, gripping it tightly with my thighs before extending a hand to Anna. Though a quick glance at the rest of the course didn't show any more walls, we might need to cooperate in the future. Other women were scaling the wall using ropes that had been placed along it at regular intervals. A few managed to vault it with no help. Others were following Anna's lead and trying to find someone to boost them. A few yards away Lily was getting a leg up from some poor woman who would no doubt be left behind.

Anna grabbed my hands and walked her feet up the wall until she could safely grab the top. Once she'd gotten a grip, I hopped down and continued to the next obstacle, not bothering to wait. Anna was fast. She would catch up. Before me was a maze of wires, as if a large, angry spider had spun a tangle of metal instead of silk. Most of the wire was smooth, but some of it was barbed, though fortunately not rusty.

I ducked, crawled, and stepped through the wire blockade, sacrificing care for speed, and paying for it with a few cuts on my arms and legs. My jeans were wet and uncomfortable, and worse, they were heavy. I struggled to maneuver through the web of wire in them, though they offered me more protection than some of the thin dresses my competitors wore. My wet shoes rubbed uncomfortably against my heels, and my mud-covered green top wouldn't have another chance to redeem itself after today. The barbed wired was poking too many holes to mend.

As I pulled myself through the final thicket of wires, I glanced back at the carnage behind me. Some women were trying to untangle their hair; others, who had been visions in dazzling, red dresses, were now dragging themselves through the dirt and mud as they avoided wires. I was near the front of the pack, and the finish line was within sight, brilliant green and gold pennants beckoning to me. The absurdity of it all struck me. What were all these women competing for? The chance to marry a prince? Did they want a quick ticket to Atlantis? I remembered my conversation with the mayor. How many of these women wanted to infiltrate the contest and kill the royal family? I picked up my pace and reached the next obstacle. Monkey bars were set at intervals over a shallow water pit. The muddy banks were steep, and I knew that if I fell into the water, my chances of qualifying would be zero. I'd have to wade to the end to climb out, since the intervals between each set of bars were blocked off. The only way across was over. I'd played on monkey bars as a kid. How hard could it be?

This was the final obstacle before the home stretch, and there weren't a lot of women who'd made it this far yet. Somehow I was still in the running. Another woman sprinted past me. Anna.

"Whatever you do, don't stop," she shouted as she breezed past. "Momentum is key!"

Anna was halfway across when another woman hopped on behind her, hesitated, then fell into the water below. I doubted my memory of how easy the monkey bars had been, but waiting any longer wouldn't help. Every second I delayed, my chances decreased.

I hopped up onto the first bar, using my momentum to swing me to the next and the next. About halfway across, my hands started to hurt. I wanted to stop and readjust, but Anna's warning replayed in my head, urging me on. I made it to the other side, hopped down, and broke into a run. Now that there was nothing left in my way, I could see the finish line and the giant counter beyond, ticking up as women crossed the finish line. It was changing from fourteen to fifteen, and there were probably a dozen or so women in the final stretch with me. Even better, two of the contestants were fighting, and one of them had the same auburn hair as Lily.

However, it was not Lily. As I got closer, I did recognize one of the combatants. Not-Lily had Anna by the hair and was pulling hard. I was close to the finish line now, and I could see the number slowly counting up. It had already broken twenty, meaning there were less than fifteen slots left.

Maybe it was Anna's helpful hint or the fact that the woman attacking her looked like Lily, but I decided to help. Taking a cue from Anna's aggressor, I yanked her assailant's hair, forcing her head back. She squealed, caught off guard by the attack from behind, and released Anna.

I didn't wait for Anna, but I saw her scramble to her feet in my peripheral vision. The counter was moving up rapidly, but my legs were burning with the effort. Stopping to help Anna had made it harder to get back up to speed. I was nearly there. The counter hit thirty. Anna passed me and crossed the finish line. *Thirty-one.* I stumbled under the flags seconds behind her. *Thirty-two.*

My chest was heaving, and I collapsed on the ground.

"You should get up and walk around if you can manage. Cool down a bit." Anna was panting, too, but she was smiling. She wiped a tear from her cheek, leaving a streak of mud in the wake of her hand. Then, she offered me her muddy hand and pulled me up.

"Thanks." I didn't have a lot of friends aside from Flora. I'd never been good at getting to know strangers. I liked being alone, but I chalked it up to being an only child. I was glad to have this connection to Anna, new as it was.

I hadn't noticed numbers thirty-three and thirty-four cross the finish line, but thirty-five would be close. Two women with auburn hair were neck and neck, and I wasn't sure which one I wanted to win, Lily or the woman who'd attacked Anna. No, that wasn't true. I'd take Not-Lily any day, but apparently there were limits to the luck my ruined green top was willing to bestow.

Lily managed a burst of speed that sent her hurtling across the finish line, and the counter ticked up to thirty-five. That was it. The final spot was claimed.

A buzzer blared, and it hit me. I had qualified for the Goddess Games. I would be leaving Earth very soon. Forever. I looked over at Lily, who was covered head to toe in mud. Her dress was ruined, and her feet were bare and bleeding in places. If Lily had run through mud and barbed wire barefoot for a chance to marry the prince, what were the rest of these women willing to do to win?

Seven

More orange-vested volunteers ushered us, the qualifiers, into waiting vans. Other women were still crossing the finish line, but they didn't matter anymore. We were the winners, and the losers were irrelevant. Winning felt great, even though it was mostly Anna and dumb luck that got me here.

Anna fell into stride next to me, her composure regained. "I thought I was doomed when that girl grabbed me," she said. "I—" Her voice broke, and she blinked hard. Caught up in the moment, she admitted to me, "My mom was just diagnosed. Cancer. Now the Atlanteans will treat her."

"I'm glad your mom will get treatment. And I wouldn't have made it this far without your help anyway. There's no need to thank me." Guilt bubbled in my stomach as I recalled how I'd considered leaving her behind at the first wall.

We climbed into the last van, making sure to avoid choosing the same vehicle as Lily. The van smelled like dirt with a hint of coppery blood, but I resisted the urge to roll down a window.

The blonde in front of us was examining her arms and bemoaning her scratches to the woman next to her, whom she seemed to know.

"We got lucky. Our wire tangle was nothing compared to the other side of the course," the young woman muttered to the blonde. "I don't even think some parts of it were passable!"

"It wasn't luck, Soph," the blonde replied. "The trial was definitely rigged."

I raised an eyebrow at Anna, but she just shrugged. I wanted to ask if anyone knew where we were going but decided against it. Probably back to the city to shower and grab our things. I was in the middle of worrying if I'd get to see my family soon when the van started slowing down.

"We're still outside the city," the blonde said.

"The barracks," Anna replied. "I think we'll get to clean up after all."

Anna was right. The men and women who were stationed out here had been temporarily sent away so that we could use their showers and facilities. We got extra water rations again, but because of the layers of grime, what would have normally been a luxurious amount of time was barely enough to get clean. After I finished, I put on the provided white tunic dress with gold trim and leggings. My stiff, dirty race clothes were nowhere in sight. I sent a silent prayer into the universe, thanking the green top for its service.

I had qualified. I was clean. I had fresh clothes that were soft and warm, and I couldn't stop running my hands down the sleeves as I wandered toward the sound of female voices.

There was a table laid out with various snacks including fresh fruit, bread, and even some cheese. I approached the food with the intention of eating a few bites, but those few bites turned into a full plate. I leaned against the wall while I ate, watching the others. It struck me as odd that so many of the women were uncommonly beautiful.

"All right, ladies," said a familiar voice. Mayor Russo strode into the room, and the chatter and chewing died down. "I know many of you have questions, and I'm here to give you the answers I can.

"In half an hour, you will leave this facility, and an Atlantean transport will take you to their flagship. There, you will be examined, treated if necessary, and interviewed. The Goddess Games will take place over the three-month journey to Atlantis, but only twenty of you will compete in the actual games. Twenty from the other two districts will also compete, for a total of sixty young women from Earth."

There was a small uproar at this. The mayor shushed the angry whispers. "I don't have any details on how the Atlanteans will choose the twenty. Once you leave this building, Earth's part in organizing the games is over. You will become joint citizens of the American Federation and Atlantis. Part of qualifying means that you are among the first wave to leave Earth, even if you are not among the twenty. Your families will be transported to the fleet in the coming days and receive the promised medical care."

I glanced at Anna, whose shoulders relaxed at that news.

"Do you know when we get to see our families?" one woman asked.

"I'm sorry. I do not. If you are among the twenty, remember that you represent the American Federation and Belvale District. You represent Earth. The Goddess Games will be broadcast to both worlds. Earth is watching. Atlantis is watching. If we want to have a true alliance between our worlds, we need a princess who puts her people's needs above her own. Keep that thought evergreen in your minds."

I looked down at my remaining food, a white cheese cube and a strawberry. I tried to resign myself to being eliminated before reaching the twenty. It was a miracle I'd qualified at all. Then I glimpsed Lily doing nothing more than eating a cracker, and I realized I couldn't give up without even trying. Her brother had cost me my apprenticeship, and now I was going to beat Lily as revenge. If I made it far enough, I would gain a ladyship. Doors I couldn't even imagine would open up for me. This was worth fighting for, and Lily was worth fighting against. I was set either way I looked at it.

I popped the cheese into my mouth, then the strawberry, and put the plate down on one of the tables. Time to do this. Mayor Russo had begun making the rounds, shaking hands and offering wishes of good luck. Soon she intercepted me. I almost thanked her for the tip about the shoes, but her greeting was formal. Maybe she didn't recognize me.

"Congratulations, young lady. Good luck in the trials ahead." She clasped my hand in both of hers and whispered, "Room 42B. There isn't much time."

I bowed my head in a shallow nod of acknowledgment. I walked away and grabbed another piece of cheese on my way out the door under the guise of looking for a restroom. I considered ignoring her order, but my curiosity won out.

42B was a small conference room with half-erased diagrams still on the board. After several minutes, the door clicked open, and Mayor Russo joined me.

"You're the only one of my girls who made it." She spoke quickly in hushed tones. I wasn't hers, and I didn't like the way she said "girls," as if I was still a child. I didn't have a chance to voice my objections before she continued. "The rebels may have infiltrated the contest too. You need to be selected among the twenty from Belvale District and stay in the contest as long as possible, or at least until you find the rebel and report back to me. As a contestant, you may see and hear things that the royal guards can't."

Russo was making a lot of assumptions. I crossed my arms over my chest. "What makes you so sure I'll agree to this?"

"I know that you're willing to do what it takes to get what you want. Our goals are aligned. If a rebel murders the prince, you'll lose any chance of gaining a noble title on Atlantis. Your friend Flora will be trapped on Earth. There will be no further evacuations. I'll make sure that you get all the help Earth can offer when completing the trials."

"What? I don't want your help. I don't want to cheat."

"Really? Then why did you take my advice and wear your work shoes?"

"I, um—" That wasn't really cheating. Russo had told me to wear comfortable shoes. She hadn't warned me about the race or explained which side of the obstacle course was easier to get through. Had Russo had a hand in getting me into a good starting position? Had she and others been pulling invisible strings throughout the process? "I wasn't the only one you tried to help, was I?"

"No, but you're the only one who made it to the top thirty-five." The mayor trained her cold, green eyes on me, and I knew then that I had not been her favorite to qualify. I was the unfortunate product of hedged bets. "Plus, I know all about the weather analyst exam." I took a breath, ready to set the record straight, but Russo held up a hand to stop me. "I'm not judging you, Ms. Woods. Sometimes the end justifies the means, and this is one of those cases. The deck is stacked against you, and the future of everyone on Earth depends on these Goddess Games."

"If they're so important, why did you humiliate Earth with that ridiculous race? A bunch of women dressed to the nines clamoring barefoot through the mud can't possibly make a good impression. There were cameras. Atlantis was watching."

"And so were the rebels. If everyone thought it was a beauty pageant, they would come prepared for a beauty pageant. I can only hope it prevented the rebels from qualifying, but an event as big as this is hard to keep completely secret."

"You made us look barbaric. You think the Atlanteans want a princess who gets into mud fights?"

"We need someone strong and tenacious. Someone who will crawl across the finish line scratched and bruised if it means victory, because that's what Earth needs in these games. A victory. I think the Atlanteans need to see the truth of whom they're saving. We are brutal and destructive. We've destroyed our planet, and we're still sucking the last bits of life out of it. They need to know that we need saving in more ways than one."

"That's putting a lot on their shoulders."

"Which is why we need a princess who can carry her share of that burden." Edwina Russo checked her watch and sighed. "Time to go. Take this." In her extended palm was a small card, no larger than my thumbnail. "It's an Atlantean commcard we modified that will allow us to exchange encrypted messages. Soon after you arrive, they'll give you a personal device, a tablet of some kind. Plug this into your device to contact me and check regularly for messages."

"And if I don't? I never signed up to be your puppet."

"Then I'll make sure you're removed from the games for cheating. With your history, no one would blink. Then you'll never make it to the finals, and you'll never get the freedom to explore your potential. You know, I see it in you. The potential to be more than you are."

I clenched my jaw. The compliment did little to soften her threat. "All right," I said, slipping the commcard into my pocket. "What am I supposed to do?"

"The rebels are planning something," she said. "Report anything suspicious. Protect the prince. Earth depends on it."

What was I getting myself into?

I rejoined the other qualifiers and grabbed another strawberry on my way back to Anna. She raised an eyebrow as if to ask where I'd been. "I needed a minute to myself. I can't believe we're leaving Earth right away. I didn't have a chance to give my family a real goodbye this morning." She gave me a sympathetic look but didn't say anything. A volunteer had begun herding us outside. It was time to go, and to my surprise, no reluctance slowed my steps. My destiny was on that ship, even if it wasn't the prince.

Outside waited a sleek white shuttle, clearly Atlantean in design. Inside were rows and rows of seats. An amiable woman wearing a green

Atlantean crew uniform directed us to our seats. She spoke English with a slight Atlantean accent, as had the king and queen in all of their appearances. She pointed me to a comfortable seat at the end of one of the rows next to a woman I didn't know at all.

Soon, we began our ascent. I wasn't sure if the sinking feeling in my stomach was from the g-forces or the mayor's words, but the gravity of the situation began to sink in. *Protect the prince. Earth depends on it.*

EIGHT

After the initial ascent, our ride to the Atlantean flagship was easy. A few hours later, the pilot announced our approach. I had to imagine the palatial spaceship from the news, since the shuttle offered no view. The gravity on the transport was much lighter than on Earth, but the pull was stronger after we landed. The flagship was set to Atlantis gravity, which was slightly higher than Earth's.

"You probably won't be able to perceive the difference, but you might tire easily for the first few days," the pilot said with a chuckle. "The Olympians chose Atlantis for us because it was as close to Earth's conditions as possible, and that included the gravity." His accent was subtle, but he drew out his vowels in that melodic way I was coming to expect from the Atlanteans.

The officer who'd directed us to our seats now ushered us onto the flagship. "You'll go straight to the medical wing for a health screening and other tests. After that, you'll learn Atlantean. This can take several hours."

"Hours? We have to learn another language in hours?" someone asked.

"Our process is different than what you're used to. It's how I learned to speak such excellent English. After that, the games master, Stefan Megos, and his crew will interview you. Follow me, please."

She didn't offer to answer any questions, and we took the hint. I'd expected to be cold, but the ship was the perfect temperature. We passed a few crew members dressed in brown and blue uniforms who stopped and stepped to the side to let us pass. A few gawked, one stood at attention, and one slipped out of sight through a noiseless automatic door before we reached him. What did these people think of us? Were they excited to see us or angry that some lousy Earth woman would be marrying their prince? Or did they just wonder what we tasted like with ketchup?

I smiled to myself at that last ridiculous thought and wished Flora was here to laugh with me—then my face fell with a horrible realization. Flora's family wasn't coming with us. They wouldn't be brought to Atlantis for five years. Years! Back when my family had been tenth-wave, it would have meant we'd arrive at the same time. But now it would be five years. She would be twenty-three the time I next saw her. And when would I get to see my parents? I'd barely said goodbye this morning, since my abrupt departure from Earth was the last thing I expected. What had they thought of the race? If I didn't make it to the final twenty from Belvale, would I be reunited with them for the trip to Atlantis?

I barely noticed the rest of the walk as I panicked about leaving my best friend behind for years and possibly not seeing my parents for three months. In the medical wing, we were called back one by one. The other women chatted, but I couldn't get Flora out of my mind. I was almost last, so I figured they'd gone alphabetically. Eventually, I was one of two contestants left in the waiting area.

"You're not a Z by chance, are you?" the other woman asked.

"W."

She heaved a good-natured sigh. "Oh well. It was too much to hope for, I suppose. I'm Riya Zan."

"Chloe Woods," I replied. I felt like I should say more, but I was saved from thinking of a question when a blue-uniformed woman called my name. "I'm pretty sure you're up next," I said, and Riya politely laughed at my lame joke as I headed back to get poked and prodded.

"I'm Dr. Stolos," the woman said, leading me into an exam room with a machine a little taller than I was in one corner. "This device is a scanner that will detect physical anomalies such as cancer. I'll be drawing blood to run a few more tests for common diseases and other long-term health issues."

"Like what?"

"Genetic disorders, for one." She reached out and put her hand over mine in a brief, reassuring pat. "I know it can be frightening, but on Atlantis we believe that to be forewarned is to be forearmed. If anything comes back as questionable, we may very well have a treatment. Part of my oath as a doctor forbids me from disclosing any personal information you might tell me during your exam to anyone else without your consent, including the royal family. However, when you registered for the competition, you signed a waiver giving them access to your medical information for the duration of the Goddess Games. You may refuse any diagnostic testing and treatment here and now, but that will also disqualify you from the competition and jeopardize your chances of receiving any treatment you or your family might need. To be clear, if you consent to testing, but have a condition that disqualifies you from the games, we will still treat you if we can."

This was news to me, but it was my own fault for not reading the fine print. Even if I had, it wouldn't have stopped me. If I refused, I'd be dismissed. If they tested me and found something they didn't like, I'd be dismissed, but I'd still be treated. Now that I was here, I wanted to see how far I could go. Plus, at the bare minimum, I had to beat Lily. "Right. Okay," I said, relaxing a little bit. "Thanks for explaining all that. Go ahead."

Dr. Stolos asked me countless questions about my family history, some awkward personal questions that made me feel more like a broodmare than a princess-hopeful, then finally scanned me and took my blood. She also replaced my birth control chip with what she assured me was a better Atlantean version.

"If there's anything to be concerned about, I'll let you know. Otherwise, no news is good news. Cara is right outside the door for you."

"Thanks," I mumbled. I stood and wondered if I was supposed to know who Cara was, but when I opened the door, a forty-something woman introduced herself and led me to a new room that looked like a movie theater, except the lights were on. The other women from Belvale District were already seated, totally entranced as they watched the screen. The bizarre thing was that the movie was in a different language. I couldn't pick out even one familiar word, and there were no subtitles. I found Anna in the audience. Her expression was blank, her face slack. The sight was eerie, and I balked as Cara tried to lead me along. "What is this place?"

"We normally show movies here, but right now, it's being used for linguistic imprinting," Cara said.

"Linguistic what?"

"Imprinting," Cara repeated, though a bit exasperated this time, as if she'd already had this conversation dozens of times. "We'll give you an injection that will prime the language center of your brain for reception. Once that kicks in, you'll need a lot of linguistic input. That's where the movies come in. You sit and watch until the Atlantean language starts making sense. It takes a few hours, but it's a lot faster than the old-fashioned way. Your brain will have increased receptivity to language for a few weeks afterward, but the bulk of acquisition will occur over several hours while you're here."

"Is it safe?" I asked. "Messing with our brains like that?"

"Every Atlantean you've met today has used this method to learn English. The drug makes you feel out of it, like you're standing still and the world is rushing past you like water past a rock. It's alarming for some people, but it's not dangerous. If you react badly, we're still close to the medical wing."

"What's a bad reaction look like?"

"If it doesn't work, for starters. You'd have to learn the hard way. Most people feel relaxed, but those who react badly have what is basically a panic attack. It won't harm you, if that's your concern."

I looked back to Anna. She certainly didn't look okay, but they wouldn't have brought us all here just to kill us. I watched one woman with dazzling blue eyes stand up. She was blinking rapidly, and her gait was a little shaky, but she made her way down the aisle toward us. Her face lit up with recognition when she saw Cara.

"*Atlantidisti nun lego*?" she asked in hesitating words.

"*Mehn, dia tehn thuran.*" Cara pointed at a nearby door, and I figured she was giving the woman directions.

The words were incomprehensible to me, but clearly Atlantean. The blue-eyed contestant looked at me and said in English, "It's not so bad. Just weird." She disappeared through the indicated door.

"Five hours," Cara remarked. "Perfectly average. So, are you ready?"

"I guess so," I replied.

Cara sat me down before administering the drug. The injection was painless, but in seconds my head was swimming. I gazed at the screen, trying to follow the dialog, but it felt as if the characters were speaking at triple speed. I knew they weren't, but there was something wrong with my perception. Reality was going to leave me behind in this theater, just like the women who were getting up and leaving.

Yet, I didn't care. This place was actually pretty nice. The voices were slowing down, and their words reminded me of an old song that I could almost remember the lyrics to, starting with a pair of rhyming lines, a snippet of the chorus, until it all finally came crashing back.

The man on screen was ordering a meal, and the woman was complaining about work. Both were speaking Atlantean, and their conversation was suddenly comprehensible. I didn't understand every word, but I definitely understood Atlantean. Could I speak it? I waited a bit longer until I was pretty sure I'd gotten the hang of it. I got up and found Cara chatting with another Atlantean.

"*Ehstha alehtheutika. Esti aponehros.*" *You were right. It's safe.*

Cara chuckled.

Many of the women who had been there when I arrived were still in their seats. "How long was I...?"

"Four hours."

I nodded. Somehow four minutes, four hours, or even four days all would have been believable answers.

Cara motioned me to the side door but didn't follow. I was still a little disoriented from the imprinting, but my energy was returning. I'd been through the screening, the linguistic imprinting, and now there was only the interview left.

I stood stupidly in front of the closed door, unsure how it opened and too afraid of breaking something to try to figure it out. Cara saw my hesitation and instructed me in crisp Atlantean to put my palm in front of the square.

A smooth, glossy touch pad was on the right side of the door. I held my hand in front of it, and the door quietly opened.

"Thanks," I said in Atlantean before stepping into the hallway. Another Atlantean led me down a corridor to the next room, and I couldn't help but feel like I was on some sort of assembly line. This Atlantean smiled pleasantly, but she didn't strike up a conversation. Unlike the uniforms I'd seen most of the crew members wearing so far, her outfit—a tunic dress and leggings—was similar to mine, though better tailored and brightly colored in shades of orange. She stopped in front of a door that looked like all the others, until I noticed the words written on a placard above the touch pad. I couldn't read them.

"Here you are," she said, already turning to trace her path back.

"Wait, why can't I read that?" I asked in Atlantean, pointing to the placard.

"Oh, the imprinting is only for spoken language. You'll have to learn how to read and write Atlantean. Don't worry, though. It's a lot easier to learn after the imprinting." With a shallow nod, she left me standing outside the door. I hovered my palm over the touch pad, and the door opened. No sooner had I crossed the threshold than a stern man in his forties sitting behind a desk snapped an order at me. "Take a seat until your name is called for your interview." He didn't even look up from his work.

I did as I was told. There were two other women waiting, but the room was silent. It looked like a regular office. There was a narrow hallway dotted with doors, though I could only see the first two. Each one had a placard beside it that I couldn't read. I had a feeling that this interview would carry far more weight than either the screening or imprinting when it came to deciding which twenty of the women from my group would officially join the Goddess Games. Those things could eliminate a contestant, but this interview would choose them, and I had no idea what they were looking for.

I put my hands in my pockets and picked my way to an unoccupied, comfortable-looking chair. The commcard from Mayor Russo was still there, and though I didn't risk pulling it out, I recalled her words and considered them. *Protect the prince. Earth depends on it.*

Were they hyperbole or my burden to bear?

I wasn't sure yet, but I was certain of one thing. If I was going to join the Goddess Games, I had to nail this interview.

Nine

I'd been waiting long enough to wonder if this was an intimidation tactic. The other two women who'd been there before me had been called back, as well as one who'd arrived after me. A few more contestants trickled in and received the same cordial reception I had, so I didn't think it was personal. One tried to strike up a conversation with me, but the man shushed her before she finished her question. I shrugged at her and mouthed, "Sorry." This man wanted to work in silence, and being rude and a little scary was the best way to keep our chatter to a minimum.

None of the women who'd been called before me had come back out, so there had to be a second exit somewhere down the hallway. Soft footsteps approached, muffled by the spongy flooring. This suite had something similar to carpeting, a stark contrast to the firm, composite flooring in the corridors and clinic. A woman in her thirties with impeccable blue eyeliner, blue streaks in her hair, and a colorfully patterned tunic appeared at the hall's opening.

"Chloe Woods," she called out in a shrill voice.

I promptly stood and followed her into one of the offices. There were nearly a dozen screens across one wall, displaying various images of me. It was creepy. They showed me running in the race, but a few were from school events years ago, and one was even of my parents.

"I'm Talia, the assistant game master," the blue-haired woman introduced herself. "I'm sure you're tired, so we'll dive right in. Stand here please." She pointed to a small X taped to the floor. "Turn slowly." I complied, trying to ignore the judgmental humphs that came as I did. She jotted some notes on a tablet, which I tried to read when she stepped in close to examine my face, but they were all in Atlantean.

She finally put some space between us, settling down into a comfortable chair. I was not invited to sit, though a quick glance around the room revealed two other chairs. And this was supposed to be an interview?

"Ms. Woods, why do you want to enter the Goddess Games?"

"To marry the prince." That was the answer they were looking for, right?

"Any other reason? A sick relative, perhaps?"

"No, I—" What part of the truth could I tell that didn't make me look bad? Nothing about Lily or Brett Vasquez. Nothing about becoming a finalist to join the nobility and find a meaningful career. The mayor's words suddenly came to mind. "I want to help Earth. If I can. This alliance is important for both our worlds."

"Hmph," she replied skeptically, typing a few words into her notes. She didn't press me on my answer. "Do you have any special talents?"

I fumbled for something I was good at. "I'm good at organizing inventory. I suggested some improvements to my manager in the ware—"

"This isn't a job interview," she snapped. "It's a games interview. The prince can decide if your skills are adequate. I'm supposed to gauge whether you'll be entertaining or pleasing to watch on the screen."

"Then what do you mean by talents?"

"Singing, dancing, painting."

I shook my head. I had almost no chance of making it to the actual competition if those were the qualities they were looking for. "I think I can still do cartwheels."

She peered down her nose at me. "Cartwheels?"

"It's been a while since I last tried."

Talia underlined something in the notes she was taking. "Are you a rebel?"

"No." I scrunched my forehead in confusion. "But why would I tell you if I was?"

"One woman already confessed today." My mouth gaped open. "She wasn't from Belvale," Talia added when she saw my shock. "What about conspiracy theories? Is the prince a cannibal?"

"Uh... no?" I looked at her like she was crazy, and I hope she noticed. Was this really happening?

"A human trafficker?"

"What? No."

"A hideous alien."

"Well, he's definitely not hideous," I quipped, shifting my weight from one leg to the other. Her lip trembled, but before I could tell if she was suppressing a smile or a scowl, I continued, "I suppose he's not an alien either. I believe the Atlanteans originated from Earth."

"I hardly can," she muttered, casting a disdainful glance at the images from the race. Had that really been earlier today? The exhaustion started to weigh me down like poorly calibrated artificial gravity. Or maybe it was the literal artificial gravity. They had warned us it would tire us out, though my internal clock told me it was late. Perhaps so late it was early. I stifled a yawn, earning a glare for my efforts. "If you're bored here," Talia said, "let me know, and I'll release you from the contest. You can join your family."

I stood a little straighter. "My family? Are they up here already?"

She tapped her screen a few times before answering. "No. They're scheduled for pick-up tomorrow morning."

"My parents?"

"Yes, that's the only family you listed on your registration. Is there anyone else?"

My voice caught in my throat. It would be almost five years until Flora's family would make it to Atlantis.

"Flora Simmons and her family."

"Simmons?" she frowned. "What's their connection to you?"

"Flora is practically my sister. Her parents are as almost as close to me as my own."

"Well, I'm afraid if they're not really family, there's not much I can do. I'm sorry." The warm hope I'd begun to feel boiled into anger in a moment. I clenched my jaw to hold back any retort. This woman knew nothing about family, and she didn't seem very sorry either. Maybe if I got far enough along in the contest, I could find a way to get the Simmonses into an earlier wave. That could be another perk of nobility.

The door opened, and in walked a man in his late fifties who clearly took care of himself. His salt-and-pepper hair and goatee were neatly trimmed, and his blue tunic had silver trim. His look was classic, especially compared to the excessive jewelry that Talia was wearing. This man did not want or need to flaunt his status. He took a seat behind the desk.

"Hello," he said, "I'm Stefan Megos, the games master. Please, have a seat."

At last, I thought. *Some courtesy.* Stefan pored over the notes that Talia had been making during our interview.

"Cartwheels?" He raised an eyebrow at me.

"Yes. I'm not much of a dancer. I can sing okay, but I'd never perform in front of people. Talia said you meant talents that would be entertaining to watch."

"Oh?" Stefan gave Talia a skeptical look. "Those types of talents may come in handy during the games, that's true, but our talents and interests reveal a lot about us. Is there anything else you'd like to add?"

"I'm good at organizing inventory, and I'm a decent cook. I play cards and read a lot in my free time." Saying it out loud made me sound as interesting as drying paint.

"Good," he said, adding his own notes to what I assumed was my file. "And you decided to enter the games because you wanted to help Earth. How will your participation help?"

I bit my lower lip. "I guess it's arrogant of me to suggest that I'd make a good leader." I glanced at the images of me from the race, still frozen on the screens on the wall. I focused on the one of me helping Anna over the wall. Then I caught sight of Lily in the background of another. "But I know that I could do a better job than some of the other contestants." I turned back and met Stefan's eyes. "I know what it's like to have people in power manipulate you and make bad, selfish decisions. I don't want someone like that to win."

Stefan smiled. "Thank you, Chloe. Talia will show you out."

Thin-lipped, Talia pointed to a door at the end of the hall. I opened it, wishing for a bed, but faced yet another corridor. This time there was no guide, but a crewman who directed me to the dining hall. It had been hours since my last meal on Earth, and I was famished.

The room looked much like a normal cafeteria, except instead of a buffet line, there were servers darting from the tables to the back where the kitchens were. Nine long tables were set with dishes and silverware. Dozens of women were already eating, far more than the thirty-five from Belvale. The unfamiliar women were talking excitedly while the women from my own city were easily identifiable by marked exhaustion.

I was tired, too, and I didn't feel like making small talk, even with the women I vaguely recognized. I eyed the empty tables but settled for the empty end of a table that was two-thirds full. Maybe I'd look shy instead of antisocial. The moment I sat down, one of the servers came over and offered me a menu, which was thankfully in English. There were soups, salads, and a few heavier rice dishes, but after answering so many questions, the server's polite query, "What would you like to eat, miss?" was too much.

"Whatever you recommend," I replied. He opened his mouth as if to ask something else, but he must have seen the exhaustion in my eyes.

"Right away, miss," he said.

He came back promptly with a bowl of hearty soup and a mug of coffee, steam billowing up from both. "If you don't like it, I'll find you something else."

I took a bite, smiled, and gave him a nod. "This is perfect, thanks."

"Glad to hear it, miss," he replied, moving on to another woman who had just arrived.

I took another bite and closed my eyes, trying to identify the flavors. When I opened them, Anna was sitting across from me.

"What do you really think of it?" she asked.

"Huh?"

"The soup."

"Oh, it's good. A little weird, kind of like when you try to recreate someone's signature dish. I think it's the Atlantean version of chicken noodle soup. Did you just get here?"

"No, I was sitting with the Lightbridge District women. You didn't see me when you came in."

"They're so... chipper. How come they're not exhausted like us?" I wondered out loud.

"You're gonna love this," Anna said. "Apparently each of the districts was allowed to hold their own qualifying contest, and the specifics weren't given. It just had to connect back to Artemis. Lightbridge had a scavenger hunt. Highmont District had a plain, boring footrace."

I extended my left arm and examined the scratches from the barbed wire. "I'll remember to be mad about it tomorrow. I'm too tired right now."

"Tomorrow is the opening ceremony."

"What happens to the extra women?" I asked. "I thought only twenty women from each district would compete." I looked around, unable to distinguish between the Lightbridge and Highmont women. I only recognized most of the Belvale contestants because I'd shared a shuttle with them. None of the people I'd known before had made it this far. Except for Lily.

"The Lightbridge women seem to think that the extras will be moved to a different part of the ship or a different ship altogether. Why?" She raised an eyebrow. "Do you think they won't choose you?"

"The woman who interviewed me was not impressed," I replied.

"You never know," Anna said. "They'll announce their decisions after dinner. Even if they don't choose you as a contestant, you and your family are still in the first wave now. That counts for something."

"Yeah," I said, desperate to change the subject before I could think about Flora again.

We talked about the race, the strange technology, and even spoke to each other in Atlantean a bit, which was bizarre. Being able to speak and understand a new language after a few hours was like magic, though we were still building our vocabularies. We got stuck on new words, but committing them to memory was easy.

The coffee had perked me up, and talking to Anna put me at ease. The food also gave me some energy, and after talking to a few other women who'd filled in the seats around us, I felt up to the initial round of cuts. I was never supposed to make it this far, but Anna, who was beautiful, clever, and social, would make an excellent contestant. I would be rooting for her. Maybe I could warn her to keep an eye on the prince if she was one of the twenty from our district.

After the last of the women from Belvale trickled in and ate, Stefan Megos entered and walked straight to a small podium at the far end of the room. Talia trailed behind him and took up position by his side. I'd never seen anyone with such great posture, I'd give her that.

"Welcome, ladies, to the flagship of the Atlantean fleet. As most of you already know, my name is Stefan Megos, and I am the games master. It has been a long day, so I'll keep things brief. Each district sent thirty-five lovely young women who qualified via the Artemis Trial. Only twenty from each district will compete in the games. Of the one hundred and five of you, four were found to be ineligible for competition, and the linguistic imprinting failed for another, so she withdrew. Forty of you in this room will be moved to quarters in one of the wings of this ship where your families will join you in the coming days. Sixty of you will be escorted to your quarters in the Palace Wing, where you will stay for as long as you remain a part of the competition. Those of you who make it to the final twelve will earn a spot among Atlantean nobility, but only one of you will become the next princess of Atlantis. You will receive further instructions tomorrow, so I recommend you get some rest tonight.

"I will now read the names of the forty who have been eliminated. Please exit with dignity and grace." Stefan nodded at the pair of sentries by the door, perhaps to remind us that we would be removed one way or another.

Behind him, Talia crossed her arms over her chest. Clearly she wanted the drama of a scorned Gaian woman while Stefan had different motives. I wasn't sure what they were, but I liked them better than Talia's. She seemed more concerned with entertainment than with choosing a future princess for her nation.

Stefan had been sincere in his promise to keep things brief: he began reading names. I braced myself, ready to get up and leave with as much dignity and grace as I could muster.

"Nellie Cousteau, Skylar Mink, Henrietta Siever, Anna Ko..."

Anna smiled at me and winked. "Good luck," she whispered before striding to the door. I was so surprised that I didn't hear the next few names. I'd only noticed because Stefan paused, waiting for the woman whose name he'd last called to stand. I looked around, worried that he'd said my name and I'd look like a sore loser. He repeated the name, Margot McMahon, and a beautiful brunette slowly rose to her feet and trudged to the doors. The names continued and the full tables began to thin. Finally, he stopped, and the room heaved a collective sigh of relief. I noticed with a grimace that Lily was still in the room. The injustice of Lily making it when Anna had been sent away made me doubt the whole contest. But maybe she could pretend to be charming when it suited her.

"Congratulations," Stefan said. "One of you will be the future princess of Atlantis. The Goddess Games will present a variety of challenges to test any aspiring princess. May you all sleep like the sun and rise bright."

The remaining sixty of us were escorted a dozen at a time to some other part of the ship. They couldn't magically teleport us from one place to another; rather we took transporters, which were a bit like a tram system running throughout the ship. The transporter modules could move both vertically and horizontally along hidden paths in the walls. When we emerged, we were in a completely different part of the ship. I stepped out of the elevator into a small vestibule, and our guide turned back and grinned with pride as he opened a final door.

"Welcome to the Palace Wing."

Everything seemed grander here. We moved into a high-ceilinged ballroom with a massive chandelier. Well, not quite a chandelier. More like a massive light with an ornate covering, decorated with figures as if a modern artist had been inspired by ancient Greek pottery. The varying opacity of the covering sent dim shadows across the floor, creating distorted shadows on the white marble of the ballroom. A staircase centered at the back of the room led into the Palace Wing itself, but I was entranced by the view opposite the staircase.

A circular window at least twenty feet in diameter looked down on Earth. I wanted to stay and view my home from orbit, but the assembly-line experience wasn't quite finished. Our guide herded us up the stairs and through the large, open doorway. Green banners emblazoned with a golden, double-headed ax framed the door. Two guards in green uniforms, a man and a woman, stood on either side of the entrance. Beyond the entrance was a small atrium with doors on either side, but our guide led us across the threshold straight ahead.

Before me stretched a majestic dining hall with colonnades along either side supported by columns with incredible foliage crafted from thin pieces of colorful metal. The tables were mostly empty, though a handful of people sat together near the kitchens in the back, laughing and talking over a late dinner. The diners watched us with interest. The colonnade on each side of the dining hall was marked at intervals by doorways. The ones on the right were flanked by guards, but the ones on the left were unattended. Our group headed left, then went up two more sets of stairs until we spilled into a corridor split in half by the staircase.

"These are your rooms," our guide said. "You'll find your name on the placard above the palm pad. You'll have access to a common room and recreation area on the floor below, as well as access to the dining hall, but you must remain in the Palace Wing unless escorted elsewhere. You may have noticed the guards on the other side of the dining hall. Those areas are reserved for crew and are also off limits unless you are escorted there. The Palace Wing is under video surveillance, so please know that you are safe. In the morning, you'll receive a proper tour after the opening ceremony. Please find your rooms and get some rest. Tomorrow is a big day!" Our guide clasped her hands together and smiled. I heard the next group of women on the stairs and figured I should find my room before more people showed up and crowded the hallway. My door was close to the stairs, and I slipped inside without saying good night to anyone.

On my bed lay my race outfit, clean but torn from the barbed wire. I pulled out the pants, which were stained with mud despite their dark color. The green shirt couldn't be saved either, but I decided to keep them as mementos from my last day on Earth. I slipped Mayor Russo's commcard into one of the pockets and shoved the clothes into the back of my closet.

Standing inside my room, I was grateful that this was the final stop of the day. I didn't bother changing out of the comfortable white and gold dress before collapsing into bed. I shut my eyes, expecting sleep to come easily, but my mind was spinning. I had made the cut. Tomorrow the Goddess Games would officially begin.

TEN

I COULDN'T SLEEP. THE coffee must have been the culprit, and now in a strange room on a strange ship, all of my negative thoughts took the helm. *Five years.* Five years before I would see Flora again, and I hadn't even gotten to say a proper goodbye.

"Guess I'm sleeping like the moon instead of the sun," I muttered, recalling Stefan's parting words. I got out of bed and walked around my room for a bit, but the pacing only made me more agitated. I recalled the window at the entrance to the Palace Wing and the brief glimpse I'd gotten of Earth. I racked my tired brain, but I couldn't recall being forbidden from leaving my room. The ballroom was still in the Palace Wing, so it had to be allowed. I slipped on a pair of soft shoes, ran a hand through my messy, loose curls, and calmly left my room. I barely made a sound as I walked down the stairs and through the dining hall. A few crew members were having drinks or a meal, probably after a late shift. I doubted this room was ever truly empty. They were sitting on the far end, and I was glad I didn't have to walk past them. The sentries at the entrance to the ballroom were another story, but my options were limited. Their backs were to the dining hall, so it wasn't until I'd made it down a few steps that they said something.

"Miss, where are you going?" the sentry asked, her tone firm and alert.

I picked up my pace and trotted quickly down the slippery stairs, running headlong toward the window. Another set of footsteps echoed after my own. The chase was anticlimactic, however, when I stopped abruptly in front of the window. The sentry who had caught up to me didn't know what to do. I half expected her to grab me and drag me back to my room, but she just asked, "Miss, are you all right?"

I started to answer her, to beg for a few minutes at the window, when another voice, this one male, rang out close behind. "Back to your post, Captain Thrace. I'll handle it." The sentry, Captain Thrace, began to speak, but her superior must have cut her off with a gesture. I still didn't turn around. The captain's footsteps faded as she strode toward the stairs.

The man was silent a moment, then said, "Is this all you wanted to see?" He sounded surprised I had bothered.

"Is this all?" I shot back. "This is the only home I've ever known." I couldn't tear my eyes away from Earth.

"I didn't mean to offend you. I understand that it can be hard to leave home. I thought you might be trying to escape. Throw yourself out an airlock or something."

I laughed. "Is the prince that bad?"

I turned, and the laugh died on my lips. The man was beautiful, and his intense brown eyes studied me. Short stubble covered his chiseled jawline, and his full lips quirked in amusement. My breath hitched, but not because he was beautiful—and oh, was he beautiful. He was familiar, like I'd seen him before.

Because I had. Once. On a screen, less than a day ago, right before the Artemis Trial. I gaped in recognition.

"I don't think he's bad at all, but I am a bit biased," the man said, flashing me a crooked grin. My face grew warm, whether from embarrassment or something else, I couldn't be sure.

"You're the prince. Prince Leonidas Agathon." *Crap.* I was supposed to get him to like me, and this would forever be his first impression. A rude runaway. "I'm so sorry," I said, stumbling over my feet in an attempt to bow. Or should I curtsy?

"There's no need to apologize, Miss—" he paused, waiting for me to provide my name.

"Woods. Chloe Woods."

He gestured to the window behind me. "Chloe, let me know when you're finished, and I'll escort you back to your room."

"Thank you." I looked back out at Earth. It didn't look like the old pictures of blue and green with happy, white clouds swirling about. The land masses were dull brown, the ice caps at the poles were smaller, and a gray storm swirled over southeast Asia.

Earth was dying. I'd known that, of course, but there was something about seeing it with my own eyes that broke my heart. I put a hand on the cold glass, or whatever the material was. Flora was still down there. My eyes stung, but no amount of rapid blinking would hold back the tears. I turned my body, squaring up toward the window, trying to hide my face.

"I'm beginning to think it's not Earth you're here to see," he said softly. He put a hand on my shoulder, and the agony I'd been holding back swelled to the surface at the tenderness of the gesture.

I swallowed a sob, pressed my eyes and lips tightly closed, and inhaled a shuddering breath.

"Is it—is there someone you love still down there?" he asked. "They did explain that your family would be brought to the ship, didn't they?"

I nodded, and once I regained enough composure, I explained. "Flora is in one of the later waves. She's like a sister to me, and now I won't see her for five years. Her family and mine eat dinner together every night. Without us—" I paused, not sure how to explain. "Without us, things will be harder for them. They're a family with three children—the younger ones are twins—and we pooled our resources."

The prince stared out at Earth, eyebrows knit in thought, hands clasped behind his back. I took the moment to study him again. His posture was impeccable. He wore a forest green tunic, embroidered with a golden pattern that reminded of waves.

Finally he spoke. "I think I understand. Under the American Federation's laws, having three children makes them ineligible for certain benefits and assistance, correct?"

I nodded. "It's not like they had twins on purpose. But they won't be brought to the ship with my parents. The woman who interviewed me told me that only biological family counted."

"It sounds like your family and this other family have a *xenia*-bond, one that you're asking me to honor."

"Xenia-bond?"

"It's something you'll learn more about in the coming weeks, but on Atlantis, bonds of hospitality, like the frequent sharing of meals that you've described, carry a heavy social weight. If you'd be so kind as to give me the name of the family?"

"Simmons," I replied at once. "Miguel and Christina Simmons. Their daughters are Flora, Daisy, and Charlotte." I didn't completely understand his explanation, but if it got Flora into the first wave, I'd take it. I wiped my tears away.

"I'll update you tomorrow," he said.

"You have no idea how much this means," I said. I finally realized how informal I was being with the prince of Atlantis. "I mean, thank you, Your Highness. Is that right? We haven't gotten any etiquette training yet."

"Your Highness is correct, or even prince, if you want, but you can call me Lee when we're alone like this."

I thought Prince Lee might be flirting with me, but before I could dismiss the thought, I burst into a fit of giggles.

"What's wrong?" he asked, running a hand through his wavy brown hair.

I took a few slow breaths until I could speak properly. "Your name is Prince Lee. As in, *princely*, like a prince."

"Well, I'm glad to see you laugh, even if it's at my expense," he replied in a mock-stern tone. "And I can't say I've heard that one before. The joke only works in English."

I wasn't sure if it was the craziness of the day or my exhaustion, but I started laughing again. "I must be in a fairy tale. A handsome prince is rescuing me and my family from our dying world. Maybe I'm dreaming," I wondered aloud. The word "dreaming" triggered a yawn, my body's reminder that I was exhausted.

"Then let me walk you to your room," he said. "We'll both need our beauty sleep for tomorrow. The cameras can be brutal."

Beauty sleep. He was the most beautiful man I'd ever seen. I almost burst out laughing again, but I'd already embarrassed myself enough. As the giddiness wore off, exhaustion set in, and I stifled a yawn. "I think you're right." As he walked me up the stairs, I couldn't help but apologize. "I'm sorry. I normally have a better poker face."

"Poker face?"

"Oh, it means not giving away what you're thinking."

"Poker. That's a Gaian card game, right?"

"Yes, how'd you know?"

"It's come up in my reading."

"Reading?"

"I'm quite enjoying Gaian novels. There's some really bizarre science fiction out there."

"I can see why you'd be interested in those," I replied. "Science fiction is tied with fantasy for my favorite genre. What about you?"

"The science fiction, of course, but I'm also enjoying the wide array of vampire novels Earth has to offer."

I laughed. "You and Flora would get along nicely, then," I replied. My tone grew serious. "I cannot thank you enough."

"Not at all. I appreciate you bringing the oversight to my attention."

We were now outside my door, so I turned to face him. I dipped into my best Atlantean curtsy.

His lips twitched in amusement. "No need for those formalities without an audience. My father and I don't stand on ceremony as much as my mother, and luckily for you, she's back on Atlantis."

"Sorry for running out to the window. Maybe you could pretend tonight never happened?"

"I could, but I'm not sure I want to. I've got a lot of women to meet tomorrow, and now I know at least one of them has a sense of humor." He leaned in and whispered, "Best not to tell anyone about meeting me tonight. It might look unfair to the other contestants." My pulse quickened. The prince was handsome, and something about our interaction was electrifying.

"I understand," I said. "Well, good night, *Princely*."

A relaxed smile crossed his face. "Good night, Chloe," he replied. "Unless, of course, you're already dreaming."

The door closed, taking away my view of the prince, but not before I caught the mischievous twinkle in his eye. He was teasing me. Now that I was alone with my thoughts, I realized how ridiculous I had been the entire time.

In the minute or so before I fell asleep, a stern, internal voice chided me: *Don't get attached, Chloe. Remember Brett. You weren't even competing against another person. You were competing against no one then, and you lost. Guard the prince, but guard your heart too.*

Eleven

THE NEXT MORNING, I awoke to a knock on my door. My heart fluttered. Could it be the prince? Had I overslept?

"Ms. Woods?" chimed a mellifluous female voice. "May I come in?"

I scrambled out of bed and took a quick look in the mirror. I was a mess. "Um, who is it?"

"I'm your personal assistant here to help you get ready for today."

I relaxed a bit. "Oh. Come in. Sorry, I didn't know I would have an assistant." She wore a fitted, red tunic over black leggings. Her black hair was pulled back in an elegant braid and tied with red ribbon. Her eyes were sapphire blue, and a few freckles dotted the pale skin of her nose.

"Well, you do. I'm also your stylist and apparently your server this morning, too, since you slept through breakfast."

"Slept through breakfast? Was I supposed to know?"

"Everyone else figured it out."

Was I sleepy or was she as rude as she seemed? "I'm Chloe. Nice to meet you."

"I'm Melissa. Here's breakfast," she said, setting a large muffin on my bedside table. "I suggest you eat it in the shower—they want you ready by fifth hour."

Fifth hour? That made no sense. It had to be past five a.m. if I'd missed breakfast, but surely I hadn't slept so long that I was in a rush to get ready for an afternoon event. "What time is it now? What time zone is this?"

"We're on Atlantean time, same as the capital city of Atlantis. It's third hour already."

"I'm still lost. Can you translate for me?"

Melissa sighed and pointed at the muffin. "You eat. I'll explain." I happily complied, and took a bite of the muffin, which smelled strongly of cinnamon. "Minutes and seconds are still the same, but the Atlantean day is divided into twenty-eight units. There are eighteen hours in the day and ten watches at night. Each hour or watch is fifty minutes long. This comes out to a little more that twenty-three Gaian hours."

"What time is fifth hour in Earth terms?"

"Around ten in the morning."

I took another bite of muffin and winced as I tried to do the mental math. "I'm sorry, Melissa, but I'm a little fuzzy this morning. How many minutes do I have?"

She put one hand on her hip and sighed loudly. "One hundred minutes, which sounds like a lot of time until you realize that I'm one person and I have to do your hair, makeup, and get you into your dress. This will be your only chance to make a good first impression on the king, Atlantis, and, most importantly, the prince."

Memories of last night flooded my alert, conscious mind, and I cringed. Too late for that. "I'll get straight in the shower," I said, popping the last bite of muffin into my mouth. I wasted a few precious minutes trying to figure out how to turn it on. As pleasant as the warm water was, it couldn't wash away my embarrassment as I replayed the events of last night. I had cried, made a joke about the prince's name, and botched more than one curtsy. I would probably be sent away at the next opportunity. I'd lose to Lily. I'd lose the chance to win a ladyship. I'd fail to uncover any leads on possible rebels infiltrating the games. But, assuming it had all been real and not a dream, Flora and the Simmonses would be coming to Atlantis with me.

Three quick thumps sounded on the bathroom door. "Today is not the day for a long shower, Chloe."

"Do these not shut off after five minutes?" I asked.

"No, they do not," Melissa grumbled.

I'd been so lost in my thoughts that I'd been in the shower for over twenty minutes. Normally, I didn't zone out in the shower. The few times I had back home, it meant getting caught all soaped up with no way to rinse off. It happened occasionally, but each instance was an irritating reminder to be vigilant.

I shut off the water and dried myself with the fluffiest towel I'd ever used. A robe was already on a hook nearby, so I put it on and went out into my room where Melissa was waiting. She appraised my face, then ordered me into the chair in front of my small vanity. She anointed my hair with fragrant products, working out any large tangles with her fingers. Then she dried it with a special towel that absorbed most of the excess water, leaving my hair only slightly damp.

I wanted to ask her a million questions about the ship and Atlantis, but she was intent on her work. Instead, I studied my room via the mirror. My bed was large and comfortable with luxurious bedding. The bed frame and matching bedside table were decorated in a simple yet beautiful geometric pattern. There was a small closet where I'd stashed my ruined race clothes. I marveled that this space, which was at least twice the size of my bedroom back home, was mine for as long as I remained in the contest.

Whatever Melissa was doing to my hair hurt, but I didn't complain. She'd probably just hurt me more. Instead, I closed my eyes and tried to think of a way to salvage my chance at staying in the competition long enough to accomplish any of my goals.

"Keep your eyes closed and relax your face," Melissa said. "We're almost out of time, and you need makeup." I obeyed. "Stay still," she said, applying a thick layer of eyeliner. A makeup brush tickled my cheeks and eyelids. She painted my lips with a thin brush, and when she told me to rub my lips together, I finally looked at myself in the mirror. I was in shock. My hair was half up in a complicated knot of braids and half down in soft, tame curls. The makeup was much more than I usually wore, but I still looked like me, just better. That was the startling part.

"Wow. I look amazing."

"Almost unrecognizable," she quipped, though I thought the corners of her mouth had turned up into a pleased smile at the compliment.

"After yesterday, that's probably a good thing. I was afraid you were going to make me look ugly because you didn't like me."

"I take my responsibility seriously," she said. After a moment of hesitation, she added, "And I don't have anything against you. Time to get dressed, or you'll be late."

She rolled her eyes when I asked her to turn around while I put on some underwear, but she complied. She pulled a cream-colored dress from the closet. "This is a more traditional peplos-style dress," she said, directing me to step into it. She pulled it up, clasped it over my shoulders with golden brooches engraved with the same doubled-headed ax symbol I'd seen on the banners outside the dining hall.

"What's this symbol?" I asked as she was tying the thin, golden belt at my waist and pulling some of the material from the skirt up and through.

"It's the Agathon family crest," she replied. "How does it feel? Secure?"

"Yes," I replied.

"Good. It's not formfitting, but it's traditional for the opening ceremony. Now go. You've only got a few minutes."

"Thanks for all your help," I said, then rushed out of the room to see one other contestant in the hall who was also running late.

"Chloe!" she said.

"Riya?" I asked. "You're stunning!" She truly was. Though we were wearing the same ceremonial dresses, her lips and nails were painted a dark red that complemented her medium-brown skin tone. Her brown eyes were barely lined, and her eyelashes were full. Her shoulder-length hair had been slightly curled and pulled back into a messy updo with a few gold and crimson ribbons woven in. If I'd woken up earlier, Melissa might have had the time to do something fancy like that with my own hair.

"You look gorgeous too!" she said. After a lukewarm morning with Melissa, Riya's sincere compliment lifted my mood. "These PAs are incredible, right?"

I suppressed a snort. "Mine surprised us both with her skill, I think."

"We should hurry. There's a parlor down this hall..." She trailed off, and I followed after her.

We were the last two to enter. Talia glared at us, but Stefan nodded in our direction. They were running this show. After all, that's what it was. There would be cameras on us for the entire ceremony. Talia looked ready to stir up drama, though Stefan seemed less enthused by the prospect.

"The ceremony will take place in the throne room. The majority of the games will be held in both Atlantean and English for your benefit. First, you will swear allegiance to Atlantis and become dual citizens of Atlantis and Earth. Then the prince will welcome you and initiate the games with the lighting of the sacred fire. After that, you will take a seat, and the prince will call you back for a brief one-on-one introduction. When he dismisses you, return to your rooms and change for lunch where we'll announce the first trial of the Goddess Games."

That was all the direction we were getting. They lined us up in no particular order. Assuming the ballroom was the front entrance, they marched us deeper into the Palace Wing. We went up two flights of stairs and found ourselves in a hall even more richly decorated than the dining hall. Rows of seats were full, though three rows near the front had been left empty for us. Our guides took us past the seats and directed us to stand in neat rows in the gap between the guest seating and the dais where the king and prince sat.

The king occupied a large throne on the top of the dais with the prince at his right. Once we were in place, King Darius led us in the Atlantean pledge of citizenship. He was warm and charismatic, and I found myself eager to become one of his citizens. Prince Agathon stood and scanned the group of women as if looking for something or someone, but he made sure not to let his eyes settle on anyone for too long. Maybe he was checking us out. After all, he was stuck marrying someone in this room. How did he feel about that? Last night I hadn't thought to ask.

What if I had sixty men from a different planet, all vying for my affection? I must have been staring, because when the prince looked my way, we locked eyes for a moment. I looked down, still embarrassed by the state he'd seen me in last night.

The prince stood. He wore a tunic the same color as our dresses, presumably as traditional as our own. His shoulders were broad, though not as broad as the king's. His brown hair was slicked back, and his jawline had none of the stubble of last night. From the looks on the faces of the women around me, they thought he was hot. I couldn't disagree.

The smiling prince held out his arms and spoke in English. This address was for us. "Welcome! Atlantis is honored to have so many beautiful and talented women from Earth participate in the Goddess Games. I am gratified to have the opportunity to unite the two divergent lines of humanity born on Earth. Though we don't worship the Olympians as true divinities, we respect and emulate their greatest qualities. Through your outstanding race performances and willingness to leave your homes, you all have demonstrated the athleticism, tenacity, and independence of Artemis. I am looking forward to meeting each of you.

"Fellow Atlanteans," he continued, switching back into his native tongue and looking into one of the cameras hovering nearby, "I hope you will enjoy getting to know these young women over the next few months, as one of them will become our princess."

At the top of the stairs to the dais stood an unlit brazier raised up on a plinth. An attendant with a small torch came from the wing and handed it to him. The prince stepped forward and touched the torch's flame to the waiting coals, which burst to life. He returned the torch to the attendant and lifted his hands once more, booming out in Atlantean, "Let the Goddess Games begin." Then, he winked at us and said in English, "Good luck, ladies."

Everyone in the hall clapped and cheered. A few of the women giggled and blushed. On screens depicting Earth and Atlantis, we could see crowds cheering and waving. The screen displaying the Atlantean capital erupted in green and gold. The prince was grinning, and his enthusiasm made me smile, but I caught a glimpse of King Darius sitting far behind on the dais, a concerned frown wrinkling his forehead as he looked out at us. Did the king not want his son to marry a Gaian woman?

The prince turned, and King Darius's features changed, now a mirror of the prince's joy. Perhaps it had been fatherly concern for his son's happiness. The prince disappeared into a side chamber where he stood ready to personally greet and welcome each of us. We were directed to the reserved seats and then called one by one to introduce ourselves to the prince. We'd been told about the introductions, but Stefan had omitted one tiny, important detail. These introductions were being recorded and transmitted everywhere, including to the throne room where we could all watch.

I was glad I didn't have to go first. That honor went to a woman named Juliet Porter, who looked like she could handle the pressure. Her brown skin was flawless, and she wore her tight curls loose, pulled back from her face on one side with a small, golden comb in the shape of a scallop shell.

She stepped into the side room, but the moment the door closed behind her, she reappeared on the screen above the dais. Juliet's dark brown eyes lit up when she met the prince, and her full lips opened into a warm smile. She curtsied and bowed her head slightly as if she'd been trained in the art since birth. Her voice was clear and sweet when she introduced herself.

"I'm Juliet Porter, Your Highness," she said. "Of Lightbridge District."

"Welcome, Juliet," the prince said. "Tell me something about yourself." His deep voice held all the warmth I remembered from last night.

"My family was the one that welcomed your scouts into our home over a year ago."

The prince nodded as if impressed. "Then I am truly pleased to meet you," he said. After a few more exchanges, Juliet left the room to cheers from the Atlanteans in the throne room. The capital was going wild as well. I was calling it now, two minutes in. Juliet would be the next princess of Atlantis.

The thought deflated me for a moment until I reviewed my goals. I didn't have to win. I only had to stay in the games long enough to stop any rebel plots and earn a noble rank. Juliet and I could both win this in our own ways. Once I thought of it like that, my nerves eased.

If I could appear poised and undo a little of last night's damage, that would be enough for today.

I studied the other women as they were called. Petra Colvin looked like Aphrodite herself, and the prince seemed pleased to meet her. Colleen Blackthorn was regal and elegant, with warm, brown hair and a peaches-and-cream complexion. Willowy Carla Vanderwaal tripped when she entered. The prince helped her to her feet and put her back at ease. In fact, he seemed sincerely pleased to meet everyone, including the statuesque Lily Vasquez, caryatid on the outside, gargoyle on the inside.

He invited each woman to tell him some detail about themselves. Some were singers, painters, and even businesswomen. Others shared more modest talents. Between studying their curtsy form and trying to learn a bit about them, I struggled to think up an interesting detail about myself. I was a competent worker, but I didn't have many hobbies. I read books and played cards, but the prince already knew those things about me. They wouldn't make me stand out either. Last night he'd learned a bit about me, but I'd hardly learned anything about him. That gave me an idea.

When my name was called, I tried to emulate Juliet's calm, confident walk and smooth curtsy with moderate success. "Hello, Your Highness," I said, smiling sweetly. "I'm Chloe Woods of Belvale District."

His eyes lingered on my face, as if searching for the unkempt, red-eyed girl he'd met last night. "Lovely to meet you, Chloe. What detail would you like to share with me?" Today his voice was deeper and his tone formal for the benefit of the camera. He was playing a role as much as I was.

"My favorite pastime is reading," I replied. "Fantasy and science fiction, mostly." He smiled politely and opened his mouth to thank me for my participation, just as he had with all the other women, when

I spoke again. "Your Highness, would *you* be willing to share a detail about yourself?"

He cocked his head, caught off guard. "I suppose it's only fair," he said, beaming at me, then the camera. "I enjoy painting when I can find the time. Thank you, Chloe, for asking about me."

Once I was out of the room with the prince, I was immediately set upon by Talia. A camera drone was hovering over her shoulder, and she spoke into a handheld microphone. "Chloe, tell us, in one word, what's your first impression?"

One word? Should I describe His Highness from today or Prince Lee from last night? *Handsome. Tall. Gorgeous. Kind. Hot. Argh! Think!* I recalled his promise to help Flora's family. With nothing better to say than "I think the prince is kind and handsome," I decided to double down on my joke from last night. Looking past Talia and straight into the camera, I grinned and replied, "Princely."

It might have sounded like a stupid answer to some, but if Prince Agathon watched these, he'd understand my meaning perfectly. I continued past Talia to my room to change. If this really was a game, I would figure out how to play.

TWELVE

I RETURNED TO MY room, where Melissa was waiting for me.

"You came off as boring but nice," she said. "Could have been worse."

"Hi, I'm fine, thanks. How are you?" Melissa was about to say something, but I kept talking. "I get it. You're not paid to be nice to me. We don't have to be friends. You made me look as pretty as the other contestants today, and I'm grateful for that."

She wordlessly handed me some leggings and a tunic and motioned for me to go change. I obliged. The design was similar to the white outfits we'd worn right after the Artemis Trial, but this was much more comfortable and more flattering. The leggings were a shimmery golden brown, and the tunic was dark green with gold trim. The fabric hugged my waist and hips, and the neckline, well, it would have attracted unwanted attention back home. My hair and makeup were still intact, and I looked great.

When I emerged, Melissa was standing, hands clasped in front of her, eyes downcast.

"What's wrong?" I asked. I'd tried to keep my tone light before, but maybe I'd come off as harsh.

"I was rude this morning and just now. I really have nothing against you personally, but I've been unprofessional. For that I apologize. It won't happen again." She looked me in the eyes, and I could tell she meant it.

"Thanks, but will you tell me what's wrong? It may not be personal, but you're clearly upset about something."

"It's Earth," she replied. "I applied for this job because I wanted to see my ancestral home, where I came from. I knew things were bad, but the Gaians destroyed it. I realize it wasn't your fault and that you've suffered because of it, too, but your people broke something that didn't belong to them. That's why I'm upset." There was passion in her voice, and I suspected she was toning down the outrage.

My heart held that same anger. "The people who are largely responsible for destroying Earth are all dead. Hate them. Hell, most of us Gaians do. Seeing Earth from up here was... heartbreaking."

Melissa nodded. "I'll be nicer from here on out."

I chuckled. "At least when you were insulting me I knew you were telling me the truth. Feel free to throw in a brutal comment here and there."

"If you insist," she smiled back. "You should head to lunch. They'll be announcing the first trial soon."

"Thanks," I replied, heading out the door.

The dining hall was filling up, and trays of sweet and savory pastries had been placed at intervals down the long tables. Missing breakfast had cost me the opportunity to meet the other women this morning, so I looked around for Riya, the only person I knew aside from Lily.

"Chloe, over here!" Riya waved and motioned to a seat opposite her. Though we'd just met, she seemed genuine. I took the open seat.

"This is Lexi Callahan," Riya said, pointing to the redhead with freckles next to her, "and that's Carla Vanderwaal."

Carla was sitting next to me, and though I remembered her from the introductions because she tripped and fell, bringing it up might not be the best idea.

"Hi, nice to meet you. I'm Chloe," I said. I caught a whiff of the buttery pastry, and my mouth watered. One muffin was hardly enough after the morning's activities. "So what's for lunch?"

"Try this one," Riya said enthusiastically, handing me a triangular pastry. "Spinach and feta cheese."

I'd never had feta cheese before, but taking her recommendation wasn't much of a risk. I doubted anything that smelled so good could taste bad. After one bite, I was sold. "This is amazing."

"This one's curried vegetables," she said, pointing to a semicircular one, "and those little square ones are spiced fig."

I tried the curry, which was also excellent, and had a few of the small fig ones, just to be sure.

I didn't join in the conversation much, but I learned about the other women. Riya and Carla were from Highmont, and Lexi was from Lightbridge. Carla had been apprenticed to a teacher. Lexi had been an administrative assistant, and she'd hated it. Riya had applied to a nursing apprenticeship but hadn't gotten it. Instead, she'd been working as a receptionist for a pediatrician.

"What about you?"

"I missed out on an apprenticeship too," I said. "Weather analyst."

"I'm sorry, Chloe. I was so bummed when I didn't get a nursing spot, but I ended up enjoying working in the office. The kids who came in were so cute. And now I'm here! Can you believe it?"

I looked at her. Bright smile, bright eyes, and a kindness that reminded me of Flora. She belonged here. "I absolutely can."

By the time we'd finished eating, I knew Riya and Carla were looking for love. They kept wanting to talk about the prince. Lexi joined in, but she didn't share their enthusiasm.

Was that how I seemed? Was it obvious I wasn't that interested? I'd have to do a better job of faking it than Lexi. Sure, the prince was charming, handsome, and generous, but I wasn't looking to fall in love. I wouldn't make that mistake again.

Their swooning over the prince was brought to an end by the arrival of Stefan, Talia, and the camera drones. Stefan wore tailored pants and a tunic-style top, though it was shorter than the tunics I'd seen most women wearing. Both were dark purple with silver embroidery down the sleeves. Talia looked out of place next to him in a bright orange dress with a giant pink flower on one shoulder to match her pink leggings.

They led us up to the second floor, giving us a tour of the gym and the lounge, the two main common areas for the contestants. The gym contained all sorts of machines and equipment I had no idea how to use, but the lounge, full of books and comfy chairs, was cozy. Once we settled in the lounge, either leaning against walls or seated in cushioned chairs, Stefan revealed what we'd all been waiting for.

"Contestants, the first official trial of the Goddess Games, the Aphrodite Trial, will take place in two weeks at the Feast of Aphrodite. She represented love on ancient Earth, but also beauty. For us, the visual and performing arts are all connected to her by their beauty. She was a famous entertainer among the Olympians. She was rumored to have taken a few lovers during her time on Earth, so perhaps some of you can claim her as an ancestor! For the first few trials, including this one, you'll be working in teams of five.

"At the Feast of Aphrodite, each of the twelve teams will perform a dance in her honor. The members of the winning team will all get dates with the prince. The members of the three lowest-ranked teams will be eliminated from the games and moved to another part of the ship."

Talia stepped forward and picked up where Stefan left off. "You'll have your first meeting this afternoon with your team and a choreographer, who will help you bring your vision to life. You'll have practice every afternoon for the next two weeks until the feast. Starting tomorrow morning, you'll have classes in the mornings covering Atlantean history and culture, language, and etiquette."

Talia stepped back, and Stefan spoke once more, silencing the grumbles and giggles with a raised hand. "We know there's a lot to do in the coming days, but something we hope will take the edge off is knowing that the prince will meet each of you for one date before the feast. It will probably be short, considering there are sixty of you, so think about the impression you want to make. Also, as one final word of advice, the prince isn't the only one watching. Your dates will be recorded, and all of the trials during the games will be recorded. In order to win the Goddess Games, you must not only be Prince Agathon's match, but the right match for both Atlantis and Earth."

Talia read out the team assignments, and I listened for my name with only one thought on my mind. *Not Lily, not Lily, please, anyone but Lily.*

When my name came up, I was thrilled that not only had the universe put Lily on a different team, but I would be working with Riya and Lexi, two women I already knew and liked. Then there was Petra, whose blonde hair, blue eyes, and curves had evoked Aphrodite that very morning. That had to be an asset, right? The other woman's name, Trinity, was unfamiliar, and I guessed I'd have to meet her once we got to our assigned studio, number five.

Riya, Lexi, and I walked over together. Petra was already there, stretching. A few minutes later, a petite woman with olive skin and brown hair arrived. I recognized her from the shuttle that had brought me to this ship. She was from Belvale, though I'd never met her before and didn't remember her from the morning's introductions.

"Trinity?" Riya asked sweetly.

The woman nodded, and we all went around and introduced ourselves before our choreographer, Maia, showed up. She walked us through the expectations: our performance would last two or three minutes or less; costumes were expected; we could choose a Gaian or Atlantean style of dance, but the theme should be appropriate for the Feast of Aphrodite.

"Meaning what exactly?" Lexi asked.

"Your movements should be controlled, graceful, and alluring. Your song should be about love," Maia replied.

Maia showed us a few popular Atlantean songs and dances. Originally, Petra wanted to do something from Earth, but after seeing some of the Atlantean options, she found them acceptable. The new problem was the complexity of the dances. Petra, who claimed to be an excellent dancer, wanted to perform something complex. Lexi was on board, but I was hesitant, as was Riya. Trinity didn't voice an opinion.

Finally, even Maia's patience was growing thin. She forced us to settle on a song, so we chose an Atlantean pop song called "Waves of Love." Then she offered us three difficulty options for the choreography: easy and boring, challenging, or impossibly difficult. Petra chose impossibly difficult, probably to match her personality. The rest of us chose the challenging one, except for Riya, which surprised me. She wanted the easy and boring one.

"I'm not a great dancer," she said.

"Neither am I," I replied. "We've got two weeks to figure it out, though."

"I'm *not* doing the boring one," Petra said, crossing her arms over her chest. "The middle one will be dull enough as it is."

"Okay." Riya sighed. "I'll do my best."

Maia left to finalize the choreography for the following day, and the rest of us returned to our rooms exhausted despite not having actually danced at all.

I was wondering what I'd do to kill the thirty minutes or so before dinner when I noticed a sealed, square envelope on my vanity. My name was written across the front in Atlantean script. I recognized it from the name placard by my door. The note inside, however, was in English; more importantly, it was from the prince.

Thirteen

As I read the neat, English print, my pulse quickened. The prince had written me a letter. Even if my goal wasn't to marry him, the attention itself was gratifying.

Dear Chloe,

Meet me tonight in front of the window at fifth watch.
This is not a date.

Lee

I reread the note a dozen times before shoving it in my vanity drawer and heading to dinner. Despite the sumptuous aroma, I didn't have much appetite. When Riya asked, I attributed it to the ungodly—ungoddessly?—amount of food I ate at lunch. Truthfully, I wasn't sure why I felt so anxious. All I expected from the prince was good news about Flora. There was nothing in his words last night or his brief note today that indicated something had gone wrong. But if I eliminated that as the concern, I could only be bothered by the last line: *This is not a date.* There was no good reason that declaration should be so upsetting.

After dinner, Melissa dropped off my schedule and supplies for tomorrow's classes, including a watch that told Atlantean time and a tablet. I could take notes using a stylus, and they'd get converted to text and stored. It was amazing. I wished I'd had this when I was preparing for the weather analyst exam. On the side were various ports, one of which matched the commcard Mayor Russo had given me.

"It charges and connects wirelessly to other devices like displays. Eventually, you'll be able to make calls to your family, but not until things are more settled." A pang of longing hit me. I missed my parents. I wanted to see them, or at least talk to them, but with so many Gaians being brought aboard, calls with family had to wait.

Melissa continued, "A wired connection is sometimes needed, especially if the ship is caught in a storm."

Storm? Was there weather in space? I thought about asking what she meant, but instead I let my thoughts spiral. In hindsight, missing out on the weather analyst apprenticeship shouldn't have mattered so much to me. I would have been leaving Earth in a few years, but it had been *my* dream in a world where so little was actually mine, a chance to pursue my own career and make a difference beyond my family. Then the whole thing with Brett happened. I shook my head. Falling for him had been a glimpse at a life I thought would make me happy, but now his memory brought me nothing but shame.

Melissa left, and I messed around with my tablet to kill time until fifth watch by trying to imitate my name written in the prince's elegant Atlantean script. I checked my closet for other outfits and was not disappointed by the selection of dresses and tunics. In the end, I stayed in the fitted green tunic I had worn that day.

Finally, fifth watch, a little after midnight in Earth time, came around. The corridor was empty, and the lights were dim. They must have put the ship's lights on a day and night cycle to give people some idea of the time of day. The dining hall was once again dotted by a few diners, and a cluster of off-duty guards looked to be playing dice at the far end. I tentatively approached the top of the steps to the ballroom, glancing across the expansive mosaic that covered the floor.

The prince stood in front of the window, looking down on Earth. One of the sentries saw me and put out a hand to stop me, but the prince waved me over. With another motion of his hand, he dismissed the sentries, who fell back to stand inside the atrium. I descended the steps and crossed the ballroom to meet him.

"If anyone asks, you're just here for the view," he said.

Which one? The prince was captivating. Lee was dressed casually tonight in the men's version of what I was wearing, his fitted, blue tunic shirt showing off his muscular chest. His pants, though not leggings, were well tailored. His wavy hair was no longer slicked back, but tousled.

"It is nice," I said, having yet to so much as glance out the window. If I believed in love at first sight, the prince would have been a strong candidate.

He smiled, quickly looking me over before he said, "You look like you're feeling better today."

"Yeah, yesterday I was a little ridiculous from lack of sleep."

"And here I am keeping you up late again. I'll get to the point. I wanted to meet to give you an update on Flora." I fidgeted as I waited for the news. "She and her family have arrived, and they'll be situated near your parents."

"Did you talk to them?"

"No, I figured it was best if it didn't seem like I was directly involved, but Stefan will be arranging calls with family soon. I believe the Simmonses will be there for your call."

I threw my arms around the prince in a hug, pressing my cheek to his warm chest. My family—my *whole* family—was safe, and they'd be coming to Atlantis with me. I'd get to speak with them soon. Lee's body went rigid, and he gave me a clumsy pat on the back. I released him and stared at my shoes, heat rising in my cheeks. Even if the prince didn't stand on ceremony, I'd crossed a boundary. If he dismissed me tomorrow for my breach of protocol, I'd still have Mom, Dad, and Flora.

"Sorry. I didn't mean... I'm just grateful," I said apologetically.

He took my hand in both of his. "I'm honored I could help you in this way."

He was still holding my hand sending waves of warmth through me. This tension needed relief. "Maybe they'll teach us about prince-hugging etiquette tomorrow."

"I'm pretty sure it's right after curtsies in the curriculum," he replied, releasing my hand. "I do have a favor to ask, though."

"Oh?" I racked my brain, trying to figure out what I could possibly offer to a prince.

A lock of wavy, brown hair fell against his forehead. "It was nice of you to ask about my hobbies today, but I don't think it was fair."

"Why not?" I asked tilting my head to the side.

"Because you learned something new about me, but I didn't learn anything new about you. You already told me about reading."

"And cards," I agreed. "Not much else. I don't dance or paint or sing. I don't design engines or genetically modify crops. My job on Earth didn't leave me much time for hobbies." As I'd learned earlier in the day, a few of the other women had left impressive jobs to compete for a chance to marry the prince. Or rather, I imagined, to be the next queen of Atlantis.

"There must be something."

There wasn't, but if I didn't come up with something, I'd look boring. Hell, I was boring. I spent most of my free time with my family. In middle school, I'd played soccer and sung in chorus, but those pastimes didn't stick. The only exceptional use of my free time lately had been studying for the weather analyst exam. Though only slightly above boring, it was all I had.

"I was studying to be a weather analyst on Earth." I kept it vague. No need to mention that I didn't get the slot.

"What does that entail?"

"The weather in general has been bad for a while—floods, tornadoes, that sort of thing. So weather analysts watch storm patterns, call for necessary evacuations, and advise the government on where to invest resources."

"That sounds incredible. What drew you to it?"

I stared out at the planet. "Flora's grandparents had a farm that got completely wiped out in a flood thanks to some incompetent analysts. That's how her family got relocated and stuck in factory work."

"That's terrible."

"Yeah." I couldn't think of anything better to say. We both stared out the window at Earth in the silence that fell between us.

"That gives me an idea."

"About what?"

"Our date. I'm supposed to go on a date with each contestant, but there are only so many new places when you've got to plan sixty first dates on a spaceship."

"Well, it is a big ship," I teased.

"A big ship with lots to oversee." He sighed and checked his watch. "I'm afraid I have some duties to attend to." He walked me to the bottom of the stairs. "But I enjoyed our conversation. Good night again, Chloe."

"Good night, Princely."

He smiled at the nickname. His gaze followed me up the stairs like the sun through a magnifying glass, but I didn't dare turn to catch one more glimpse of the prince.

Once I was safely back in my room with the door closed, I sprawled out on my bed.

Lee was kind. I liked talking to him. And, as much as I hated to admit this part to myself, he gave me butterflies. The last time I'd felt like this, I'd made the mistake of trusting Brett. He had been kind and fun to hang out with too. No matter how much I enjoyed flirting with the prince, I couldn't get too attached. This was a game, and I wasn't going to win the prize I wanted by actually falling in love with Lee, though his charm would make it easier to play the part. Plus, soon he'd meet all the other women and fall for one of them. Maybe Juliet or Riya. Then our banter would become friendly, not flirty, but he'd keep me around until the end anyway. As odd a fantasy as it was, maybe I'd come out of the games with a ladyship and a friendship with the prince.

Fourteen

Melissa woke me up in time for breakfast the next morning. She dressed me in a dark blue tunic and leggings and left my hair down. When I reached the dining hall, Riya was practically floating she looked so happy.

"Chloe!" she squealed. "I get to meet the prince today! Our date is during dance practice, though."

"That's fantastic!" I said, grateful he had picked Riya as one of his first dates. He'd fall in love with her, and any guilt I had about my real motivations for entering the games would be irrelevant. "I'm sure we'll survive without you for one day."

"What about you?" Carla asked. "Did you get an invitation to meet the prince?"

I took a giant bite of the honeyed cake I was eating to bide a little time. Technically the answer was yes, but I wasn't supposed to share that information, and it hadn't been a date. That part was very clear.

"No date for me yet," I replied. Technically true was my favorite kind of true.

"Me either." Carla sighed into her eggs, and I turned to glance in the direction of the ballroom.

"Oh, I'm sure he'll invite you both out soon," Riya said. "I heard Juliet is his first date today, right after breakfast."

Juliet was at the next table, and she looked radiant. A bright blue, off-the-shoulder dress clung to her curves when she moved. She wore her tight curls down once more, and her makeup and jewelry were subtle. She was naturally beautiful, and her PA was capitalizing on it.

"Anyone else today?" I asked.

"Harmony," Lexi said, sitting down next to me with a cup of coffee in hand. "And Corinne." She pointed the two women out. They were pretty but paled in comparison to Riya and Juliet.

"Four dates in one day?" I whistled. "He's going to be busy."

"Even accounting for the fact that Atlantean weeks have eight days, not seven, if he's going to fit us all in, he's got to go on three or four dates a day," Lexi replied. "I feel bad for the women who end up with dates at the end of the week. He'll be exhausted."

Soon we all trickled out of the dining hall and headed to our various classes. My first class was on the Atlantean language with Riya. We could understand and speak it well enough, but this was an opportunity to expand our vocabularies and learn how to read and write the language. Today was relaxing because we learned the alphabet and how to write our names, or as close as they got. Atlantean used a different alphabet, and some names were better suited than others to the unfamiliar letters and sounds. The teacher, Ms. Viola, was impressed when she saw me writing my name in the flowing, Atlantean cursive the prince had used.

We also learned the basic Atlantean calendar. The first part I'd already learned from Melissa. Every Atlantean day was divided into eighteen hours and ten watches. Each hour or watch lasted fifty minutes, and minutes were fortunately the same as on Earth. An Atlantean week had eight days: Protomera, Deuteromera, Trimera, Tetramera, Pentamera, Hexamera, Heptamera, and Octomera. Most of their prefixes were Greek and commonly found in English, so I didn't have much trouble keeping them straight.

Every month was exactly four weeks, or thirty-two days, and there were twelve months, just like on Earth. We were currently in the

Month of Aphrodite, which would be followed by the Month of Persephone. Even though Atlantean days were slightly shorter, there were more of them in each year. I did the math, and an Atlantean year was about one week longer than an Earth year. A little more math told me that the prince was twenty in both Earth and Atlantean years. The Olympians had done an impressive job of picking out a new Earth-like planet.

Next, I headed to etiquette class, which was its own hell. A grumpy man named Mr. Phlox taught us about titles and curtsies, so if we didn't learn about hugging royalty tomorrow, I'd have to give Lee a stern talking-to the next time I saw him. Our date would occur sometime in the next two weeks, but I had a feeling it would happen sooner rather than later.

Culture and History was last, and I was happy to take a seat next to Lexi. We were learning about xenia today. After all, my family's xenia-bond had saved the Simmonses.

Our instructor, Ms. Angelos, was informative but dry. "When our scouts first came to Earth a year ago, their ship was damaged in a terrible storm while landing, and they needed a place to shelter. You all know the story, but your very own Juliet Porter and her family were the first to welcome them. This created a xenia-bond between our two worlds that had to be honored.

"This tradition was handed down to us by the Olympians. In fact, every Atlantean relocated by the Olympians first offered them hospitality. Xenia means offering food and shelter, no matter how humble, to a guest in need. This principle guides us, and now, it must guide you."

Lee had been right. His retrieval of Flora wasn't so much a kindness but a duty. He was bound to honor my friendship with her family like a xenia-bond now that I had been sworn in as a citizen of Atlantis.

After a long morning of classes, I'd worked up an appetite. Riya was missing at lunch, probably getting ready for her date. I was happy for her to begin with, but once dance practice started, I was thrilled she was elsewhere. Petra was impossible to please. She kept arguing with the choreographer until Lexi shut her down. I followed Trinity's example and kept my mouth shut as I tried to keep track of the moves.

I was not a good dancer, but with some practice, I thought I could get our routine down. I wouldn't make it look as good as Petra, or even Lexi, but they could stick me in the back. I didn't need to be the star of the performance. We just had to place high enough to stay in the games.

After dinner I spent some time practicing Atlantean letters in the lounge. I thought I'd find something to read, but all the books were in Atlantean, a detail I hadn't noticed the last time I was here. Instead, I copied interesting words and looked them up. I much preferred to get lost in my task than listen to Harmony recount the details of her date over and over again to anyone who'd listen. Petra finally told her to shut up because no one cared about how the prince had pulled out her chair for her like the perfect gentleman. The others kept their encounters private, but Riya kept zoning out and giggling. I reminded myself again that I was happy for her, then warned her what dance practice was like with Petra.

⋙ ⋘

The next day passed in much the same way. I vowed to spend time in the lounge later and get to know some of the other women. Today, Colleen, Lily, and two other women I didn't know had dates.

In Atlantean we practiced letters, a rote task I found soothing. Etiquette had yet to reveal anything about how to hug a prince, though we did learn the correct way to hold a teacup. History and Culture was a lecture on Aphrodite, whose month it was. Apparently she had an eye for design. She was an entertainer aboard the Olympians' ship who'd been elevated by her work as an artist. Dance and the visual arts, in particular, were her strongest domains. She'd been quite inspired by Earth's beauty during the Olympians' visit and had spent much time planet-side painting, sculpting, and creating other digital masterpieces that Ms. Angelos showed us. She'd also had affairs with several of the locals, which had caused her association on Earth with romantic love.

Overall, classes were good. Dance practice, on the other hand, was a disaster.

Riya, the prettiest of us all, was hands down the worst dancer I'd ever seen. I tried to help her when Petra screamed at her, but I couldn't do much since I struggled with the moves myself.

"We'll get the choreographer back tomorrow for costume directions, and she can walk you through it. I'm sure that will help," I said. That cheered her up a bit, and we went to shower before dinner. As I washed off the sweat from practice, I contemplated the inevitable prospect of coming in dead last.

After dinner, I was back in the packed lounge, skimming a picture-heavy book of fairy tales—socializing via osmosis, as I liked to think of it—when Lily strode in, looking glamorous in a black gown that showed off her figure. Her hair was still pinned in an intricate updo, though it looked a little loose. Her fair skin was glowing. She was a vision, and I hated her for it. I couldn't handle listening to her talk about her date. I quietly closed my book and tried to slip away.

"We had an *intimate* dinner in one of the smaller parlors," Lily was gushing, "and then we danced. He held me close and—"

Thump.

In my escape, I'd knocked a heavy book off the table near the door. Every head in the packed room snapped in my direction.

Lily was not pleased to lose the attention and be reminded of my existence. "Chloe, you're ruining my story."

"Oh, forgive me, Lily," I said in mock sincerity, "but I'd never be able to do *that* as well as you. I'm pretty sure a lady doesn't kiss and tell."

A few of the women laughed, and Lily's face grew dark. She struck back. "I doubt you'll ever have the opportunity. You have to get kissed first. If my brother didn't want you, what makes you think you stand a chance with the prince?"

"Simple," I replied, clenching my fists. "Prince Agathon has better taste."

I didn't wait for a reply this time. Laughter erupted in the lounge as I stormed down the hall. I'd let her get the last line by leaving, and I worried what she might be telling the others about Brett and me. I couldn't ignore her; whoever had come up with that bit of advice deserved to be left on Earth permanently. Her words cut deep because she was right. I didn't stand a chance with the prince. Sure, he'd been really nice so far, but I hadn't been chosen for a date yet. Plus, even Brett had been nice once.

That night I decided to visit the window again, more out of habit than hope that the prince would be there. At least that was what I told myself. Seeing Earth calmed me, as if it were an anchor. Earth was home, yet home wasn't on Earth anymore. The people that mattered to me were on this ship somewhere, and I was a citizen of Atlantis. Earth was a cautionary tale now, fit for fables and fairy tales—a cradle of life that had withered and endured a tragic and untimely death.

At first watch, I slipped out of my room. The dining hall was more crowded than the previous nights, but I'd come down much earlier tonight, around nine o'clock in Earth time. When I reached the top of the ballroom stairs, the sentries were missing. Two figures stood silhouetted against the window, gazing out at Earth.

The prince and one of his dates, still out together, stood in front of our window. No, not our window; *the* window. The woman must have said something funny because their laughter echoed through the ballroom. I retreated unseen from the entrance way and returned to my room. An uncomfortable tightness settled in my chest. I told myself it was because I wouldn't be able to see Earth tonight, and that it had nothing to do with the prince's date. Nothing at all.

Fifteen

By the next day, I'd settled into my routine. Melissa would prep me for the day, I'd go to class and lunch, and then we had dance practice before dinner. Today our choreographer was back to help Riya and to get our input for costumes. Petra, who was from Lightbridge, thought we should wear something bikini-inspired since the song was called "Waves of Love."

"We're supposed to look *alluring,* not trashy," Lexi said.

"Bikinis aren't trashy," Petra replied.

Lexi rolled her eyes. "On a beach, no, but at a dinner party?"

Inclined to agree more with Lexi than Petra, I turned to the choreographer. "Are bikinis over the top?"

"Yes, Ms. Woods. We're not especially conservative on Atlantis, but a bikini would be inappropriate for the setting. I'd go with something colorful and fitted. Short and low-cut would be acceptable."

"Then let's do that," Petra said. After some more arguing, we settled on sleeveless leotards and short, flowy skirts with layers of blue and green fabric for the twirling parts. The choreographer suggested bronze and gold accents that pulled the look together. The costumes were fun, like we weren't taking ourselves too seriously. We'd leave the serious costumes to the better dancers.

Riya had another rough day. We tried subbing in a few easier transitions, but it didn't help. Petra looked annoyed, but I kept the heat off Riya by asking Petra for pointers and corrections. She delighted in criticizing me, and Riya got some space to practice with a kind teacher. I, begrudging as I was to admit it, benefited from Petra's advice.

I wondered if the other groups were having this much trouble working together. From the looks of things at dinner, Lily's group seemed to love her. I wondered if this meant they hated me in solidarity. Another woman came back from a date, and she was swarmed by the others asking her questions. She was positively giddy, and I wondered if he'd kissed her or something.

Which would be fine, I reminded myself. *He doesn't have to fall in love with you—you shouldn't even expect him to. He just has to like you enough to keep you around.*

"I heard Harper was crying after hers," Riya said. "She wouldn't say what happened, only that it didn't go well."

"Do you know everyone?" I asked Riya.

"No, but if you stopped staring at books in the lounge all night, you might know a few more," she replied. "We know you're not reading because they're all in Atlantean."

"Hey," I said, crossing my arms. "They have pictures too."

Riya rolled her eyes and we both laughed, but she was right. As much as I might pretend that sitting in the lounge counted as recon, I hadn't learned anything that might help Russo—or protect the prince. I wasn't good at making new friends, and I hadn't been trying much since I got here.

"I get your point," I said. "I'll try harder."

When I returned to my room, Melissa was there. She handed me a square envelope with my name in a familiar scrawl across the front.

"It's from the prince," she said. "Is your date tomorrow? If you've got any details that will help me pick your outfit for—"

I missed the rest of what she said as I reread the note more slowly.

Chloe,

Not a date. If Melissa asks, this note is an update on your family. She's a brilliant PA but nosy. We leave Earth's orbit tomorrow, and I thought you'd like to take one more look. I've told the sentries to take a break at fifth watch again if you're interested.

Lee

I placed the card back in the envelope. "Not a date," I said. "Just an update about my family."

Melissa looked so crestfallen that I felt bad for concealing the truth, so I offered her some consolation. "Don't worry. I'm sure by the weekend the prince will be ready for boring, so he'll send for me."

Melissa put a hand on her hip. "That's not what I meant."

"I'm fine, really."

"It's early in the games anyway," she said. "I'll let you get some rest then."

I was too agitated to focus on Atlantean letters that night, so I cleaned my room. Melissa had made it clear she was my assistant, not my maid. I was putting away an abandoned outfit choice when I saw my Artemis Trial shirt and pants tucked away in the back of my closet.

With a jolt I remembered the commcard that Mayor Russo had given me. I'd been so overwhelmed and busy that I hadn't even tried to use it. I pulled it from the jean pocket where I'd hidden it and plugged it into my tablet. A small window appeared on the screen. There were two messages. The first instructed me on how to use the device. I could send and receive messages, and once opened, the messages would automatically be deleted after I logged off.

The second message was from Mayor Russo: *The first trial is a dance competition. Make friends and look for signs of a rebel.*

"Thanks for the thrilling update," I muttered to myself. If all the messages were like this, I wouldn't have to worry about getting any hints for the trials. I didn't want her help, but if she could get me to finals? Well, that would be tempting. With nothing of substance to report, I sent a quick reply: "Acknowledged." I might not want to work for Russo, but I'd still share any suspicions I had about contestants who might be rebels. I didn't want anything bad to happen to Lee. He was a good person. I stuck the commcard back in its hiding spot and found a different pair of jeans and a cute top. I wanted to wear Earth clothes for my final farewell to the planet.

When I reached the window, I was alone, just me and Earth. Had I misunderstood? I shrugged and stared, leaning up against the glass. I must have zoned out, lost in memories of birthdays in the park and how the rooftop garden of our apartment building changed from cloud gray to mud brown, then to glossy green. There was plenty of life still on Earth, but we hadn't done enough to stave off the apocalypse. Despite what I'd told myself when I used to dream about Brett, I'd never had a future on Earth, but maybe up here and on Atlantis, I would.

"May I join you?"

Lee had come after all.

"It's your window," I replied, shifting to the side. "But don't get any ideas. Remember, this is not a date." *Let's see how you feel about that reminder.*

"That's right. I only get one date per contestant these two weeks, and I'm planning something special for yours. I need a few more days, though."

I turned to face him and raised my eyebrows. "Is that why you kept writing that in your notes?"

"Of course. Why else would I write that?"

"I thought maybe you didn't want to go on a date with me."

He looked abashed. "That's not the reason at all. Though meeting you like this has reminded me of sneaking out of the palace when I was younger."

"Was it to meet a girl then too?"

"Of course," he said, this time with a grin. He grew quiet, and I wondered if he was thinking about her, this mystery woman. I didn't ask, though. It was a dangerous topic. He might still have feelings for her, or worse, he might turn the question around on me. "What about you? Did you ever sneak out?"

"It's hard in a small apartment. Can't go out the window a dozen stories up, and for some reason parents find a teenage girl oiling the creaky front door to be suspicious." He rubbed his mouth with his hand, suppressing a laugh. "Flora and I did manage to sneak out once to go to a concert, but we got busted when we came home."

"Was it worth it?"

"It was one of the most incredible nights of my life. We danced, we sang, we splurged on diner food and talked all night. I don't know what we talked about, but the memory of how I felt is stronger than any single piece of the evening."

"I know exactly what you mean. My best friend back home snuck me out of the palace for my sixteenth birthday. Lysander. You'd like him. Everyone does."

Lee grew silent, and I got the distinct feeling he was lost in some memory. A minute later he broke the silence. "This has to be our last non-date for a while, and though I doubt it's been the second most incredible night of your life, I want you to know th—"

"Chloe!" A shrill voice echoed across the ballroom, and I flinched. *Lily*. God, I didn't need more reasons to hate her, but the list kept growing anyway. She was dressed in a nightgown that left little to the imagination. Lee was checking her out as she approached, and I could hardly blame him. Even my *very* uninterested eyes were drawn to her cleavage and curves. She was effortlessly sexy, I'd give her that.

"Lily!" I returned her greeting, acutely aware of the details—or lies—she could spill about Brett. I should play nice, but I couldn't help myself. "You're looking rather, um, perky for such a late hour."

Lee caught my meaning but turned his laugh into a warm greeting. "Lily, it's nice to see you again so soon. Are you here to look at Earth before we leave?"

She nodded, moving to stand in between us, but the prince placed a hand on her lower back and guided her to his other side.

"Your Highness," she said. "Is it true we get calls from family tomorrow?"

I straightened, eager for his answer.

"Yes, I believe so," he said.

"Good, I can't wait to speak with my brother! You remember him, right, Chloe?"

I put on my best poker face. "Yeah, I remember him." Noncommittal. Polite.

Lee furrowed his brows. "You two knew each other on Earth?"

"Only a little." I yawned covering my mouth with one hand and arching my back in a stretch. That caught Lee's attention, and he offered to walk me back and give Lily a chance to say her farewells undisturbed. In a surprise to no one, she'd finished looking at Earth and joined us.

Back at the contestants' hall, my room was the first stop. From behind him, Lily smirked at me as if she'd won something. Maybe she had. He clearly found her attractive.

"Good night, Chloe. It was a pleasure to run into you."

"Good night, Your Highness," I said, dipping into a decent Atlantean curtsy. When I looked back up, his eyes locked with mine. The next moment, Lily was pulling him away. The last glimpse I caught before I stepped inside my room was Lily's arm wrapping around his like a treacherous snake as he walked her back to her room.

Sixteen

Lily was bragging at breakfast about how she'd run into the prince last night and that he'd found her irresistible. She left me out of the story, which was fine by me. I would happily continue under the radar. Instead, I studied the women around me, wondering if any of them could be a rebel. How would a rebel even act? Aloof? That made me a prime suspect. Trinity too. She was reserved, but that didn't make her guilty. If Riya and Lexi hadn't befriended me, I would have stayed in my room a lot more. Lily sought status, so her motives for joining were probably becoming queen. What about Harmony? She'd made a show of how much she'd enjoyed her date a few days ago. Maybe it was an act to make her seem genuine. I was about to take Riya's advice and try to get to know Harmony a little better when the table of contestants began to empty.

"Calls to family!" one woman squealed as she hurried past. After barely having a chance to say goodbye back on Earth, I raced back to my room and grabbed my tablet. Directions on how to make calls had been sent to all contestants. I practically vibrated with excitement when the vid-call went through. My parents looked healthy and happy as ever, and the Simmonses were there with them.

"I can't believe they moved us up to the first wave because of you!" Charlotte said.

"Yes, I didn't think that we would count as family by their defini-tions," Mrs. Simmons said. "Of course that's exactly how we think of you all."

I returned her smile. "It has to do with something they call a xe-nia-bond. It's hard to explain."

They asked me about the contest, and if I'd met the prince, but I stayed vague. He was nice. The food was great. I'd made some friends. I was still waiting on my date with the prince. All true. I omitted how awful Lily and Petra were and my secret not-dates with Lee. There was no time to talk to Flora alone, and I didn't want to reveal these details to the whole family. The call was over too soon, but seeing them all safe and secure filled me with a peace I hadn't known I was missing.

Each morning Melissa reassured me I'd get my date soon. I used the days of waiting to talk myself out of whatever I had started to feel for the Atlantean prince. That warm, fuzzy feeling he gave me was gratitude and nothing more. In fact, it was easier to stay focused on my goals when Lee wasn't around, though the mayor hadn't sent any new messages.

After a full Atlantean week, we got to see the first episode of the prince's dates. The opening ceremony and introductions had been livestreamed, but the dates from the past week had been recorded and edited into a short program. The show started off with a montage of the prince and the contestants, then our answers from when Talia asked us to describe the prince in one word. Most went for things like handsome, strong, charming, but no one else had said princely. It had sounded funny in my head but seemed a bit stupid on air. Oh well. Can't win them all.

We watched clips of the prince on his dates: dancing with Lily, dining with Colleen, and joking with Riya. A few women had been given more time than the others in the episode and on dates, but Juliet was clearly the featured contestant. She and the prince were strolling arm in arm down one of the hallways, no buffer activity needed to make the other's company bearable.

"What made you join the competition?" he asked her.

"Earth and Atlantis need union. I love Earth and its people, and I'm getting to know Atlantis. I want to love Atlantis too."

From the tone of Juliet's voice and the way she was looking at him, one could safely substitute "you" in place of "Atlantis" and preserve the meaning. At the end, we were promised more tantalizing footage next week, followed by live coverage of the Aphrodite Trial.

I felt off the whole day. I tried to pinpoint the reason—some bad food, not enough sleep, Lily's continued existence—but the answer was staring me in the face. I was upset because it had been five days since I'd heard from the prince. It wouldn't be the first time I'd misjudged a guy's interest in me. I worried that my time in the games was limited.

Finally, on the tenth day of dates, just over halfway to the Aphrodite trial, I got the invitation. Melissa played it cool, but I knew she was excited.

"You're his afternoon date!" she said, reviewing the invitation. "Hmm, casual attire, but we can dress it up a bit, I think."

"If I nail this date, maybe I'll miss part of dance practice," I quipped.

"It can't be that bad. Isn't Riya doing better?"

"Barely. She's getting the general idea, but she's terrible when it comes to individual moves. Not that I'm great either, but she's way off."

"Want me to hide contraband in her room and get her kicked out?" Melissa was deadpan, but the second my eyes went wide, she burst out laughing. "Kidding, geez!"

Class was the same old thing. I enjoyed learning Atlantean, etiquette was a necessary evil, and History and Culture was interesting, if at times boring. Today's lesson was on culture. The Atlantean word on display was my only preview, but from the letters, it looked like we were going to learn about something called *ah-reh-tay*.

"Since you're all in this competition, I think it's important that you understand the Atlantean concept of *arete*. Though the concept has changed over the years, arete is excellence in mind, body, and spirit. The future princess is expected to embody arete."

Everyone glanced toward Juliet, who pretended not to notice. She did seem to be excellent in every way. I'd only talked to her a few times, but she'd been warm and funny. I liked her, but so did everyone else. She was always surrounded by people, which meant I hadn't gotten a chance to know her well. I had safely crossed her off my list of potential rebels.

Ms. Angelos put up some prominent examples from Atlantean history of men and women who embodied the ideal, and from her description, they sounded like thoughtful, talented people.

"Arete doesn't mean that you are flawless. It means that you have the drive and ambition to better yourself each day. To curb your vices and cultivate your virtues. I often think of arete as a mindset rather than a destination."

I cocked my head, thinking it over. Arete. I liked it. Maybe that's what I'd felt when I was studying for the weather analyst apprenticeship. I hadn't fully realized the sense of purpose it gave me until the dream was gone.

I had a quick lunch, then went to meet Lee. Melissa had put me in a bright blue dress, with stylized ships embroidered in silver along the hem. Lee was standing by the window in a white tunic shirt and Agathon green pants. Stefan and Talia stood nearby with the camera drones, ready to capture our greeting.

"Ms. Woods," he said, nodding in my direction. "You look lovely."

So formal. But with the cameras here, I understood. We weren't supposed to know each other beyond our brief introduction after the opening ceremony. "Thank you, Your Highness. Lucky for me, my PA has a real eye for these things."

I turned my attention from the prince to the window. We'd left Earth days ago, and I hadn't had a reason to return to the ballroom until now. I'd assumed the view would be endless black, but it was the opposite: a mesmerizing rainbow of light streaked past as the ship sped to Atlantis.

"It's beautiful," I said.

"More beautiful than Earth?" he asked. "The sentries mentioned you'd come to gaze out the window before we left orbit."

My eyes glittered at the memory stirred up by those words, even if our meetings at the window didn't exist for the cameras. "Earth was beautiful despite its flaws, but I've learned that my true home isn't a place. It's people. My family is aboard, and so this is my home." *You saved Flora, and I will forever be grateful.*

"Well said." He studied me, and warmth spread across my cheeks. He lowered his voice so only I could hear. "I'm sorry you had to wait so long for our date, but it took a little more planning than dinner and dancing."

"As long we're not actually dancing, I'm sure it will be great," I replied.

Talia and one of the camera drones approached, but Lee raised a hand to stop her. "I'm sorry, but you'll have to leave us here. The cameras aren't allowed into the area of the ship we'll be visiting."

Talia's eyes looked ready to bulge out of her head, but Stefan had a twinkle in his eye as he looked from me back to Lee. "Understood, Your Highness. Perhaps we could hear how it went when you return?"

"Of course, Stefan."

The prince took my hand and led me to the vestibule that contained the transporter access point. I hadn't left the Palace Wing since my arrival nearly two weeks ago. "Where are we going?" I asked, following him into the transporter. It reminded me of an elevator with a handrail along its walls, except it was larger and followed both horizontal and vertical tracks hidden within the ship's bulkheads.

"Did you know that there are storms in space?" Lee asked as soon as the doors closed.

"Melissa mentioned them once. What are they like?" I could feel subtle shifts as the transporter changed direction, though I didn't need to use the railing stabilize myself. We were now moving vertically, I thought.

"Think of them like clouds of radiation that travel through space until they dissipate. Certain areas in space are more prone to them."

"Are they dangerous?"

"In some ways. But I don't want to spoil everything. We'll be at astrozalemetry soon."

"Astro-what?"

"Astrozalemetry. It's the department that analyzes these storms and gives the ship updates and warnings."

That's when it clicked. "Like space weather analysts."

He grinned. "Exactly."

The transporter doors opened, and he led me across the hall into astrozalemetry. It was unlike any room I'd ever seen. The ceiling was high and the lights were dim. The walls displayed storm models. Workstations were spread throughout the room with most arranged in a vague circle around the center table. Projected over the table was a large three-dimensional map showing the ship's course between Earth and Atlantis.

A tall woman with black hair and olive skin acknowledged our arrival. "This is Commander Della Charis. She's in charge here, and she can do a better job explaining what they do. Commander, this is Chloe Woods."

"I'm always happy to talk about our work!" she said, her gray eyes bright with enthusiasm as she reached out and shook my hand. "We've set up buoys along this course and other routes we frequently take that can transmit local data back to us, including information about radiation storms. Some areas of space are prone to these types of phenomena, but not everywhere. Unfortunately the shortest path between Atlantis and Earth experiences quite a bit of this interference. We take the data from the buoys and use it to project where storms will be and whether or not we should avoid them."

"On Earth we had no option to avoid storms," I said. "Is there a reason you wouldn't avoid one?"

"Some areas are constantly stormy," she admitted, "so it's difficult to fully avoid any contact. But the ones that are smaller, we absolutely do. The storms interfere with many of our ship's systems, but with a little warning, it's no problem."

"Are they dangerous?"

"They can be, but anything that would pose a real threat we make sure to avoid. Life support, hull integrity, and other critical systems are well shielded."

"What do you do when there are no storms?" I asked.

"She's a curious one, Your Highness" Commander Charis said to Lee, who was leaning against the center table.

"I wouldn't send you anyone less worthy," he replied, looking pleased.

Send? What did that mean?

"Well, Chloe, we get to sort through the other data from the buoys. Like over there," she said, pointing to one of the screens. "We're just now approaching a storm-prone area of space, so in the meantime, we've been studying readings from a red giant that's close to collapsing. But that work will have to be put on hold," she said, gesturing to the 3D projection in the center of the room. She entered some commands on the nearest console. "As you can see, the forecast is about to change."

I looked at the model, which had zoomed out to show the ship's course. There were regions of pink, purple, and blue, all moving dynamically along our projected path.

"Do the colors show the intensity of the storm?" I asked, taking a step closer.

"Yes. What you see now is based on our buoy data, so it's slightly delayed, but our programs use the actual data to extrapolate where the storms will be once we reach high-activity areas."

"Incredible. Earth's programs are nowhere near as sophisticated."

"Thank you, commander," Prince Lee said, beaming at his officer. "Do you have a spare station where we could run some models or maybe look at the red giant data?"

"Of course. Back in that corner. They're on their break for another twenty minutes."

Lee and I played around with the simulations on one of the screens. The details were very different from what I'd studied to become a weather analyst, but I could feel a familiar sense of purpose radiating from the people in the room.

When it was time to leave, I gave Commander Charis my sincerest thanks. Once we were back in the transporter, Lee studied me once again.

I smoothed down my blue dress. "What's wrong?"

"I've arranged for you to come here and learn about our monitoring systems a couple of times a week. You could even call it an apprenticeship if you like." His tone was light, but I could see that he was gauging my reaction. "If you want to. This is an opportunity, not a requirement."

I opened my mouth to thank him, only to close it again. Words alone weren't enough. I hoped that hugging the prince on a date was acceptable. "Thank you," I said. His arms folded around me this time, returning the embrace. Just as I was about to release him, he pulled me closer, reassuring me that this was exactly where I belonged. Warmth trickled through me wherever our bodies touched. I was supposed to be protecting him, but he radiated safety.

I hadn't noticed the transporter slowing, but I did feel it stop. The doors opened silently, and instead of the entry to the Palace Wing, a crew member in blue stood there. Lee let me go at once, putting distance between us. The spell was broken. The crew member, who'd been focused on his tablet, looked up at the motion.

"My apologies, Your Highness. I'll take the next one." He straightened and gave the prince a salute, but the corners of his mouth curled into a slight smile.

I was blushing as if we'd been caught in a much more compromising position, and to my surprise, so was Lee. The door closed again, and Lee sighed. His face was turned so I couldn't read his expression, but I was pretty sure he was embarrassed by what his crew member had probably assumed.

"I'm sorry, but they never did teach us hugging etiquette," I said, trying to alleviate some of the awkwardness.

He laughed, and the tension dissipated. "I'll be sure to give you a private lesson later, because you'll be missing etiquette class on your astrozalemetry days."

I beamed at him. "Thank you. This opportunity is incredible. And not just because I'll be missing etiquette."

"I was afraid you wouldn't like it."

"Wouldn't like it? This is the best date I've ever been on," I said.

Lee shook his head. "I've set the bar too high for next time, haven't I?"

Too soon the transporter slowed again. Lee led me by the hand to where Talia and her camera drones were waiting. His shields went up the moment they saw us. The friendly ease of our date had been replaced with polite formality. The prince asked me a few questions about what I'd thought of the ship and crew, thanked me, and kissed my hand. I felt the performance of it, but Talia loved it. He had to get ready for his next date and left me to the production crew.

Talia asked for details, like what I thought of the prince after our date, and other questions similar to what she'd asked other candidates on the first date roundup episode. When she lost interest in what she clearly considered a boring date, Stefan stepped in. "Do you know why he took you on a such an unconventional date that, judging from your smile, you enjoyed? I can't imagine many young ladies would prefer storm watching to dancing."

I couldn't give away our conversations in front of the window. While Lee was technically allowed to see contestants outside of official dates, I got the impression it was discouraged.

"I was studying to be a weather analyst on Earth, so he thought I'd be interested to learn about the radiation storms in space and what a weather analyst looks like on this ship."

Stefan cocked his head to one side, and I could have sworn he was about to ask me how the prince knew but then thought better of it. "Thank you, Ms. Woods. We won't keep you from practice any longer. I have a feeling the prince would hate to see you eliminated in the Aphrodite Trial."

He'd meant it to be light and joking, so I smiled and agreed I should get to practice. On the inside, I panicked. I hurried off to our studio, only to pass Riya running down the hall in tears.

SEVENTEEN

"Riya!"

I tried to get her attention, but she disappeared up the stairs. I debated whether to follow her or go to practice. She seemed like she needed some time alone, and I figured the fastest way to get answers was to head to our studio and ask Trinity and Lexi. I already had an idea of what had happened, so when I opened the door, I wasn't surprised to find Lexi and Petra inches apart, shouting at each other.

"*Hey!*" All heads snapped in my direction. "What's going on?"

"Petra went off on Riya, who ran off crying," Lexi said.

"She's terrible!" Petra flung her hands in the air. "She'll ruin all our chances."

"You're the terrible one!" Lexi shot back. "Those things you said to her! Do you really think that helped?"

"Oh, please. Nothing can help her! Our best bet is for her to quit. We're not going to win or anything, but if she's in our performance, we are guaranteed last place."

"Stop!" I raised my voice again. "We'll figure something out. There must be some other modifications we can make—"

"The dance is already so boring that we'll be lucky if the audience doesn't fall asleep," Petra said, wrinkling her nose.

She was right about that. The dance was boring. We'd cut out a lot of the cool parts to make it easier, but the overall performance suffered for it. "Let's call practice for today. I'll check on Riya, but we all need to keep thinking of something we can do to make it passable."

"Whatever," Petra said, bumping into me as she stormed out. Trinity said an awkward goodbye, leaving me alone with Lexi.

Lexi sat down and put her fingers to her temples. "I would never say this in front of the others, but Petra's right about how bad Riya is. Unless the other teams are worse than us, we're going to lose the Aphrodite Trial."

I wasn't ready to leave the games yet. I had Lily to beat, a new sort-of job, rebels to uncover, and maybe some feelings that I didn't want to think too hard about. "We just need to find our angle," I said. "Maybe Riya can stand to the side and play the tambourine or something while Petra dances circles around us."

Lexi chuckled. "I bet the prince would still be impressed. Riya is the prettiest one on our team."

"She really is." I sighed. "I'm going to go check on her now if you want to shower and get ready for dinner."

"Thanks."

I braced myself. I didn't know what to say to Riya. Platitudes raced through my mind. *If at first you don't succeed, try, try again. Hard work pays off. Everything works out in the end.*

Bullshit. All of it. She'd been trying. She'd been working hard. It was not working out. I ended up at her door with nothing to say, but I knocked anyway. I'd follow her lead.

Her PA opened the door, and the sound of running water told me Riya was in the shower before her PA could. "I guess it's not a good time. Could you tell her Chloe..." I trailed off, listening. Riya was singing in the shower. Not just singing, but belting out a trendy pop-rock song from a year ago, "Frenemy." I recognized it immediately because she was at the chorus.

Get out of my face, stop wasting my time
I don't need a friend who only whine whine whines
Sometimes I just gotta scratch that itch
and call you what you are: a—

Her PA loudly cleared her throat, but I already knew what the next word was. I was shocked, not by the colorful lyrics from such a sweet person—the song was fitting for the afternoon—but rather by how amazing she sounded. Her voice was clear and powerful. When she'd said her talent was singing, I'd never expected this.

"Please tell her I stopped by, and ask her to come to my room before dinner if she feels up to it."

"I will, miss," the PA said, closing the door and muffling the volume of Riya's song.

I walked back to my room, wishing we were in a singing contest instead of a dancing one. I wasn't much of a singer either, but Riya, not Petra, deserved to shine in front of the prince. The thought gave me an idea, so I messaged Melissa with a few questions. While I mentally plotted out the details, Riya knocked on my door.

"Come in."

She entered and sat down on my hastily made bed, getting right to the point. "Practice was awful," she said. "Without you there to distract her, Petra went on and on about arete and how I was a terrible dancer and how I would make an awful queen, how the prince wouldn't like me once he realized how terrible I was, and—"

"Slow down," I said, putting a hand on her shoulder. "Forget everything she said to you. She's a terrible student because the whole thing about arete today was that we're striving to be *our* best, not to be the *literal* best. No one who's watched our practices would dare accuse you of not trying."

"I'm still dragging the team down."

"I'd argue that Petra and her sour attitude are the real drag." Riya stopped fidgeting, her eyes wide in silent agreement. "I'm not going to lie to you," I said. "You're a terrible dancer, but the rest of us aren't that great either. We need to find a different way to stand out."

"Oh, I think we'll stand out," Riya muttered. "On the wrong end of the spectrum."

"I'm not sure about that. I heard you singing in the shower when I stopped by earlier. It was amazing! You can really sing."

"Thank you." She looked back up at me, eyes sparkling. "I learned from my mom. I'm not as good as she is, but I've sung at a few small parties. Mostly for family and friends."

"How would you feel about singing at the Feast of Aphrodite at the end of the week?"

"I don't know. Is that even allowed?"

"I asked Melissa, my PA, and she thinks so. She checked the fine print for me. I wanted to see if you'd even be up for it before I asked the choreographer. If you're in the center singing, you'll do more limited dance moves, and if you get flustered, you can just stop moving and pretend you're really focused on singing or something. Or start one of those over-the-head clap things."

Riya wrinkled her forehead in thought. "Petra will never let me be in the center. The singer is the star."

"I've got an idea to keep her in check. So, if I can get Petra on board, you'll do it?"

She nodded. "Anything to avoid having to dance."

"Great. I'll figure things out with the choreographer tonight and share the details at practice tomorrow."

She stood to leave but hesitated at the door. "Thank you. For the first time since we started practicing, I feel hopeful."

"Don't thank me yet. We've still got a few hurdles to get over."

"I know, but not many people would be willing to put someone else in the spotlight."

"I have to confess that it's a selfish idea," I said. "I want our team to do well enough to move on, and that means playing to our strengths."

"That's still a totally different mindset than Petra's. She'd never come up with an idea that took the attention away from her."

I gave her a reassuring smile, and once she left, I got to work. I asked Melissa where I could find Maia, our choreographer. I caught her right as she was leaving her office. Her face fell when she saw me, and I didn't blame her. Our group had been very high-maintenance so far. She must have sensed my desperation because she heard me out. By the end, she'd agreed to come to our practice again tomorrow.

I grabbed a quick dinner and collapsed onto my bed, exhausted. Between my date and the dance drama, the day had been long. If my plan worked, I might have a chance to go on another date with the prince. To find the rebel. To stay in the games long enough to earn a ladyship. That was why I was doing this, right?

⟫⟫⟩ ⟨⟪⟪

I was worried that no one would show up to practice after Riya and Petra's fight the day before, but everyone was there—even Petra, though she came in and started stretching on the far side of the room. Trinity arrived last, and I sighed in relief.

"I was thinking about how to fix our dance, and the muse struck me," I said.

"Upside the head with a bat?" muttered Petra, loud enough for the rest of us to hear.

I ignored her and continued. "Riya can't dance, but she could sing water from a rock. If we do our dance like a live musical performance,

Riya can do limited movements while she sings. We'd do the regular moves."

"And let her steal all the glory?" Petra stalked over and shot a dark glance at Riya.

"If we don't make a change, we're leaving the Goddess Games at the end of the week. We all know it. Our options are to either give Riya the spotlight or lose, and I hate losing. Riya, will you sing the chorus so they get it?"

I expected her to look nervous, but singing was her element. She didn't even wait for me to start the music.

Waves of love, crashing down
Got my feet pinned to the ground
Waves of love, you come and go
But I can't take this ebb and flow
Anymore

Riya's eyes had been closed while she sang, but now she popped them open expectantly.

"Wow," Lexi said.

"That was great," Trinity chimed in.

Petra folded her arms. "She can sing. We agree on that," she said. "But this isn't fair."

"Petra, you are the best dancer on the team. We're not questioning that. During the instrumental bit before the final refrain, you'll have a chance to take center stage and show off what you can do. You and Riya would be carrying the team."

Petra mulled it over. "Fine," she said.

Lexi scoffed, but I addressed her too. "Lexi and Trinity, if you want, we can spotlight each of you for the verses."

"What about you? There are only two verses."

I shrugged. "I don't think I want the spotlight on this one. If we make it to the next trial, hopefully it will be better suited to my talents."

"Oh, please. Your list of talents is so long that reading was the most interesting hobby you could share with the prince during your introduction on day one." Petra smirked.

I bit back my retort. I needed Petra's cooperation today with the choreographer more than I needed to have the last word.

Lexi and Trinity learned a few special sequences for their verses once Maia showed up. Things were coming together. By the end of practice, we were exhausted but smiling. That had never happened before.

We had five rehearsal days left, and we made each and every one count. The night before the Aphrodite Trial, all sixty contestants gathered in the lounge. Stefan and Talia showed us the episode of the second week of dates. I was barely a blip in the roundup episode. Carla, a short blonde named Isabelle, and Petra were featured. The rest of us got ten seconds of footage and a few lines of dialogue if we were lucky. There were a few seconds of the prince leading me off to the transporter and then the performative hand kiss upon our return. They had cut out my interview entirely. I didn't know whether to be grateful for the privacy or upset at the slight. Between my date footage and the sense of impending doom surrounding tomorrow's performance, I doubted I would be a part of the Goddess Games much longer.

EIGHTEEN

AT BREAKFAST THE DINING hall was abuzz with conversation and speculation about the day's trial. My friends, to my relief, didn't want to talk about dancing anymore.

"I realize I never asked about your date," Riya said. She stabbed another pancake off the platter with her fork and set it on her plate. "What did you do? I couldn't tell from the episode last night."

"He showed me some of the ship and took me to astrozalemetry. It's kind of like the spaceship version of weather analysis."

"Oh, that sounds..." She trailed off.

"Interesting," Lexi finished for her. "He took me to the gardens, just like everyone else."

I'd been jealous of the dates in the gardens, since they reminded me of my rooftop garden back home, but maybe Lexi had a point. The date had been perfect—uniquely planned for me.

"But the gardens are lovely," Riya said playfully. "And as long as you had fun on your ship tour, Chloe, that's what matters. Plus, starting tomorrow, they're going to let us visit the gardens whenever we want. Juliet asked for permission for everyone."

"I'll have to thank her." It didn't hurt to be in the good graces of the front-runner. My motivations weren't entirely pure, but my gratitude was sincere. I was in awe of Juliet. I suspected Juliet would be the next princess. From everything I'd seen so far, Juliet had been born for the role. Sure the prince seemed to like me, but he was nice to everyone. The date episodes proved it.

Melissa took her time getting me ready. She'd coordinated with my teammates' PAs to make sure our group's look would be cohesive. Stage makeup involved more glitter than it had a right to, and though I found the look over the top, she assured me it was perfect for the performance.

I assumed we'd be in the ballroom, but instead, a large reception hall had been decorated for the occasion. We'd been arranged out of sight in an adjacent room that connected directly to the stage, but we took turns peeking into the reception hall from behind the curtains. Guests dressed in fine Atlantean clothes crowded around circular tables spread throughout the room. I caught sight of Talia with a couple of crew members off to the side, controlling the handful of camera drones hovering near the stage. The event would be livestreamed, so she needed the extra help.

Right in front of the stage was a rectangular table with four seats. I wondered if it was for the royal family, but Stefan stepped on stage, and I didn't have to wonder much longer. He was the emcee for the evening, and he introduced the judges who filed in and took their seats at the table.

"We are honored by the presence of our three judges. Please welcome Benton Elgos, son of the queen's advisor Deltor Elgos and junior advisor himself to the king." Benton's black hair was cropped close to his head, and he looked about twenty-five. *Guess that's why he's a junior advisor*, I thought.

"Next, Marlena Cintera, known for her record-breaking dance performances at the Atlantean Cup." Marlena, a lithe blonde, waved to the crowd. "And finally, Mario Ligata, responsible for popular dance fads like the Crackle." Mario stood and did a brief dance move I assumed was the Crackle to whooping and applause from the audience.

A politician and two dancers. Benton looked amused, Marlena's smile was tight and polite, and Mario was leaning back, a crooked smirk across his face.

Stefan continued. "And of course Prince Agathon must have a good view."

Mario wolf-whistled when Lee made his entrance. His wavy, brown hair had been tamed into an off-center part, and he looked incredible in a formal, green tunic and tailored pants with intricate, golden embroidery. Lee shook hands with Mario and Marlena and gave Benton a shallow nod. As Stefan kept talking, Lee took a seat at the judges' table. Once the attention moved away from him, he glanced up at the stage and smoothed down his tunic. Was he nervous?

Stefan calmed the crowd and introduced the first team without further ado. They had chosen an old, well-loved classic from Earth that the judges seemed to enjoy. The second team chose a catchy, upbeat Atlantean song.

Stefan was gracious and efficient, and the performances ran smoothly from one to the next. I was able to watch from the wings along with the other teams who had yet to perform. Lily's team, clad in skintight shorts and low-cut crop tops, performed a song from Earth that I thought was too vulgar for the setting, but the younger judge, Mario, loved it.

"Sounds like something you might sing in the shower," I whispered to Riya. She giggled, relieving some of the tension.

Juliet's group went next, and even though they were only the third group, I knew they were the winners. Juliet and Colleen were perfectly poised, as were the other women in their group. More importantly, their song was a remixed mash-up of an Earth song and an Atlantean song. The two melodies and lyrics worked perfectly together, and their performance was flawless. The significance of the fusion of Earth and Atlantis was not lost on the judges. Marlena and Benton clapped enthusiastically while Mario whooped and pumped a fist in the air.

Carla's team was next, and they were a disaster. Carla's clumsiness had been endearing during the opening ceremony, but now it threw her whole team off. The next few performances went well, but only one of them stood out.

Out on stage with the lights shining in my face, I couldn't see the judges or Lee. I could almost pretend that he wasn't watching. Almost. My stomach fluttered, and my pulse thrummed in my neck as I got into position and put on my brightest "showbiz" smile. I was in the back with Trinity. Petra and Lexi, the two best dancers in our group, were on either side of Riya.

When the music started, my nerves calmed as muscle memory took over. Lexi performed her showcase well, as did Trinity. I messed up a few steps, but the errors were small, and with Petra in front of me, I doubted anyone was paying much attention to what I was doing.

During the instrumental part at the end, Riya stepped aside, giving Petra center stage. She nailed her part, and after a particularly spectacular sequence, cheers rose up in the crowd. I was glad that her performance, followed by one last chorus from Riya, would be the judges' final impression.

Chests heaving and grins wide, we took our bows and left the stage. The audience was clapping and cheering, and even though their praise wasn't for me personally, I was proud of my team. We didn't get to see the last two performances, but I thought our chances of making the cut were good. We'd been better than Carla's group certainly, and there had been a couple of other groups that didn't impress. The last group's music stopped, and after the applause, Stefan returned to the microphone.

"I'd like to invite all the contestants back to the stage for one final bow and round of applause as we wait for the judges to make their final decisions."

We obeyed. The judges had their heads bent and were discussing our performances in whispers. I couldn't help feeling nervous. What if they'd considered Riya's singing a distraction rather than an asset? We'd been the only group with a singer, and from the looks a few of the other women were giving us, I could tell they didn't think it was fair.

Marlena waved to Stefan, who retrieved a palm pad from her. "Ladies and gentlemen," Stefan began. "I have the results. I'll begin with the teams that have been eliminated. Everyone is welcome to stay for the party, no matter their team's ranking." He gave us a genial smile.

To no one's surprise, Carla's team came in last. She looked disappointed, but I hoped she'd stay for the party. I wasn't familiar with any of the women on the other two eliminated teams. We came in sixth place, which was six places higher than I'd expected to be a week ago, so I was thrilled. Lily's team came in third, and Juliet and Colleen came in first, to no one's surprise.

"Congratulations. I'm sure the prince will be in touch soon to arrange his dates with the winners." With that, Stefan ended his announcements, and the trial was over.

Attendants cleared away the stage to make room for a dance floor and some tall tables, perfect for socializing and eating canapés. While the guests, a mix of important Atlanteans and Gaians of all ages, had gotten a proper meal, we were left to graze on the bite-size snacks set up on a buffet table. Petra, Riya, and Trinity filled their plates with a socially acceptable amount of food. Lexi piled hers as high as she could, and for every morsel I put on my plate, I popped one right in my mouth first. Dancing was hungry work, and now I was in for an evening of small talk, another exhausting activity.

I was surprised to find that my team chatted amiably. Petra was in such high spirits she was actually bearable. While the others listened to Petra give a play-by-play of the competition we'd just survived, I surveyed the remaining contestants. Across the room, Colleen was grinning up at the prince and when he excused himself, she watched him go with starry eyes. She liked him. Not that I could blame her. I liked him too. Then she caught me staring at her. The stars in her eyes went out, replaced by a grimace. I took a sip of my water and looked around some more.

A dark-haired woman named Yvonne was brooding in corner with her team, the rest of whom looked pleased to still be in the contest despite placing ninth. She scanned the room, looking for someone. Or a sign. Could she be the rebel? Then a tearful blonde approached, and the two hugged. Yvonne broke down in tears, and I averted my gaze. I recognized the blonde from Carla's team. The two friends would now be separated. No wonder Yvonne was upset.

Enough spy work for me for the evening. Maybe I'd lucked out and the rebel had been eliminated in the trial. I'd barely touched the food that had made it onto my plate when Lee approached our group.

"Riya," he said in a congratulatory tone, "hearing you sing 'Waves of Love' made me reconsider disliking it."

"You're joking," she said, putting a hand over her mouth. "We picked a song you didn't like?"

"Until today. I've changed my mind, thanks to you. Petra, your showcase was mesmerizing. Absolutely incredible. Lexi, Trinity, you must have worked very hard on your verse spotlights. Well done." Finally he turned to me. He tilted his head as if reaching for some compliment he could give me. "You didn't have a spotlight. Would you allow me to fix that?" He held out his hand, and there was no choice but to take it. His touch was magnetic, and I was running out of reasons to deny my attraction. He led me onto the packed dance floor where a number of couples were twirling around, dresses fluttering, laughter ringing, tensions hot and high.

"There was a reason I didn't get the spotlight," I said, growing anxious that I would have to dance in front of the prince. Again.

He squeezed my hand. "Oh, I know. Don't worry."

Moments after we stepped onto the dance floor, the upbeat music slowed. He pulled me close, interlacing his fingers with mine, placing the other hand low on my back. When I turned, his face was so close to mine his cheek brushed against my hair.

"Did you plan this?" I breathed.

"Maybe. I figured a slower song might be more manageable for you," he teased. "Are you free later?"

"There's no Earth to pretend to look at." I could feel eyes on me.

"How about we—"

The lights went out. A few people cried out in surprise while others giggled wickedly, taking advantage of the temporary darkness. Lee kept one hand on my back and moved the other to stroke my cheek. I longed to melt into his arms and embrace the secrecy of the darkness, but my senses were already heightened. The hairs at the back of my neck stood, and every cell in my body was screaming the same thing at me. Something was wrong. Suddenly, the prince's proximity was suffocating. I shoved him back, and from the startled yelps, I guessed he'd crashed into the other couples. The force sent me reeling backward, too, in the opposite direction.

The dark was no longer fun or appealing once people started getting jostled around, and thankfully, the lights came on after a few more seconds. I looked around to get my bearings. A very confused Lee was staring at me from the floor, but before I could explain why I'd pushed him away, a woman screamed. There was someone else on the floor a few feet away from me, and they weren't moving. It was one of the judges. Mario. Some sort of dart was sticking out of the back of his neck.

Guards immediately pulled Lee away, and the party was over. Guests were escorted out of the hall and contestants were led to their rooms, but not before I saw the somber head shake of the medic who'd attended the young judge. He was dead, and I was certain that the dart had been meant for Lee.

Since we were all locked down in our rooms, I guessed I wouldn't be meeting with Lee that night. Around third watch, a note from him confirmed it.

Chloe,

I have to cancel our non-date. I've been locked in my room. You looked beautiful tonight. I'm sorry if... well, that's best said another day. In person.

Lee

I was disappointed, though I tried to convince myself I didn't mind. My goal wasn't to win him over, it was to—

The commcard from Mayor Russo. I'd been so busy with preparing for the Aphrodite Trial, I hadn't checked it for a few days. I pulled it from its tattered pocket to read the new message: *Rebel in games confirmed. Identity unknown. Attack expected at Aphrodite Trial.*

My stomach knotted with guilt. I'd been negligent. I'd gotten so caught up in my rivalry with Lily and the charm of the prince that I'd forgotten my real mission. I was here to find the rebel and protect Lee. Without the prince, our alliance would crumble. And if a games contestant killed an Atlantean royal, what would happen to the rest of us?

I sent my reply: *The prince is safe. No leads on rebel's identity yet.*

I'd been lucky tonight, but it was close. Maybe if I'd seen Russo's warning in advance, I would have noticed something out of place, a clue to the rebel's identity. I had to keep a closer eye on the other women if I wanted to start a new life on my own terms once we reached Atlantis.

Nineteen

The next morning, breakfast was served in our rooms. I'd received no more updates from Mayor Russo. As I ate my muffin, my tablet dinged. It was an alert informing us that the security sweep was complete and the contestants could return to classes that day. A few minutes later, there was a knock on my door. I assumed it was Melissa, come to get me ready for the day, but a pair of very large, somber guards blocked the exit. They escorted me to the king's office. I wasn't sure what I'd done.

Was it Russo's commcard? Or maybe it was because I'd pushed the prince last night. No one had seen it in the darkness, but I was positive that Lee knew it was me and not the bustle of the crowd. We hadn't explicitly covered it in etiquette, but I was pretty sure that assaulting the crown prince was a crime.

I gulped and followed them into the office, arms pressed to my sides and head bowed.

I'd expected an immaculate chamber with ornate chairs and walls covered in regalia, but the king's office looked modern and lived-in. Several monitors and screens were set up around the room. There was even a fair bit of physical paper, and I recalled how the prince preferred to send me paper notes rather than digital ones.

I expected a stern face, but the brown eyes that met mine were kind and crinkled at the corners with crow's feet. The resemblance to his son was strong, though he looked a bit sturdier. I somehow had the presence of mind to curtsy and mumble, "Your Majesty." I'd been paying attention in etiquette class, though I never dreamed I'd speak to the king himself.

"Ms. Woods," he said, "you look utterly terrified. I'm not sure what they told you to make you so pale, but please take a breath and relax. Or perhaps you're not feeling well?"

"I'm fine, thank you. I'm not sure why I'm here."

Lee opened the door and strode in. "Sorry I'm late. Father," he said, dipping into a shallow bow. "Ms. Woods." He nodded in my direction but didn't meet my eyes.

"Ms. Woods," the king began. "We've reviewed the events of last night and determined that Prince Leonidas was the target. He avoided the poisoned dart just barely, thanks to you. What exactly happened?"

I decided to stick to the facts and keep my feelings out of it. "I was dancing with the prince when the lights went out. When they came back on, one of the judges was on the ground."

"As was I," Lee muttered, giving me a sidelong glance.

"Did you see anyone suspicious nearby?" the king asked.

"I don't think so. Can't you look at the security footage?"

The king looked to the prince who shrugged. "I told you she didn't know," Lee said.

"Know what?"

"The radiation storms that we track interfere with some of our systems. We shield everything vital like engines and life support, but shielding is costly and finicky, requiring significant maintenance so we don't use it on all systems. Surveillance is most affected."

"Oh. I knew they interfered with some systems, but I didn't know surveillance was affected. What about Stefan's camera drones?"

"They are shielded, but he shut them off after the trial ended."

"Okay. Did the storm knock out the lights?" I guessed.

"No, the storm wouldn't have affected the lights," the king said.

"Sabotage," I whispered. My eyes widened, and I looked up at the king. "You thought I might be involved. Because I knew about the coming storms."

King Darius pursed his lips. "I mostly wanted to know if you'd seen anything, but I'll admit the thought crossed my mind."

Lee came to my defense. "If she were involved, it would have been easy for her to poke me in the dark with that dart. Plus, if she hadn't pushed me, I would have been hit."

Lee still wouldn't look at me, but the king cocked an eyebrow, amused. "Pushed you, eh? What'd you do to deserve it?"

"Nothing." I spoke before Lee could attempt to answer. "I got scared in the dark. The prince has been nothing but kind." I turned to Lee. "I'm so sorry, Your Highness."

"No need to apologize." Lee gave me a quizzical look, but at least he was looking at me.

"Right," the king said. "Well, thank you, Ms. Woods. If you remember anything, please let us know. Lee, there are a few more young women to interview, if you have the time."

"Of course." This would have been the perfect opportunity to share any suspicions I had about the identity of a rebel, but with no leads, I had nothing to offer the king.

One of the guards escorted me to astrozalemetry for my first shift. The crew's joking and smiling from last week had been replaced with terse replies. Even Commander Charis was efficient and businesslike, barking orders and questions in Atlantean.

"Sorry, Chloe," she said. "After last night, we're calculating some course corrections to avoid the worst of the storms."

"That sounds difficult."

"It is. I'm afraid I won't be able to explain much today."

"I understand." So I watched. The storms were predictable up to a point, and they had to do constant corrections. This set of storms would only last a few more days, and if Charis's crew stayed on top of adjustments, there would be minimal interference with the ship's systems.

Amplified by the focused mood, their operation was seamless. No quibbling or griping, just succinct feedback. They were a well-oiled machine, and I longed to be a part of it or something like it. Things in the warehouse had been frantic, with people moving around from one task to another, and if there was a promotion up for grabs, the only rule was to trust no one.

With everyone's attention on course corrections, I was able to work at an empty station in the back. I revisited the red giant data that Lee and I had looked over together, and then my curiosity about the storms took over. Not wanting to interfere with their current work, I searched through old storm data from their trip to Earth. I might not understand all the technical jargon in Atlantean, but I had gleaned a general understanding of the models. I was deep down a rabbit hole of past storm data when I found myself trying to access a restricted file. The dissonant chime jarred me, and I glanced around to see if anyone had noticed me trying to gain access. It was about Earth, that much I could tell from the file name, but the reason for its confidentiality eluded me. I quickly backtracked to permitted files, hoping my accidental foray wouldn't get me in trouble.

Right before my shift ended, Lee arrived. The commander gave him an update, and then he offered to escort me back. This would have been exciting if it wasn't for my guilt about pushing him away.

"I'm sorry," Lee said, keeping his distance in the transporter. "I didn't realize I was being too forward last night."

I racked my brain, trying to figure out why he thought he'd been too forward. Suddenly I remembered the feel of his hand against my cheek. In the dark, where no one could see. Hidden away. That was the truth of it, and I was only now realizing it. The prince was hiding me away. Meeting me late at night, keeping me from the cameras so there were barely any clips of our date for the episode. He liked me, but only when there was no one around to see. Publicly, he treated me like any other contestant, and I didn't know why. That was why I was having such a hard time trusting my own feelings. What if it was all an act, just like it had been with Brett?

"No, that wasn't it," I replied.

"Then why did you push me away? And don't try to tell me you're afraid of the dark."

I couldn't share my doubts, and I certainly wasn't about to tell him about the rebel among the contestants, so I settled on something that was technically true. "I'm not usually, but on such a crowded dance floor, I panicked."

He smiled, but the expression was tight, as if he didn't believe me. "Tomorrow night," he said. "Be ready at fifth watch."

With the Aphrodite Trial over, we were entering a new month, the Month of Persephone. We also had our afternoons back to ourselves. Rumors swirled about how a rebel had attacked the prince undetected. A few suspected disgruntled Atlantean nobility had used the opportunity to frame the Gaians, but most agreed it was a rebel. Some even whispered that a rebel could be hiding among the contestants, and it wasn't long until that rumor became the favorite.

I spent my first free afternoon with Riya in the newly opened garden, accessible to contestants from first hour to last. I wanted to thank Juliet for requesting access for us, but she was nowhere to be found.

"Where's Juliet?" I asked Riya.

"On a date with the prince." Riya sighed. "I hope we win the next trial so we can spend more time with him. He wrote me a card telling me how beautiful my singing was. Do you think he sends a lot of us cards?"

This revelation stung, but it was obvious. Of course he wrote notes to a bunch of the contestants. This was the reminder I needed. I was not special. I was just another contestant, and I'd been lying to myself. Even after Brett and that painful lesson about trusting someone with my heart, I'd gone and done it again.

"I got one. Same sort of thing," I replied.

"Oh." She sounded disappointed too. "Do you think somebody can like more than one person at a time?"

"I guess so," I replied. "Why, are you interested in someone besides the prince?"

She smacked my arm playfully. "No. Don't you think it must be weird for him? He probably likes a bunch of us, and meanwhile we don't have options."

"I'm sure it's weird. It's how I'd feel if the roles were reversed."

I lay back in the grass, soaking in the simulated sun, impressed by the sky's fake clouds. The rooftop garden had felt like this, a verdant patch in an otherwise lifeless, constructed environment. I saw Juliet enter, followed by Lee. They were laughing and saying their goodbyes from the look of it. Juliet curtsied a perfect curtsy, and the prince leaned forward and kissed her cheek.

The knife in my heart twisted, and I lost all desire to thank Juliet for garden access.

I thought about pretending I was sick so I could avoid meeting with him that night, but I needed to keep him close. Back to business. *Find the rebel. Make it to the final twelve. Stay in the game, but remember, that's all it is. A game.*

TWENTY

When I awoke, I'd received a message from Mayor Russo: *Find out rebel identity. Be vigilant.*

I was supposed to be doing that already, but I'd let myself get distracted. I barely paid any attention in class that day. When a rebel spy—no, murderer—could be in the room, Atlantean fine dining etiquette didn't seem like a worthwhile focus. One of my fellow contestants had tried to kill the prince and ruin any chance of an alliance, all because they believed the worst about the Atlanteans. Mario's death added urgency to my mission, even as I doubted my ability to uncover the rebel's identity.

I learned from Lexi and Riya that the prince's date that day was with Colleen. She was quiet and nice. Organized. Competent. *Probably a murderer.*

That afternoon the prince took her for coffee on one of the upper floors of the Palace Wing, which I had no reason to visit. That didn't stop me from making one pass down the hall and sneaking a glance. The camera drones were all focused on the two of them and didn't catch me.

When they went to the gardens, so did I. This was far less suspicious because most of the other contestants were there. I sat under the trees, admired flowers, and lay in the grass, sure to keep a good angle. If she was the rebel, she probably wouldn't try something with all those cameras on her, but I was hoping to catch some hint of guilt or betrayal in her movements.

In the lounge after dinner, Colleen approached me, which was odd. We'd only ever talked in groups.

"Chloe," she said with a hand braced against her hip, "why were you watching me with the prince today?"

Great. I'd been found out. "What do you mean?" I said as innocently as I could.

"You walked by during our coffee date and followed us around the garden."

I shrugged. "Everyone was in the garden. Don't you think you're being paranoid?"

She raised her eyebrows and crossed her arms. "Whatever. It was weird and creepy. We *both* thought so." She stomped off and found Juliet. The two had a hushed conversation and kept casting glances in my direction.

So they'd noticed. The prince had noticed. Wonderful. I was being ridiculous. If the last attempt had taken place in the dark, the rebel wasn't interested in murdering him in broad daylight—or rather, shiplight. I sighed. I couldn't even fool myself. I was jealous. My snooping was self-interested.

As I left, I overheard Colleen telling Juliet that the prince was letting her work with one of the chefs a couple times a week since she'd told him how much she liked cooking. Just like my time in astrozalemetry. Another sign I wasn't special to the prince. I was just another contestant. I wondered how many non-dates he'd been on with the other women.

I killed time in my room until fifth watch. I headed downstairs, assuming I should go to the window, but the prince stopped me before I entered the dining hall.

"This way," he said, leading me down a deserted hallway. My stomach fluttered, and I wondered what he had planned for this evening.

He stopped at the top of a flight of stairs. "I have a surprise for you."

"After the Aphrodite Trial, the real surprise is that you kept me around."

"Let's just say I'm not keeping you around for your dancing."

I cringed. "Yeah, our performance was a little rough."

"But you found a way to make it work, and I'm glad. I would have hated to see you go."

"Does that mean you have no control over eliminations?"

He put his hands in his pockets. "In the past, the prince or princess hasn't had any say until much later in the process. I can pull strings here and there, like mentioning how much I enjoyed your group's performance while sitting at the judge's table. But something like meddling in the Aphrodite Trial so a specific team would come in first would have been difficult. Stefan's not an idiot, though. He can tell who I'd like to keep around even without me saying it. Sometimes, even before I know it myself."

Lee smiled, like there was some joke I wasn't in on. Before I could ask what exactly he meant, he stopped in front of an unlabeled door. "Here we are. Why don't you do the honors?" He gestured to the palm pad by the door, and I obliged.

The doors opened, and I gasped, taking in the sight. The room was covered floor to ceiling in bookcases, packed with colorful spines. A glance at the nearest shelf confirmed my suspicion. They were all in English. These were Earth books.

"The journey to Atlantis takes a few months, and we wanted to preserve some of your physical books. We'll be bringing more on future trips, but we thought it would be nice for you and the others to have some books around you can read."

"There must be more than this provincial life," I muttered.

"*Beauty and the Beast*?" He chuckled. "So I'm the beast, then?"

"Wait, *how* have you seen *Beauty and the Beast*?" I blushed then, realizing the implication of my words. "I didn't mean it like that. You're nothing like the beast."

"I've taken you from your parents. You're trapped with me. I've just given you a library. Well, you and the others. I can see the parallels. You'd make a decent Belle." He looked at me not with his usual geniality, but something more. "More than decent actually." He cleared his throat. "Where to first? Fantasy?"

The walls I'd placed around my heart earlier in the day crumbled like sand in the surf. "Of course." Because if this wasn't my fantasy, I didn't know what was.

We thumbed through the spines, sharing recommendations and laughing at ridiculous titles and covers.

"Wait. If you've actually read some of these books, you can read and write English. But they told us there wasn't any imprinting for that."

He shook his head. "No, unfortunately it took a lot of time and effort over the past year."

"Impressive."

"Gaians are going to be my people soon. I take that responsibility seriously. It's why I'm holding the Goddess Games among Gaian women, not Atlanteans. Not everyone approves of that decision."

"Like who?"

"My mother, for one."

"Really? The queen disapproves, but you're doing it anyway?"

"It's the right thing to do. I believe that now more than ever." He locked eyes with me, and I couldn't help thinking when he said now, he meant *now*, here with me.

I recovered myself as we moved along the shelves. I hadn't had this much fun in a library since... I swallowed. *Since studying with Brett,* my reluctant mind finished. The sobering recollection reminded me this whole contest was a royal obligation for Lee, just as my participation was an obligation to Earth.

"Back here. I want to show you something." Lee led me to a corner where the shelves were weighed down with heavy encyclopedias. "This is my favorite part of the library," he said.

I studied the shelves, looking for the reason. "Why? I'm sorry if I'm missing something—" I turned back to find him standing so close, and the look in his eyes made my breath hitch. "Obvious," I finished.

"No security cameras. Not even the guards in the surveillance room can see us. So, I'd like to kiss you, if that's all right."

He reached out a hand and cupped my cheek, directing my lips to his. Heat flooded my limbs during the brief hesitation before we kissed. I wanted this. I wanted him. His lips were soft and lingered on mine, and my whole body tingled at the sensation. Then he took my face in both hands, bringing our mouths together once again, this time with more urgency. I put my right hand on his chest to steady myself and noticed his heart was beating as fast as my own.

An unwelcome memory pulled me from the moment. A different pair of lips. Another kiss. Would this kiss lead to the same kind of heartbreak? The spell broken, I pulled away. This was a mistake. The happy glow that had filled me flared up, and suddenly his embrace was stifling, just like it had been in the dark after the Aphrodite Trial. I had to go. I extended my arm, putting space between us. "I'm sorry," I said, not meeting his eyes. "Thank you for the tour." My tone was all business, and his was all confusion as he called after me.

"Chloe? What's wrong?"

He didn't follow me as I hurried to my room, and after a few minutes, I knew there would be no knock on my door. He'd gone to great lengths to hide his feelings for me from everyone and from the cameras.

What had I been thinking? There was no way to do this. I couldn't spend time with the prince and pretend I didn't have these feelings, but I also couldn't let myself believe that I was special. He'd sent a note to Riya, kissed Juliet affectionately on the cheek, and arranged for Colleen to work in the kitchens the same way he set me up in astrozalemetry. How many other women had he kissed in unmonitored corners of the ship? There were limits to the lies I could tell myself, and this was beyond those limits. I couldn't risk getting hurt again.

I'd focus on the trials, stay in the games, and find the rebel. Lee had confirmed that he didn't have control over the outcomes of the trials, so maybe I could stay in the competition long enough on my own. I didn't need the prince to like me to become a finalist in the Goddess Games, and that was the only outcome that mattered anymore.

Twenty-One

No one had seen the prince for two days after our library non-date. Stefan and Talia gave us a boilerplate explanation about some royal duties he had to perform for the people of Atlantis, but we all knew there was more to his absence than they were letting on. Because of my time in astrozalemetry, I knew some unavoidable storm surges were coming up and the prince's absence was meant to keep him safe. The surprise opening of the library took the edge off Lee's absence.

The women on Juliet's team whose dates were postponed as a result of his absence were devastated. Harmony sulked, though the other two women named Becca and Micaela seemed resigned to their fate. On the third morning, however, their chatter at breakfast sounded cheerful. Their dates had been rescheduled at last.

I focused on my classes. In History and Culture, Ms. Angelos was teaching us about the goddesses. "Each goddess had a variety of traits. Atlanteans don't worship them as literal divine beings, though their advanced technology originally made them seem like deities to our ancestors. The Olympians were aliens, but they were very much like humans in their emotions. We use their examples to inspire virtue and warn against vice. Take Artemis, for example. We've told you how we admire her athleticism and tenacity, but she was also cold and unforgiving. Aphrodite cultivated beauty, but infidelity and disdain for what she deemed ugly were her downfalls.

"Next, we have Athena, a favorite among Atlanteans for her strength and wisdom. We admire her strategy and craftiness, but even she could be arrogant, deceitful, and uncooperative at times. These strengths and faults are important to keep in mind, as the Athena Trial will take place in eleven days."

That was two Atlantean weeks after the Aphrodite Trial. The class was a flurry of questions, asking for details, rules, hints, anything, but the only further information she revealed made me groan. We'd be working in teams again. The same teams. I liked Lexi and Riya, and Trinity was nice, too, but I really worked best alone.

As soon as Ms. Angelos dismissed us, Lexi popped up next to me. "Have you been to the library yet?" she asked.

Though the revelation of the library had been a welcome distraction for most of the women, I couldn't bring myself to visit it. The truth was that I had visited. With Lee. But I didn't know how to explain that whole mess to Lexi, so I said, "It's only been open for a couple of days."

"Then let's go. I haven't been either."

"Not right now. I'm going to work on some Atlantean homework."

"I thought you liked reading," Lexi said, giving me a funny look.

"I do," I conceded. "Bring me back something fun."

I was playing cards with Riya in the common room when Lexi returned from the library. She plunked down a book on the table next to me. "Something fun, as requested."

"*Her Alien Prince*?" I asked. I grimaced at the cover, which featured a blue alien man, presumably the titular prince, with very nice abs.

"You did say you liked science fiction. You can always go get something else." Lexi was smiling, and Riya was laughing so hard she was at the point of tears.

"Thanks, Lexi," I said dryly. "You know me so well." I rolled my eyes and cracked open the book. I got a couple of weird looks and a few laughs, but it was nice to read a book in English, even if it wasn't my style. Plus, it reminded me of Flora's roof books, and I welcomed that scrap of familiarity.

Prince Leonidas had emerged again that evening to take Becca out on a date, but judging from her spirits when she returned to the common room, it hadn't gone well.

"He barely talked to me," she sobbed to Juliet. "I don't think he likes me."

"Oh, Becca, he's probably worried about something unrelated, like whatever he's been up to the past few days."

Harmony and Micaela's dates in the following days didn't go much better from the sound of things, and I tried not to be happy about it.

Soon it was time for the third episode of the Goddess Games to air. There was a recap of the Aphrodite Trial, which had been livestreamed to Earth and Atlantis already. There was some generic footage of women in the garden and the library, but the focus was on the prince's dates with the winning team, especially Juliet's and Colleen's dates. I wasn't sure what the point of these episodes was, beyond introducing the potential future princess of Atlantis to both of her peoples, but I was not making much of an impression in them.

Just like that, the third Atlantean week, twenty-four days, of the games had passed. The Athena trial would occur in eight days, and we still had very little information about what to expect.

⟫⟫⟫ ⟪⟪⟪

I still refused to go to the library, so Lexi had returned *Her Alien Prince* and brought back *Her Alien Protector*. Apparently it was a series, and I wondered how many I'd have to read before there were no more left. Or maybe I could convince Riya to bring me something else. Despite my objections, I was still up reading when my door notification went off around fifth watch. It wasn't Melissa. She'd never come this late before. Maybe Riya or Lexi needed something?

I put the book down on my nightstand and opened the door. Lee was standing there in a dark blue shirt and a matching pair of loose pants. I gaped at him.

"Can I come in? I need to talk to you." He cast a desperate look up and down the corridor. "Please? I'd rather not get caught out here in my pajamas."

I stepped aside and motioned him in before closing the door behind him.

"Are you even allowed to be here?" I asked.

"It's not the best idea I've had, but I couldn't sleep. I feel like ever since the Aphrodite Trial, I've been doing the wrong thing. I'm sorry about misreading the situation in the library. Can you explain what happened?"

Considering I was now, definitely, only in the competition to earn a place in the nobility, the fact that he was ashamed of me shouldn't have mattered. But it did. I was tired of being hidden away.

"If you're worried someone might have seen you come here, you could have just sent a note." I folded my arms across my chest. "Apparently you send a lot of those."

"What?"

"You kissed Juliet in the garden in front of the cameras, but you hide me away in a corner. You were embarrassed when that crew member saw us hugging—just hugging—in the transporter. You set Colleen up to learn from the chefs just like you got me shifts with Commander Charis. I know you write to the other women too. You parade around with the others through the gardens, dancing, playing games, but you sneak me away from the cameras to the astrozalemetry lab."

Lee gave me a puzzled look. "Commander Charis says you've been enjoying your time there."

"How many women have you taken on 'non-dates' and only kissed in secret alcoves?"

By the end of it, I'd backed myself up against my vanity, creating a rift between us. This whole concept of the Goddess Games—competing for the prince's attention—was stupid.

Lee took a step back. "So that's why you're upset? I thought you understood."

"Understood what? That this is an awful game?"

"That I'm playing the game too."

Reluctantly, I uncrossed my arms. "What do you mean?"

"I'm careful about what I let the cameras see. Yes, there are surveillance cameras all over the ship, but that footage is for security purposes. Stefan and Talia don't have access to it. I accept that there are some things my security crew will see—my visit here tonight, for example—but I handpicked the team working in our security room. I know they'll be discreet."

"Can't you tell the cameras to go away like you did when you took me to astrozalemetry for our date?"

"At this early point in the games, not really. And to answer your other question, none."

"Huh?"

"I haven't taken any other women on 'non-dates,' unless you count that time Lily showed up when we were at the window. You're the only one I feel like I know well enough to see outside of the competition. The only kisses have been the ones on camera, except for you in the library. So this was the reason you ran? You thought I didn't really like you, so when I kissed you, you ran?"

When he put it like that, my reaction seemed absurd. *I was afraid you were using me like Brett did.* "I don't want to talk about it. It's complicated."

"Then," he said, his eyes flickering down a moment, "it was a bad kiss?"

I shook my head. "No, definitely not bad." That sounded lame, but I wasn't about to tell him that the memory of it kept me up at night.

He smiled in relief, then caught sight of the novel propped open on my nightstand.

"What the hell is this?" He crossed the room and picked up my copy of *Her Alien Protector*.

Oh god, why? Why was this happening? "Lexi's idea of a joke." A quick glance in my vanity mirror confirmed that my cheeks were bright red.

He smirked as he thumbed through the novel. "You've almost finished it."

"And?"

"And it's book two in a series."

"I'm broadening my horizons."

He set the book down and held up his hands in a defensive gesture. "No judgment here. But you do know we're not aliens, right?"

"So you say," I teased.

"I'm only human, as I'm sure you're realizing." He stepped closer. "Just remember that what the cameras see is what I let them. I've enjoyed the freedom to be myself around you. The rest is a performance, a part of the games."

"So you'll have to kiss a bunch of the others?"

"Yes, and I'll have to do it on camera as the games progress." He grimaced, as if dreading the anticipated public displays of affection. "I may not have to pass the trials, but like I said, I'm in these games as much as you are."

"At least you don't have to perform a group dance."

He tilted his head and sized me up. "I think the Athena Trial will be better suited to your talents than the Aphrodite Trial was."

"I hope so."

He hesitated in front of my door, turning back. "I really do like you, Chloe. Navigating the games is hard for me too."

The prince left, and I considered his words. When I was with him, it felt real. Laughing and joking with him had already become familiar. Maybe I could trust these feelings after all, and see where they led.

TWENTY-TWO

My morning was spent in astrozalemetry, so I was out of the loop when I came back to lunch to find the dining hall abuzz. Becca and Harmony were talking excitedly, and Lily was moving so swiftly, eyes fixed on her tablet, that she didn't see me. I stepped to the side, but she sensed my movement, looked up, and bumped into me anyway as she went past. *Charming as ever.*

"What's going on?" I asked, sitting across from Riya and Lexi, who were discussing something over their tablets.

"That's right! You missed it," Riya said. "Hang on." She tapped a few buttons on her tablet, and mine vibrated with a notification.

"There are three riddles to solve that can earn you a date with the prince this week. Like a warm up for the Athena Trial," Lexi summarized. "Each riddle gives you a location, and at that location, you'll find a token with the double-headed ax, the Agathon crest."

"But you're working together?"

"Yeah, you can work with a partner, and if you win, you each get a date," Riya explained. "Lexi and I already paired up. Sorry."

"That's fine," I replied, quite happy with the prospect of working alone. "Let's see these riddles."

I opened my tablet and read the first one.

What creature has one voice, yet goes on four legs in the morning, two at noon, and three in the evening?

"This first one is familiar," I said out loud.

"It's the riddle of the Sphinx from—ouch!" Riya yelped. Lexi had nudged an elbow into Riya's side. "Sorry, we're not supposed to be a group of three."

I grabbed a sandwich and got up. "It's cool. I'll go work on these in my room. Good luck!" If there were three tokens to be found, I'd much rather Riya and Lexi find them than Lily.

In my room, I discovered the answer to the first riddle was man: crawling on four legs as a baby, walking on two as an adult, and using a cane in old age as a third leg. So what was I supposed to do, find a man? I snorted. I had no idea how to find a man, riddle or otherwise, so I moved on to the other two.

Where hearts and vines tangle, follow love's gaze.

Maybe somewhere in the garden? I read the final clue.

In lifeless woods full of life, search for romance.

That was puzzling. Was it in the garden too? That seemed unlikely. At least these two had actual directions, even if they were painfully vague. The first clue had been nothing more than a classic riddle. How did "man" give any indication of what we were supposed to do with that answer?

The hunt was on, and I had to admit, it was fun. When I got to the garden, it was full of other contestants wandering around. There were a lot of vines climbing up arched trellises, the gazebo, and even a few of the statues.

Where hearts and vines tangle. The vines were probably literal, but what about hearts? Some of the leaves were heart-shaped, but those areas were swarmed. If the token was there, I wouldn't have much chance of finding it. I started at the gazebo, then moved on to the statues. Maybe one had to do with love?

I headed toward the nearest lonely statue of a woman. The statue was painted, and the eyes were inlaid with colored stones. Her pink dress had been sculpted so realistically that I almost mistook it for fabric, and her hair hung in brown ringlets so lively I could imagine them bouncing.

The statue was exquisite, but I didn't recognize her as one of the goddesses, let alone Aphrodite or someone else associated with hearts. After another twenty minutes of three dozen women searching the garden, I had a feeling it was the wrong place. And if the last clue had referred to the garden, we'd have found that one by now too.

Many kept searching, but I was among those who left to search elsewhere. As I walked out of the garden, I glanced at a mural of Demeter cradling her daughter. It always caught my attention as I left, but today it stuck out for a different reason.

What if the hearts and vines were in a painting?

Though tired from roaming around the garden for so long, I decided to give myself an art tour of the Palace Wing. There were a lot of rooms that were open to us now, but most of my fellow contestants typically stuck to the lounge and the gym—or their own rooms if they wanted privacy. I'd seen a few teams that got along well meeting in the lounge every now and then. My team hadn't all gotten together since the Aphrodite Trial, and I was grateful that the Athena Trial didn't require any sort of practice. The less I had to interact with Petra, the better.

I walked around the halls, admiring the various paintings. Some looked ancient, with stylized figures and geometric patterns; some were extremely realistic; and others used various techniques that I couldn't name. The subject matter was just as varied. There were depictions of the gods and goddesses I recognized, but also more modern figures, including prominent Atlantean athletes, scientists, and artists.

A photograph of Atlantis from orbit caught my eye. I'd never noticed it before, but the contrast to Earth was stark. Atlantis looked alive. Its swaths of land, the color of emeralds but far more precious, were unfamiliar shapes, and I wondered what they were called. The clouds were wispy, white swirls over cerulean oceans and trailing archipelagos. No matter what happened in the games, I'd be able to share this world with my family. Our most recent call a few days ago had assured me they were all doing well, but I missed them.

When the Atlanteans first arrived, I had imagined their home as a parallel Earth. This image showed me what I'd already learned from History and Culture. Atlantis was its own civilization and culture, elevating concepts like xenia and arete. What had Earth elevated? Greed. Short-sighted greed. The people who stole my birthright were long dead, but their legacy served as a cautionary tale. After the chaos and devastation, Earth could never recover.

My reverie was broken by angry voices. The door to a nearby room had just opened.

"You can't do that!" declared a familiar voice.

"Then stop me." I recognized that one. Shrill and venomous. Lily.

"Give it back, or I'll tell them."

"You'd have to prove it, and I hear the storms are messing up their surveillance again. Good luck."

How would Lily know about the timing of the storms? I burst in, ready to accuse the brazen witch of being a rebel, but she was pinning one of the challenge's tokens to her tunic. She wasn't a rebel. She was a cheater. *Must be a family trait.*

"You're too late Chloe. I'll give the prince a kiss for you."

I clenched my jaw, unable to think of a reply. She brushed past me, and my firsts curled. Once the sound of her footsteps had faded, I approached Juliet. She was sitting in a chair, her tight curls up off her neck and pinned in place in a loose bun. She wasn't crying, but she did have her face in her hands.

"Juliet?" I asked tentatively. "Are you okay?"

She put her hands down and straightened up. "Yeah. I guess."

I glanced around the room, and the second I saw the painting on the wall, I knew this had to be the right place. In the painting, an elderly couple was holding hands, but they were turning into trees unlike anything I'd seen. Vines wrapped around them, entangling the two, and Aphrodite was looking down from above. It was beautiful, and the perfect answer for the second riddle: *Where hearts and vines tangle, follow love's gaze.* Aphrodite was associated with love on Earth, so I followed her gaze to a small table beneath the painting that had a single drawer.

I pointed at the table. "It was in there, wasn't it?"

"Yep," Juliet replied.

"I heard what Lily said. She stole the token, didn't she?"

"She took it out of my hands. She came in right after I found it like she'd been watching me. I promised to share it with Colleen, so I couldn't share it with her when she asked. Otherwise, I would have."

"If you want someone to back you up, I will. I knew Lily back on Earth, and she was awful."

Juliet laughed bitterly. "She says the same about you. Guess I know who to believe now."

"I mean it. I'll back you up."

"You can't even be sure I'm telling you the truth. You hardly know me."

"You're right, but I know Lily. This is totally in character for her. And from what I overheard, the implication was definitely that she was going to get away with something."

"I don't want to cause a fuss. I've already gotten a couple of dates with the prince. I'll be fine."

"If that's what you really want." I would have done everything in my power to get Lily eliminated if I were Juliet, but I got the sense she was a better person than I was. If only there was proof! The surveillance cameras were in and out because another cosmic storm had shifted.

But how did Lily know that? While the general knowledge that the storms caused surveillance issues had leaked after the Aphrodite Trial, I'd only found out about today's storms in the astrozalemetry lab this morning. Maybe Lily was bluffing to discourage Juliet from pursuing the issue.

"It is," she said. "There are still two more tokens to find. I should get back to Colleen and tell her I had no luck. Will you keep this to yourself?"

"Sure," I replied. There was something about Juliet. I wanted her to like me even if we weren't friends. She had a calming and captivating presence, and I couldn't figure out why the prince didn't spend more time with her—or just pick her outright and call off the games.

"Thanks." Juliet walked out the door, and I took a seat, mulling over the next clue. After ten useless minutes, I got up and headed to the dining hall. Maybe a snack would help. My watch told me it was nearly dinnertime, so I returned to the dining hall.

I was loading my plate with roasted vegetables when Riya and Lexi joined me. From their faces, I could tell they hadn't found a token.

"Lily got the first one," Lexi grumbled.

"I know," I said.

"How?"

I remembered my promise to Juliet and shrugged. "A disturbance in the force."

"I don't like her much either, but why do you hate her, Chloe?" Riya asked.

"I don't want to talk about it."

Lexi complained about how Lily had sauntered into the garden bragging loudly and waving the token around. "There's no way the prince will enjoy his date with her."

"Oh, she's got a few assets I'm sure he can appreciate," I murmured. "Even if integrity isn't among them."

Riya rolled her eyes, and Lexi laughed.

"I'm going to go search in the lower levels. Want me to return your book?" Lexi offered.

"Sure, thanks. And go ahead and get the next one. I'm invested now."

"In the plot, I'm sure," she said, giving me a wicked grin.

"What are you implying?" I asked, putting a hand to my chest as if scandalized.

I'd kept the clue about a lifeless forest in mind as I'd examined the art, but nothing had jumped out at me. After learning the first token was hidden somewhere near a painting, I was even more convinced that the others would also be near works of art.

After another fruitless forty-five minutes, I passed by the lounge, trying some closer-to-home locations since nothing else had panned out. I glimpsed Trinity inside, the only one there. *Might as well take a break and say hi.*

"Trinity, how are you?"

"I'm good. The change of scenery is nice."

I cocked my head to the side. "You know you can come in here whenever you want, right?"

"Yeah, it's overwhelming. I like being in here alone."

Was that a hint to leave her alone? Probably. "Yeah, it's dead in here right now thanks to the riddles. Well, I'll leave you to it."

As I was walking out the door, something clicked. Dead. Lifeless. The lounge was full of Atlantean books made from paper, and paper was made from dead trees. *A lifeless forest.* Books were full of stories. *Full of life.* That had to be the library. *Search for romance.*

I claimed to love reading, and I couldn't figure out a clue for library? Embarrassing. I hurried down to the library, avoiding the section where Lee had kissed me. This was a clue that had to make sense for everyone, not just me.

I caught sight of Lexi and Riya whispering and giggling in one of the aisles. The joy on their faces made my heart sink. They had found the token. I put a smile on and joined them.

"Did you find it?" I asked.

"Yes!" Lexi said. "I did. I went to get the next book for you, and it was sitting right there in the gap where your book should have gone. I guess there was a convenient space there when they were placing the token."

Grinning, Lexi held it up for me to see. It was a small, golden pin with a delicate etching of the Agathon crest.

"That's fantastic," I said. "I can't believe how long it took me to figure out the clue meant the library."

"Well, I'm glad you're not boycotting the place anymore," Lexi replied. "You can get your own books from now on." She handed me the final installment of the series: *Her Alien King*.

I shook my head and tucked the book under my arm. "Fair enough. So, I guess you go tell Stefan and Talia?"

"Yeah," Riya said. "Let's go, Lexi. Good luck with the last clue, Chloe!"

"Thanks," I replied.

I stayed behind, running my fingertip along the spines of books, tracing their embossed titles. Had Lee put the token here for me to find? Or was it purely coincidence? After his comments on my reading choices, I was certain this was intentional. This was his way of offering me a proper date and proving that he wasn't embarrassed, and I had blown it. Now I really had to find the last token, but there was so little to go on. *Man*. I'd passed dozens of pictures of men. What if it meant man in a more generic sense, like a human? That was even worse, opening up the field to an impossible scope. I returned to my room to think in peace.

One clue was a painting. The other was a book. Both clues had to do with love, hearts, and romance. So, a man that had something to do with love? Maybe Cupid, or Eros, as the Atlanteans called him.

But Eros wasn't a man. Eros, like all the Olympians, had been an alien. Very, very humanlike, but not truly human. Back to the drawing board.

My door chimed, and Melissa entered, tapping away at her tablet. "Tomorrow the prince is arranging to have the contestants share his meals with him in the royal dining room. Three teams per meal."

"Please tell me mine is breakfast," I said.

She looked puzzled. "You are. But why would you want that? Most of the women would want dinner."

"I don't want it hanging over my head all day."

"Why would you dread it?" Melissa raised an eyebrow. "I've seen the way you look at the prince, and I've seen the way he looks at you."

"I think you must be biased." She wasn't. The prince liked me. He'd told me himself. Now I had to decide what to do with that knowledge.

"Maybe. All the PAs think their contestant is special. Well, most of them. But I heard that a curly-haired brunette was seen meeting him in the ballroom by the window."

"Juliet has curly, brown hair."

"Fine. Keep your secrets. The prince is a good man. Worthy of love."

Whatever heartfelt praise Melissa sang next, I didn't hear. The prince. He had the token. I'd seen it, the Agathon crest, pinned on his collar.

"I need to find him. Where is the prince at this hour?" It was nearly first watch, around nine in Earth time.

"Whoa, when I said follow your heart, I didn't mean right this second."

"Melissa, I'm sincerely sorry to tell you I missed about the last thirty seconds of whatever you said. But I figured it out. The riddle. I need to find the prince."

She narrowed her eyes at me, then shrugged. "He was in the kitchens giving directions for tomorrow's meals. But I don't know if he's still—"

"Thanks!"

She called after me, but I was already out the door, barreling toward the dining hall. I'd never visited the kitchens, which were in the back. The dining hall was full of guards, crewmembers, and other palace employees getting off their shifts, so I didn't seem too out of place there. I hesitated before opening the door to the kitchens to search for the prince.

I found him back in a quiet part of the kitchen, gesturing at the head chef. I got close enough to hear he was speaking in Atlantean. I hadn't heard anyone speak that much Atlantean outside of my language class since my arrival, and the sound was musical. I could understand his requests for sautéed vegetables, roasted fowl, and five different flavors of cakes, but the language still felt new and strange and lyrical. I stood apart, just out of his peripheral vision, soaking in the sound.

Then the chef focused on me, causing Lee to turn and discover the disturbance for himself. Now that I was here, in front of him and the chef, I fidgeted.

"Your Highness," I said, curtsying. "May I have a word?"

Lee nodded and thanked the chef, who returned to his work.

"How can I help you, Chloe?"

"Well, I'm here about the riddle of the Sphinx."

"Oh?" he replied, all of a sudden playful.

"Yes. It's you. You're the answer. That pin there is just like the tokens." I pointed at one of the pins on his chest over his heart.

"So it is." He unfastened the pin but held it in his hand. "Before I hand it over, tell me. Did you find any other tokens today?"

"Not in time, I'm afraid. And no need to rub it in. I already feel like a colossal idiot for missing the library one."

"I wouldn't dream of it. Glad you figured this one out. I'd hoped someone would figure it out tomorrow during one of the meals, but it's too late to cancel them now, I suppose. Here," he said, placing the token in my hand. His fingers barely brushed my palm, meager contact that wasn't nearly enough. I closed my fingers around the pin, which was still full of his warmth.

I fumbled for something else to say and extend our conversation: the token I'd missed, the others who'd found the tokens. My thoughts turned to Juliet, who should have gotten the first token. An unplanned question popped into my head. "Can I request one more thing?"

"Like what?"

"Can I share this token with Juliet and give her the second date?"

"Was she your partner? I didn't think you two were close."

"We're not close, and I worked alone. It's a long story, and I can't explain it, but I'd like to share this with her."

Lee raised his eyebrows. "I'm not sure if I should be worried that, after complaining about me flirting with the other women, you're now trying to share me with one of them. Hmm, on second thought..."

My eyes grew wide. "Oh, trust me. I almost didn't say anything. In fact, I'll probably regret it in the morning."

"If you're sure, then request granted." He lowered his voice so no one else could hear. "You should go before I do something I'll regret, like kissing you in front of half the kitchen staff."

The prospect of another kiss gave me butterflies, and I tried to embrace that feeling instead of fighting it. "As you command, Princely," I said, curtsying once more.

As I returned to my room, I kept turning over one thought in my mind. If the meals were to get someone to figure out the riddle, he'd wanted me there at breakfast. At breakfast, I would have had the first chance of the day to notice the token. If this really wasn't an act on his part, then I needed to figure out if *I* was leading him on and how far I could let things go while I was still uncertain of my intentions in the games. If I made it to finals and the prince picked me, would I choose him?

Melissa was right. The prince was a good man, worthy of love, but I wasn't sure I was ready to risk my heart again.

Twenty-Three

MELISSA ARRIVED FAR BRIGHTER and earlier than I expected, but that's what I deserved for running out on her last night. She noticed the token on my vanity. "So you really did figure out the last riddle." She was already pulling my hair into a messy fishtail braid. It didn't seem formal enough for a meal in the royal dining room, but I wasn't sure how to broach the subject with Melissa.

"I'm not questioning your skill, but is this the right look for a royal breakfast?"

"When the prince sees you today at breakfast, I don't want him to imagine the future princess. I want him to imagine his future wife, the woman who'll throw her hair into a messy braid, put on a comfy tunic, and join him for breakfast."

She put me in a green dress that stopped a few inches above my knee and cinched it at the waist with a gold belt. The hem, sleeves, and neckline were lined with wide stripes of white accented with gold thread.

"These are his colors, aren't they?"

Melissa nodded, and I could see her vision had come true. I looked beautiful and put together but casual, like the women in old pajama ads. No one looked like that at bedtime or right after waking up, but the illusion sold more pajamas. As I was leaving, a note came from the prince: my invitation to join him on a date in a few days in honor of finding a token.

In the center of the royal dining room stood a long, rectangular table made of rich brown wood with gold inlay. It had been set with gold-rimmed plates and more silverware than anyone could possibly need at breakfast.

Lee hadn't shown up yet, but Riya and Lexi strolled in at the same time. Both wore more formal looks than me. Riya's arms were bare in a sleeveless, purple dress with an A-line skirt that almost brushed the floor. Lexi's goldenrod dress clung to her hips and stopped at her knees to reveal Greek-style sandals that snaked up her calves.

"You both look amazing!" I said.

"Our dates are tomorrow!" Riya said. "Lexi's afternoon. I'm evening."

"That's awesome! I actually found the last token, and mine is in a few days."

I looked around for Trinity, but she hadn't arrived yet. Petra was talking to Juliet and Colleen, whose group was here too. I was profoundly grateful to see that Lily would be sharing a different meal with the prince today.

When Lee arrived, we all stood and curtsied. He gave a slight bow, then motioned for us to sit. He went around the table greeting each of us by name and somehow managed to speak with everyone, even Trinity. I hadn't seen her slip in.

The meal began in earnest with pastries, potatoes, fried greens, and even some bacon. I'd noticed that Atlantean meals were light on meat, which had been a reality on Earth for a while.

I picked up a pastry with a cheese-and-vegetable filling and proceeded to cut off small, bite-size pieces. Halfway through the pastry, I looked up to find Lee looking at me, lips pressed together in a smile. He'd chosen the same kind of pastry, which he picked up with one hand. "Breakfast isn't usually a formal meal on Atlantis," he said.

I shook my head and continued with my knife and fork. "I spent a lot of time studying which utensils to use at a royal meal, so I'm going to use them."

"Suit yourself." He shrugged, took another bite, and turned to someone who'd called his name.

Then I noticed Juliet giving me a weird look. I smiled, and she returned the gesture, though it looked a little strained, before replying to Colleen right next to her. Their conversation seemed a little tense, so I looked back to Lee. His brown waves were styled back out of his face, and his brown eyes sparkled with laughter. He was talking to Trinity, and she was laughing. The sight surprised me, but I was glad for it. He glanced my way, and I looked down. Had I been staring?

I avoided looking at him for the rest of breakfast, which ended shortly thereafter. We'd only exchanged a few words, but even so, the morning had been fun.

Our language and culture teachers teamed up to assign us some Atlantean children's books, full of fables teaching moral lessons. They were similar to fables on Earth, but Atlantean fables had a strong emphasis on stewardship of the planet. Or maybe they were giving us those particular fables for a reason.

After lunch, Juliet found me. She didn't look as pleased as I thought she'd be.

"You didn't have to share your token with me."

"I didn't think it would upset you," I replied.

"I'm not upset. It's Colleen."

Things clicked into place. "She thought you were secretly working with me or betrayed her or something."

"Yeah. I caved and told her about Lily. We're fine now."

"That's good. Sorry. I didn't think it would cause any problems."

"Why did you do it?" she asked. "We're not close, no offense, and I didn't help you at all. I don't even know where you found it."

"I don't know. I guess I did it because you didn't deserve what happened with Lily. Or you can consider it a thank-you for getting us access to the gardens."

"No, I owe you one. Want to go to the gym with me? We can be workout buddies. Colleen is more of a yoga girl anyway."

Most of me wanted to say no. I hadn't done this to get in Juliet's good graces. I did it to spite Lily. But I'd gotten weaker in recent weeks without the routine exercise of my warehouse job, and I didn't like it.

"Sure," I replied.

"Great. Change and meet me there."

I did as I was told. In the previous weeks, I'd tried a few of the VR treadmills, but the scenery always made me wish I were in the garden with real sights and smells instead. To my surprise, Juliet bypassed the cardio machines and went straight for the weights.

"They're programmable to pretty much any reasonable weight. The prince tried to explain it to me, but I don't fully understand. I know they work in a similar way to the artificial gravity on the ship."

"Neat," I said, programming a set of dumbbells for about what I thought I could handle. Then Juliet showed me some exercises for different muscles in my arms.

We stood in front of the mirror doing shoulder presses, and I couldn't help admiring Juliet's steady form and strength.

"What's it like in Lightbridge?" I asked.

"Probably a lot like Belvale," she replied.

"Do you miss it at all?"

"I can count on one hand the things I miss about Lightbridge and Earth."

"Like what? The beach?"

"My friends. Don't you miss your friends?"

I hesitated. "The only real friend I have is in the first wave."

"Then you are one of the luckiest people I know." Juliet put her weights down. She blinked hard and set her jaw. It didn't take a genius to figure out she'd left someone behind and didn't want to talk about it.

I stuck to lighter topics for the rest of our session, and Juliet was laughing again after another set of reps. To be exact, she was laughing at my attempt at a pull-up, but I'd gladly be a distraction. I didn't want to think about how I'd feel if Flora was still on Earth.

At the end of our training session, I thanked her. I hadn't done more than a few pushups and crunches since getting the warehouse job, and this was my first time using weights. Their versatility allowed me to work out muscles I didn't even know I had, and the following day, every time I moved or thought about moving, those muscles made sure I remembered exactly where they were.

Juliet's evil plan to incapacitate me had worked nicely.

Twenty-Four

THE NEXT NIGHT, MY two friends gave their reports. Lexi and Lee had played an Atlantean board game and later gone swimming.

"I can't believe he took you swimming!" Riya exclaimed.

"Best view on the ship," she joked, but something was making her uncomfortable. "I mentioned that I loved swimming on our last date."

"He's thoughtful like that," I said.

Lexi stayed uncharacteristically quiet while Riya gushed about her discussion of music with Lee. He'd sung a duet with her, and then they'd gone for a walk that ended with an impromptu dance in the ballroom. Riya yawned. "I'm exhausted. Think I'll call it a night."

After she left, I checked in with Lexi. "You okay?"

"I probably shouldn't say this, but I know you won't tell anyone."

"Yes, but if you're a rebel, I'm screaming for the guards."

Lexi rolled her eyes. "The prince is great and all, but I don't think I like him in a get-married kind of way."

She seemed disappointed, and I grasped for something to say. "No one expects you to fall in love immediately. Maybe you just need to spend more time with him?"

"That's what I thought after our first date, that things would fall into place as time went on. He's kind, funny, and looks really good in a swimsuit." She raised her eyebrows. "Have you seen Atlantean swimsuits? Because—"

"Lexi, stop!" I covered my mouth with my hand, trying to stifle my laugh. I shamelessly hoped that footage would make it into the date episode.

"My point is, there isn't a spark. I wish there was, but I'm relieved that he doesn't seem to feel it either," she said.

"How do you know that?"

"I've seen it in the way he looks at some of the women. Not leering or anything. It's hard to describe, but it's the way he looks at Riya and Juliet sometimes."

"Oh," I said. "I think I know what you mean."

"You'd better. He looks at you that way the most. You never told us much about your first date, but you must have made quite the impression."

"I guess so."

"So, do you like him?" Lexi asked. "I can tell Riya does, but she's an open book."

I paused. I found Lee charming. He was easy to talk to despite being a prince, and I replayed our kiss in my mind every night before I went to sleep. "I do. I wish sometimes I felt like you do, warmly disinterested, but I like him." I frowned. "A lot, actually." Saying it out loud terrified me. I couldn't keep waffling anymore. I couldn't take it back.

"I'm pulling for both you and Riya. How do you feel about harems?"

I groaned. "I feel like I'm glad I'm picking out my own library books now."

Lexi cackled at that, but the conversation had worn us out, so we headed to our rooms. It was a relief to know that Lexi's heart wasn't in the competition, but a concern that mine absolutely was.

⋙ ⋘

The next day, Lee began to honor the token dates. He gave Juliet a tour of the engine room, a part of the ship where the cameras couldn't follow. That evening, he took Lily dancing again.

When it was time for my date, I was ready for the cameras. Melissa dressed me in a rose-pink, off-the-shoulder dress and pinned my hair up in braids and flowers. Lee had invited me to play an Atlantean board game, then have dinner in a private parlor.

"That sounds nice," Melissa said.

And that's all it was. Nice.

He greeted me politely, explained the rules of the game, and proceeded to handily beat me while inquiring about my family. The camera drones hummed steadily overhead while Talia sat in a corner, mostly out of sight. He asked me if I wanted to play another round, but I declined. "Too much like chess; not enough like rummy or pinochle."

"You'll have to teach me those sometime. Dinner?" he asked, standing and offering me his arm.

"I guess so." He walked me from his sitting room to a private dining area. "Are you mad at me?" I whispered as we settled into our seats.

The question startled him into being himself for a few moments. "No, I—" He turned to Talia, who was settling into another corner in our new location. "Talia, could you give us five minutes?"

"Your Highness," she said, putting a hand on her hip, "you agreed to allow us to film all your dates with the contestants, and this is not a restricted area of the ship."

"Talia, please." He was extremely polite, but it was clearly a command, not a request. Talia sighed and followed her drones out of the room.

"I can't do this in front of the cameras," Lee said. "Especially with you."

"Why not? You'll have to open up on camera eventually."

He drew back. "That's laughable coming from you. You act like this all the time, even we're alone. Sometimes I'm talking to you; other times you block me out. At least you know when my walls will be up."

"That's not fair," I objected.

"No," he said. "It's not." He trained his intent, brown eyes on mine.

My rebuttal died on my lips. He was right. The most honest I'd been with him was the first night when I was crying. Ever since then, I'd been pushing him away, literally, like after the Aphrodite Trial when we were dancing. Or in the library when he kissed me. I wasn't avoiding prying eyes like he had been in the transporter. I was avoiding him. Every time he got close, I pushed him away.

"I'm sorry," I said softly. "You deserve to know the truth. But first, I think you should tell Talia and Stefan no more cameras. They get a few shots at the beginning and end, and then you're left to enjoy your dates as yourself."

"I can't—"

"You're the prince. You can do whatever you want, and before you go on about the people needing to see you, they already have. Just stage a few minutes instead of the whole date. You'll be happier being you."

He was still mulling it over when Talia returned with Stefan at her side. Stefan gave me a sidelong smile while Talia finished a tirade she'd clearly begun in the hall. "See? He sent us away."

Lee put his own mask back on, the polite, regal persona he showed the cameras. "Talia, I think you've gotten enough unlimited access. From now on, I'll give you fifteen minutes at the beginning and end of the date and the opportunity to return at certain points if the activity warrants it. I understand your need for content, but the constant presence is too much. You and your cameras have been interfering with the Goddess Games, even if it was unintentional."

"Your Highness," Talia said, her pitch higher than I'd ever heard it, "I wish you'd recon—"

"Effective immediately," he said.

Talia looked ready to give the prince a piece of her mind, but Stefan stepped in. "Talia, he has a point. We'll have to make the most of the footage we get." He turned back to Lee and bowed. "Thank you for your patience this past month, and I trust that if we are interfering moving forward, you'll let us know."

Lee nodded, his expression still serious. Talia was red-faced, but I swore Stefan winked at me when he turned to leave.

A minute later, we had the room to ourselves. "You know? I feel lighter. Thanks for the suggestion." He checked his watch. "It's still a little early for dinner. Maybe a cocktail?"

"I don't really drink," I said. "Alcohol was a luxury good on Earth. Can you recommend something that's not very strong and tastes good? I don't like the wine they serve at dinner, but I don't think it's the wine's fault."

"Sure," he replied. "I know just the thing." He opened his tablet, made an order, then invited me to sit with him on a couch in front of one of the walls, which was actually a giant screen. Using his tablet once again, Lee brought it to life. Waves crashed on the shore, and small birds chirped and flitted about the sand, hunting for crabs or sandworms. Back from the shoreline were scrubby bushes and trees with long, feathery leaves.

"It's beautiful. Is this Atlantis?" I could almost feel the sun on my skin.

"Yes. I used to spend a lot of time at this beach as a kid. Now that the cameras are gone, will you tell me what you've been hiding? Is it a boyfriend back on Earth?"

"No. Nothing like that. I promised you I'd explain, but you need to understand that this story also kind of involves Lily."

"I'd be lying if I said I wasn't interested to understand the, uh, dynamic you two have."

I looked at him and held his gaze. "What I'm about to tell you—it's humiliating. Flora is the only one who knows the full story. Every time I come close to the memories in my head, I slam the door and run away." If I wasn't good enough for Brett, why would I be good enough for a prince? Brett had fooled me, so anyone could.

He frowned. "You don't have to tell me. I don't want to force you to relive something painful."

"No, it's all right. I want you to understand. You were right when you said I haven't been fair to you."

"I promise to keep it to myself."

I focused on a spot on the beach. "Over the winter, I started studying for the weather analyst apprenticeship. I went to the library every night I could after work, taking notes, reading up on past storm responses, all of it. The books I needed had to stay in the library. I couldn't check them out and take them home.

"One day, the study guide I needed was already being used. After a little sleuthing, I found a guy named Brett Vasquez was using it. He was Lily's brother, though I didn't really talk to her until later. Brett and I studied together the whole winter. I started to have feelings for him, and he flirted back. I thought he liked me, too, though he was more reserved when Lily was around. She was always awful to me on the rare occasions she stopped by the library."

I chanced a look at Lee. He was frowning. "So Brett didn't return your feelings?"

I shook my head. "Worse. He pretended to. He kept hinting that once the entrance exam was over, we could both work as weather analysts"—I swallowed—"and basically live happily ever after. The day of the test, he sat next to me. About halfway through, I noticed him glancing at my answers. At first I shrugged it off, thinking I'd imagined it, but once I got that suspicion, every glance was painfully obvious. I tried to block his view, which must have tipped him off. The rules said I was supposed to turn him in, but I couldn't do it. I liked him too much."

Lee reached out and put his hand on mine.

"Just as I was finishing up, Brett turned his test in and spoke with the test proctor. He must have claimed I was the cheater because the proctor tossed my test and informed me I was disqualified."

Lee leaned forward. "That's outrageous! Without any sort of investigation?"

"Nothing. I've relived that moment so many times in my mind. I should have called him a liar, made a scene, punched him, done something! But I couldn't. I still cared about him. I thought it must have been some misunderstanding, that he'd explain it all to me."

"But he didn't."

I shook my head. "Atlantis was just a fantasy then. They hadn't assigned waves yet, so I didn't know how long I'd be on Earth. Brett and that test represented every hope, plan, and dream I had for the future. It wasn't that he rejected me, it's that he used me. I believed that his feelings were real, and by the end of it, I couldn't even trust myself. That's what makes it so awful. Not the lying or cheating. It's how he made me feel about myself and how hard it still is to shake those feelings, like there's a traitorous part of me always whispering that I'm worthless."

A few tears rolled down my cheeks, dripping onto my dress. Lee offered me a handkerchief, then held me as I got my breathing under control.

"I know my opinion's not the one that matters here, but I think you're incredible. I wish you could see yourself the way I do." His words were a light that banished some of the darkness that had crept into my thoughts. "I suppose it's too late to accidentally leave him on Earth," Lee said thoughtfully.

I laughed and wiped away the last of my tears. "Is there a habitable planet in between Earth and Atlantis? We could make a pit stop, and I'm negotiable on the habitable part."

Lee released me and laughed, only to grow serious once again. "Your frustration at feeling hidden makes a lot more sense now. I'm sorry that I made you doubt yourself."

"It's not your fault. But I want you to be able to be yourself. It must be hard to choose a princess in front of the whole world. Two worlds, I guess."

"Especially when there are still a lot of eliminations to come. I wasn't supposed to get attached to anyone this early in the games. There are a lot of contestants that I enjoy spending time with or who are interesting in some way. Then, there's you—"

Our conversation was interrupted by the arrival of our drinks. In honor of the relaxing beach scenery, he'd ordered us something called "Beach Nectar," which was a mix of tropical flavors: pineapple and coconut with barely a hint of alcohol. We sipped our drinks and talked freely. I began to relax, but my drink was so weak—as promised—that I didn't know whether the cause was the alcohol or the fresh openness between us.

Dinner without the cameras was just as nice. Lee told me about his best friend back home, Lysander, and I shared stories about Flora. I was looking forward to our next call with families, which was tomorrow.

"Oh no! Flora's birthday. It's..." I counted the days we'd been on the ship. "Today. I completely forgot to keep track of the Earth calendar. She's turning eighteen."

"Want to call her right now? I'm curious to meet this Flora."

A part of me did, but I also didn't want to interrupt our date. "No, we get calls tomorrow. She'll understand. But I have an idea. If it's not too much to ask."

Lee listened, a gleam in his eye as he conspired with me to send Flora a birthday gift. "I'll make the arrangements right after our date."

Conversation meandered back to his life on Atlantis until we hit a lull. The prince grew quiet, lost in thought. "I hate to bring it up again, but was Lily involved in helping Brett cheat? Because if so, I'll have her removed from the games."

"No, she wasn't involved in it as far as I know. She's just..." I didn't want to sound petty. "We don't get along."

"I won't mention any of this to her. It's jarring to hear your description and compare it to my own experience. She's been very, uh, sweet to me."

"Oh, I'm sure," I said, grimacing at the thought of the two of them together.

A chime indicated someone at the door. I raised my eyebrows at him in question.

"Must be Talia. I sent for her."

"Why?"

"I promised her access if the activity warranted it. Please don't push me away this time."

Lee opened the door and greeted Talia.

"I'm going to give Chloe a good-night kiss, which you may record."

Talia looked at me as if disgusted by his choice, but she directed her cameras into position.

"I had a wonderful time getting to know you today," Lee said, taking my hands in his. We both ignored the cameras, though I struggled with it more than he did. "May Tyche smile upon you in the coming trial."

He leaned down and kissed me, his lips moving gently on mine. Despite being staged, this kiss was genuine. I hoped the camera couldn't see the goosebumps on my bare arms. Lee pulled back and smiled. He walked me back to my room, but with the cameras rolling, I didn't want to ask who or what Tyche was.

Even if Lee changed his mind tomorrow, today was real. That mattered. Even though I'd misjudged Brett, that didn't mean I was wrong about the prince. The Goddess Games made it hard to distinguish sincerity from performance, but I was finally beginning to trust myself again.

Twenty-Five

The day before the Athena Trial, the next episode of our dates aired. They played it in the common room after breakfast since our classes for the day had been canceled.

Lexi's date was probably the best one, and not just because he was shirtless. Lee seemed most like himself, though I got what Lexi meant when she'd said there were no sparks.

"The only reason there's so much footage of my date is because Talia couldn't bear to cut out any of those abs," Lexi muttered. Riya and I laughed, and Talia glared at us, as if she'd heard her name.

Next, we watched the prince and Riya enjoy a romantic duet and stroll. Lee was a competent singer, but Riya outshone him to no one's surprise. She looked radiant, and he'd kissed her on the lips, though it was brief. He'd unfortunately kissed Lily, too, and she'd seized the opportunity to clutch him in her harpy's grasp. I couldn't stop myself from making a face.

Juliet's date ended with a kiss on the cheek once again, but hers was the most remarkable to me, even though much of it was in a part of the ship where the cameras weren't permitted. They spoke so easily, mainly about Earth and Atlantean politics. She asked questions I never would have thought of. In the clip, she asked about labor laws and forced labor. The prince assured her that worker protections on Atlantis were strong and that forced labor of any kind, like slavery, was strictly forbidden. He and Juliet didn't have the chemistry that he shared with Riya and Lily, but they had a different sort of bond. They were both leaders.

My date was played last. Just as with the first, there wasn't a lot of footage. There was some polite back-and-forth as we played Atlantean chess, then a dramatic cut to our kiss. As far as telling a story, my date contained a gaping plot hole. Where was the laughter over dinner, the drinks at the "beach," and the buildup to the kiss? Not recorded. But from the reaction of the other contestants, they'd seen something in our kiss that they hadn't in the others.

"Whoa, Chloe," Lexi said. "Is that what happens when you let him win at chess, or whatever you played?"

"I wouldn't know. I didn't let him win. He wrecked me."

"I bet he did," Lily snapped, looking me up and down. "Your dates seem to involve a lot of off-camera activities. How *do* you spend your time together?"

"Eating dinner. Visiting the beach in an immersive experience," I replied, acting confused. "Wait, what are you suggesting about the prince?"

A shadow passed across her face, but then it was gone. She stormed out of the room, and a few other women followed.

"Good riddance," Lexi muttered.

I wasn't so sure. Looking around the room, suspicious eyes met mine. Petra looked like she believed Lily's unspoken accusation, that I was sleeping with the prince, and she wasn't the only one. Micaela and Colleen were muttering to each other. Juliet didn't look my way. Even Riya seemed upset, but that was for a different reason. Unlike Lexi, she had real feelings for the prince.

All of a sudden, I didn't want to be in the lounge anymore. "I'm going to get ready for my family call." Was it that bad? Had I actually done something wrong? I didn't think so, but the way the other women were reacting gave me doubts.

When I got to my room, Melissa was there to set up my call with my family. She was practically vibrating with excitement. "He gave *you* the kiss of Tyche!" She'd apparently watched the episode air.

"Yeah, I meant to ask what that was. What's Tyche? They haven't covered that in our classes."

"She's the embodiment of luck. On Earth, Tyche was the goddess of luck, but there wasn't an actual Olympian counterpart for her. I think she was actually an ancient deity from the Olympians' own pantheon."

"Oh, so a good luck kiss? That's sweet." I smiled at the memory.

"In the games, it's something special. It's like a token. He wants you to win the next trial."

"How big a deal is it?" I asked.

"It's not a declaration of love or anything like that, but it's a big deal that he did it so early in the games. It's his way of signaling that you are a worthy contestant."

"Ahh, probably because there's so little footage of our dates. The others weren't pleased with that. They're right, though. There's a big disconnect between what's been shown in the episodes and our actual interactions."

"Well, not everything gets recorded, as you said."

"But you're not bothered by it?" I pressed her. Melissa busied herself with smoothing my hair. "Melissa?"

She sighed. "Fine. I was organizing your things, and I found the notes he sent you. You really ought to destroy them, you know."

I jerked my head in her direction. "What! I thought you weren't my maid, and it wasn't your job to clean up after me." A jolt of panic swept through me, but if she'd found the commcard, she would have already turned me in.

"I was *organizing*, not cleaning. Don't worry, my lips are sealed."

"I should report you or something. Snooping like that has to be illegal."

"It's not. And I would know. Back on Atlantis I'm a lawyer."

"What? And you're doing my hair and makeup? How'd that work out?"

"Hair and makeup are a hobby of mine, and you've learned about arete by now. I'm sure they gave you the 'strive for excellence' talk, but Atlanteans love to learn, and we love art. People are my medium. A lot of practice on a lot of patient friends gave me the skills I needed to earn a spot to see Earth. And work as a stylist and PA in the games. Many of the other PAs have other jobs back home. Some of them wanted the prestige while others were curious to see the planet we left behind."

"That's amazing. So, if you're a lawyer, any tips on how I destroy the evidence?"

"You mean the letters? There's a setting on the trash disposal. See?" She pointed to a button marked with a small horseshoe shape.

"So that's what the little omega button does. Thanks." I lowered my voice and looked her in the eye. "Nothing inappropriate happened. I promise."

"I believe you. It's not the prince's style, and I don't think it's yours either."

"Hearing that means more than you know."

"I'll leave you to your call. Let me know if you want lunch delivered today."

As soon as Melissa left, I called my family, eager to learn how they were settling in. Mom and Dad looked a little grim, and even Flora looked reserved.

"My parents and the twins send their love," Flora said.

"Send mine back," I replied. "Is everything okay? You all look upset."

Flora perked back up, and my parents shared a look. "We're all doing well. The Atlantean doctors identified a few minor issues that they've treated us for," Dad said.

"You promise they're minor?" I asked, unsettled.

"We promise."

"Then what's wrong? Are they treating you okay?"

"Yes," Flora said. "They've been wonderful hosts. Just some of the other people here, from Earth, keep complaining and spreading those ridiculous rebel conspiracy theories."

"The alien cannibal ones?" I asked. "Because if they're aliens, then they can't also be cannibals by eating humans."

"Versions of that, yes, and the ones about enslaving the people from Earth. There are rumors of people disappearing, then coming back days later with no memory of their absence," Flora replied.

"Just rumors. It's nothing to worry about, Chloe," Mom said. "It seems like the prince really likes you. Is he—" She faltered and blinked hard. She was fighting tears, but I didn't know why. "Is he a nice young man? Properly behaved?"

My happiness shriveled. They thought the same thing the other contestants did about all my off-camera time with the prince, except, even worse, they assumed that I was an unwilling participant.

"I don't know what rumors are circulating out there, but the prince is a wonderful man," I reassured her. "I'm safe here. I do like him, and he likes me too."

The three of them relaxed at once. "We're glad to hear you're doing well," Dad said.

We kept talking, and I told them about the other contestants, the library, and a few interesting bits from my class on Atlantean culture. By the end of our call, I realized I'd monopolized most of our time.

"Can I have a minute alone with Chloe?" Flora asked.

My parents nodded. "Of course. Love you, pumpkin!" Dad said.

"Love you!"

My parents left, and she retreated to her room. They must have called from the Simmonses suite, which had a small common room for the family.

"So you're really okay?"

"I'm more than okay. The prince is something out of a fairy tale. Which reminds me, did you get the books?"

Her eyes sparkled with mischief. "Oh yes. The *Her Alien Kingdom* trilogy. Fortunately while my parents were out. I don't have a rooftop or access to the gardens, but at least I have my own room now!"

"You can thank the prince. He's the one who made the arrangements to send them."

"You asked the prince to send me these books?"

"He knows all about you roof books." I gave her a wicked grin.

"Traitor. Does he know you were up there with me half the time?"

"Let's just say these books come at my personal recommendation."

She shook her head. "He sounds perfect."

"I told you. Prince charming."

"I'm glad the rumors aren't true."

"Me too. Happy birthday, Flora. I wish I was there to hug you."

We said our goodbyes, and as I logged off, I couldn't help but wonder: if my own family had these doubts about the prince, what about the other people from Earth? And if others believed the rumors, then what did they think of me?

Twenty-Six

The Athena Trial was scheduled for the morning, shortly after breakfast. I decided to check again for any messages from Russo. After missing her warning about the Aphrodite Trial, I figured I should check one last time before the next challenge. Sure enough, there were two more messages waiting for me. One congratulated me on getting so close to the prince and asked for an update on any leads I had. What was I supposed to say, that I was too busy falling for the prince to figure out who was trying to kill him? I replied that I had nothing new to report. While I could report my suspicions to Russo, if I figured out who the rebel was, I might go straight to the prince instead.

There was one more message titled "Athena Trial Help."

I was one tap away from making it through the next trial. Athena had been a results-oriented Olympian. She probably would have read the message, given her close association with Nike, the Atlantean embodiment of victory. Nike was like Tyche in that she wasn't an actual Olympian, even though she'd been called a goddess in ancient Greece. Athena was always willing to do whatever it took to win. Was I?

I considered my choices. When I started the games, the only thing I'd cared about was making it to the finals so I could become a noble and choose my own path. My chance to make a difference on Earth had been stolen from me, so would it really be so wrong to steal that chance back for my new life on Atlantis? What would Lee think of me, and would any of that matter if I was eliminated today?

I sighed. If I cheated and made it to the finals, I'd be no better than Brett, taking up a spot that I didn't earn. Russo's message tempted me because I wasn't ready to leave the games for more than one reason. My finger hovered over the unopened message.

I dropped my hand into my lap. No. I wouldn't do it. I was finally beginning to trust myself again, and that meant trusting myself to do this by my own merit. The prince had given us riddles to solve, so maybe the trial would be similar. I was decent at riddles and puzzles thanks to all the fantasy books I'd read; the heroines were always solving puzzles to retrieve some powerful weapon or artifact. The prince had even said he thought the Athena Trial would suit me. Some hints would have been nice, but I'd gotten this far on my own. I'd continue through the games on my own too. Plus, there was a not-so-small part of me that worried about how Lee would react if I cheated, especially after I'd told him about Brett.

I'd just put the card back in my ratty jean pocket in the closet when Melissa knocked at the door. Cheerful and chatty today, she dressed me in a simple, gray tunic and put my hair up in a high ponytail.

"No makeup?"

"Not today. All the contestants will have the same sort of look."

I'd gotten used to the bright colors and expert hair and makeup, but I'd manage without it for a day. From the common room we were marched to a large, open room. A circular structure stood before us with doors placed at intervals. Based on the distance between the doors and the number of remaining teams, I guessed there were nine total. Stefan was once again introducing the event. Talia and her camera drones were by his side.

"Athena is one of the most respected of the Olympians," he began. "Though at times she was vengeful, Atlanteans admire her wisdom and strategic mind. Her association in ancient Earth myth with weaving is one we take figuratively, as she's known for her cunning ability to weave a lie with nothing but the truth. She does not take kindly to failure, and she was the one who trained our ancestors in much of the Olympian technology we enjoy. Her attributes are cleverness and creativity. Athena also hated to lose. She is strongly associated with Nike, the embodiment of victory, and Athena was known for wearing a ring that featured her symbol, a winged woman.

"The rules of her trial are simple. You may not interfere with the other teams in any way or you will be disqualified. Your team will pass through a series of three rooms, and each room will hold a challenge to overcome. A successful solution will earn your team a Nike token, which will allow you to open the door to the next challenge. Each incorrect attempt will earn your team a Medusa token, and one of your teammates must leave the course. Your team must decide which member will go. At the end, all rooms will open into a shared space. The first team to reach the Athena statue at the center will be declared the victor. The two teams which rank the lowest will be eliminated."

"I know who's going first if we get a Medusa token," Lexi murmured next to me, flicking her head toward Petra. I stifled a laugh, and Riya shot me an annoyed look.

"The challenges will test your knowledge of the Atlantean language, culture, and history you have been studying, as well as your knowledge of Athena. Once you've passed the three challenges, you'll be able to seize victory."

My shoulders relaxed. My Atlantean reading and writing were getting better, and I enjoyed most of the culture classes. "Good thing there's no etiquette involved," I muttered.

Lexi smiled, but Riya huffed.

"Riya, are you okay?" I whispered. She ignored me.

"Your wit will be tested alongside your knowledge," Stefan proclaimed. "Remember that while many answers may look like a solution, each puzzle has a single best answer."

A crew member led my team around the circumference of the room to a door marked with the number six. A bell chimed, and the door clicked open. I followed my four teammates into the first puzzle chamber, accompanied by a camera drone. The trial had begun.

In the center of the room stood a table scattered with rectangular blocks. Six Atlantean words were inscribed on its smooth surface. At a glance, the words were familiar, even in Atlantean letters. They were the names of a few Olympians, and each name had a corresponding indentation in the same shape as the scattered blocks. The scattered blocks also held words in Atlantean, but these were less familiar.

"We're supposed to match the blocks to the right Olympian," I said, grabbing the nearest block and beginning to decipher it.

"Obviously." Petra rolled her eyes.

While we were nearly fluent in spoken Atlantean thanks to the imprinting, reading was still a challenge. We all had the alphabet down and common or familiar words came to us easily, like the names of the Olympians. But many of these words were unfamiliar in writing, and even pronouncing them out loud didn't always help. Without context, it was hard to get a sense of an individual word. But there was another layer of difficulty. As we went through the blocks, we put them near the Olympians they best matched, but the answers weren't clear cut.

"I feel like there are a lot of ways we can solve this," Lexi said, rubbing her temples.

"Yeah, but there's supposed to be a best answer," I replied. "Look at Aphrodite. We've got *philia* and *kallos*, love and beauty. But philia isn't romantic love. So it would have to be kallos."

"There's also a difference between the Atlanteans and the ancient Greeks in how they view the Olympians," Trinity said. I was surprised she spoke, but I was glad for it. "I've been reading Greek and Atlantean versions of the same stories, and the Olympians are much more reasonable in the Atlantean ones. Aphrodite is primarily associated with beauty and art on Atlantis."

I picked up the stone labeled kallos and offered it to Trinity, but she shook her head. I would have to be the one to place it in the slot and hope for the best. The heavy tile fit perfectly into the indentation, and after a few tense seconds, a blue light glowed under the tile, reflecting off the smooth edges.

"Nice work, Trinity," Lexi muttered, eyes fixed on the blue glow.

"Okay, so we have to think like Atlanteans for these," I replied, moving on to the next one. As we went through the Olympians, Trinity's reasoning proved itself again and again. After we had narrowed down Hermes to "guide" and "messenger," "guide" seemed the obvious choice. Messenger was his primary role in Earth mythology, not Atlantean canon. He had been the navigator on the ship that brought the first humans from Earth to Atlantis. Hera was "ambition," not "queen." She had been the first officer on the Olympian ship, one of the youngest among her people to achieve that rank. Her role as queen was a human interpretation of her subordination to her ship's captain, Zeus. Artemis was "huntress," not "archer." "Huntress" encompassed her drive and competence as a defensive pilot.

Now that we'd knocked the easy ones out of the way, we had only Zeus and Demeter left.

"Let's do Zeus next," Lexi said. "Demeter looks impossible."

"Well, both of the words for Zeus mean 'power,' so I guess we just have to pick one," Petra said, reaching for one of the tiles.

"They can't mean the same thing, though. There has to be a difference," I argued.

"Then what's the difference?" Riya asked sharply.

"You okay?" I asked again, wondering why she was so irritable, but she ignored me. I refocused on the tiles, reading them both aloud. *Dynamis. Sthenos.* Instantly, the difference clicked. "Sthenos is more like strength than power. I've heard them use this word to describe the strength of radiation storms. It must be dynamis. Maybe that's more like command power."

"How convenient that your special little job helped us out!" Petra said, her voice bubbling with mock enthusiasm. "Is this trial rigged too?"

I had been leaning over the table to get a better look at the tiles, but at her words, I straightened and met her eyes. "What?"

"You heard me," Petra said.

I looked at the others. Trinity was studying the Demeter words, Lexi looked ready to throttle Petra, and Riya was glaring at me with her arms crossed like she wanted an answer. I thought about the unopened message from Russo and wondered if any other teams had gotten help.

"If it is rigged, I'm not in on it. Can we get back to this, please?"

"Fine," Petra said. "But I think you're wrong." She whirled around, picked up the tile inscribed with the word "sthenos," and placed it in the slot.

From the look on her face when the tile glowed red, she'd really thought it would be right. On cue, a gentle click sounded from the table. Following the sound, we found a small opening in the table where our Medusa coin was waiting for us.

"We have to send someone away before proceeding," Riya said.

"I vote Chloe," Petra said.

"And I vote Petra," I fired back. "Your mistake earned this coin, so you should go."

"Petra," Lexi said, shrugging.

"Chloe." My eyes found the face of my betrayer. Riya.

"Really, Riya?"

"You baited her into putting in the wrong tile, probably so you could eliminate her," Riya said. "After all, you've got a history of being less than truthful."

"That's literally insane. Look, if our team wins, we all benefit, even the eliminated ones."

"Then why don't you step down if it doesn't matter? You'll still benefit," Riya said.

"Because Chloe doesn't think the team can do it without her," Petra said. "After all, the prince probably gave her the answers so he could keep someone easy to—"

"Petra," Trinity said in an even tone.

"What?" Petra snapped.

"I vote Petra goes," Trinity replied. Her voice was low but firm.

Petra wrinkled her nose. "Fine. I'll go, but remember, you're all expendable to her."

I wanted to confront Riya and work through her issue, but we had one more puzzle to solve. Trinity had placed the "dynamis" tile in the slot, which glowed a happy blue.

Demeter only deepened our group issues.

"I don't really know these words," Trinity said. "That one is something like 'growth,' and the other is... food-related?"

Everyone generally agreed with her first assessment, but the second word had us split. I said it aloud a few times. "I think it's an archaic word or something," I said. "Why do you think it's food-related, Trinity? I get the same vibe, but I don't know why."

"It shares a stem with the Atlantean word for food," Trinity replied. "I've seen the word for food before in the dining hall, near the kitchens."

"Wait!" Riya said. "This other word. Growth. I've seen it in the gardens. It has to be the one."

"Riya's right. It's on a plaque," Lexi added.

"Which plaque?" Trinity asked, frowning.

"The one right in front of the little forest part," Riya said.

"Then I don't think we should pick it," Trinity said. "Demeter is known for controlled growth, like crops. That little forest area is wild. We know she was responsible for managing rations and food supply on the Olympians' missions, as well as colonial infrastructure. She was all about logistics."

"So we should pick the word we don't know?" Lexi asked. "What if it doesn't have to do with food after all?"

"If we pick 'growth' because we know it, that's just as careless. If we can rule out growth, the unknown word is the better choice," I said.

We took a vote, and it was unanimous, however grudging.

"Here goes nothing," Lexi said, sliding the unknown tile into the slot. Tense seconds ticked by while we waited for feedback, until we got that blue glow. Another gentle clink indicated the arrival of a new token. The form of a winged woman had been stamped onto the coin. Nike. Victory.

"One down, two to go," I said, picking up the coin and pushing it into the slot by the door. It swung open, revealing the next room.

TWENTY-SEVEN

THE SECOND CHAMBER WAS larger than the first. The walls were covered in tapestries that featured geometric patterns of varying colors and complexity. At one end was a solitary chair, and at the other were a bunch of upright posts of varying heights, no thicker than a chair leg. The posts on one side had long strips of colorful fabric twisted in between them. The other side was fabric-free, though there were plenty of colorful scraps of fabric spread throughout the room. I approached the chair and sat down. "Whoa, check this out," I said. The others were already on their way, so I got up to let someone else sit. Riya took the chair while Lexi and Trinity crouched next to her.

"Is that a wing?" Lexi asked.

The fabric was woven between the posts in such a way that it looked three-dimensional, a white wing much like Nike's in the foreground, with all the colors of the rainbow as a backdrop. The sight was stunning, but I forced my mind back to the puzzle at hand. "Do you think we are supposed to fill in the other side to match, weaving the fabric between all these stakes?"

"I guess so," Riya said. "I'll sit here and direct you all."

I held my tongue, but Lexi put a hand on her hip. "How kind of you! Next time you've got an issue, maybe you can resolve it before we're in the middle of a trial?"

"I think it makes the most sense to start with the colors in the back, then work forward so my view isn't blocked," Riya said, ignoring Lexi's comment.

"Let's just go. The sooner we finish the trial, the better," I said. *For so many reasons.*

We'd woven in the purples and blues, which were the farthest back. Looking at the other side, there were some extra twists and turns of the fabric that were unnecessary. A viewer in Riya's position wouldn't be able to see them, so why were they there?

"Something's weird back here," I said.

"Yeah," Lexi agreed. "The other side is way more complex. This is too easy."

"It looks fine to me," Riya said. "You can start with the green now."

I dropped the green fabric to the floor and stepped out of the forest of fabric and stakes. What had we missed? I peered around the room, looking for anything out of place. The token dispenser was attached to the wall near the door to the next room. I hadn't seen it at first among the designs on the wall tapestries, so I searched for anything else on the wall I'd missed.

"Of course," I said, running toward a ladder disguised as part of the patterned wall. I climbed up a few rungs and figured out our mistake. "It's supposed to be Medusa from the top. We need a second spotter up here giving directions. Trinity, can you?"

"Sure," she replied, hurrying over. We traded places, and Lexi and I got back to work, adjusting our purples and blues based on feedback from Trinity. Then we got into the greens and yellows, which were very complicated to weave correctly. The reds and oranges got a little easier, or maybe we were used to it by then. The final step was weaving in the white for the wing.

"Everything good?" I called up to Trinity.

"I think so," she replied, climbing down.

Riya stood, giving us the thumbs-up. Lexi pushed the button next to the token dispenser, but the light glowed red, and we received another Medusa coin.

"What did we miss?" Lexi grumbled, bunching her fists in frustration.

"We have to eliminate someone before we can find and fix it," I replied. "Any volunteers?"

No one moved.

"You could go, Chloe, since you should have left last time," Riya said.

"I think it should be you, Riya," Lexi said. "You just sat in the chair the whole time. You haven't been the greatest team player today."

"Team player? Really? You want to go there? Fine," Riya said. "This whole time Chloe's been lying about her time with the prince. We ask about her dates, and she says they're fine and changes the subject."

"I don't have to tell you everything," I said. "I don't like to share that stuff, and I have my reasons."

"Why? Are you doing things with the prince that would get you kicked out of the games?"

"No, and I doubt the prince would break the rules of his own Goddess Games," I replied. "I'm sorry if you think I lied to you, but I never did."

"What is it Athena is known for on Atlantis? Weaving lies with the truth? Maybe that's why this is your best trial—it sure feels like you lied."

Lexi, who'd been watching our verbal volley, interrupted. "Where's Trinity?"

I looked around, but there was no sign of her. "She left. So we could keep going."

"What?" Riya asked. "Maybe she realized she messed up." Riya climbed the ladder to identify Trinity's mistake. Lexi made a similar move toward Riya's chair.

"Right there," Lexi said. "That green bit there isn't quite even. Let me know when it's good." With that, she got up and returned to the mass of cloth. I sat, watching the symmetry of the two halves even out. Lexi returned, checked once more, and then checked the Medusa view from the top.

"Cross your fingers," Lexi said, pressing the button once more. This time, a blue light glowed behind the button, and our Nike token appeared.

Riya had been silent the whole time we were making the adjustments. "It was my mistake," she said softly. "I should have left, not Trinity."

"There's no use second-guessing it now. You were wrong, but maybe that means you'll be more careful in the next task," Lexi replied, slipping the token into the lock of the next door.

"I'm sorry," Riya said. "I've been awful today. I don't know what happened to me."

I did. Riya really liked the prince. It was hard to see him with other people, especially someone you might not have realized was a threat. "It's okay. I think I get it. Let's finish this trial, then talk it out."

"I'm going to need more groveling than that," Lexi said, "but Chloe's right. It can wait."

Riya smiled at that, and even though things weren't quite right between us, the anger that Riya had been radiating was gone.

The third room was a cluttered mess. At the center was a life-size statue of Athena, her hand held out in a familiar pose. There were dozens of small statuettes of the goddess Nike scattered throughout the room along with a lot of worn, mismatched furniture, like we'd been teleported into a thrift store.

The task was obvious. "We have to put the Nike statuette in her hand," I said.

"But which one?" Lexi asked.

"They all look the same," Riya said.

After some checking, we agreed they were all identical.

"If there's no difference in the statuettes, there must be another difference," I said.

"The material, weight, or some other characteristic we haven't thought of," Lexi added.

"Is there a significance to the number thirteen?" Riya asked. "That's how many there are spread throughout the room."

"Not that I can think of. If we can't figure it out, we get three guesses. Maybe we should look for any clue next to the statuettes."

Lexi walked around gently rapping on the statues, lifting each one slightly before replacing it, but her defeated shrug told me that she'd found no hollow statuettes. I didn't see anything special about the wicker basket or coffee table where two of the statuettes were standing. One stood in front of a mirror as if admiring the powerful span of her wings, but the mirror itself was unremarkable, just like the rest of the junk.

"Hey, there's an inscription at the base of the Athena statue," Riya said. "It's in English. Maybe it's a clue." She read it aloud. *"You must see yourself as the victor."*

I looked at my reflection, brown curls in a simple ponytail, my tunic as gray as everyone else's. Nothing to make me stand out. Could I really see myself as the victor? Did I really have a chance at winning this? What if we were stuck in this room until we were eliminated?

Come on, Chloe, think. That's what you're good at. We're all dressed plainly because this trial isn't like the Aphrodite Trial. We're not showcasing our bodies; we're showcasing our minds. Time to heed the inscrip-

tion's advice and see yourself as the victor. Imagine yourself holding one of those little Nike statues, just like Athena.

I could see one of the Nike statues in my reflection, but she was facing away from me. "The mirrors," I said, struck by a bolt of realization. "It's something to do with the mirrors and the reflections."

There were three mirrors in the room. I stayed in front of mine, Lexi took one in the corner, and Riya took the one closest to the central statue.

"What are we looking for exactly?" Riya asked.

"I'm not sure," I replied. "You must see yourself as the victor. Athena is supposed to be holding the statuette of Nike, meaning she's holding victory, literally. If we hold the same pose as Athena, maybe our hands will point to the right statuette."

"Oh, wow," Lexi said. "I think this is it. Look!"

Unlike the other two mirrors, Lexi's mirror was positioned so that it faced in Athena's direction. The statue stood in the center of the room, and when Lexi put her hand up, she was able to line up her body to cover the reflection of Athena's statue. The reflection of one of the Nike statuettes stood in her own reflection's outstretched palm.

"It has to be," Riya agreed.

"Stay here and make sure I grab the right one," I said, hurrying to the other side of the room. "This one?" I called, my hand hovering over the statuette, heart pounding in my chest.

"Yes!" Lexi replied.

By the time I placed the Nike statuette in Athena's hand, Lexi and Riya were by my side. The statue's eyes glowed bright blue, and a token clinked as it landed in a small hollow at the base. This was the final room. We were almost there. I picked up the token and hurried toward the door with my friends, placing the coin in the slot.

When the door opened, there was no finish line. Instead, we were in a cage of wire mesh. There was a small gate, but it was closed. Beyond the gate was an even larger statue of Athena holding Nike. In addition to ours, eight more cages surrounded the statue, with about fifty feet between the gates and the statue. The ceiling was much higher in here than in our puzzle rooms, but this was clearly the end, where the true winner would be decided. Even with the statue in the center, I could see into all the other cages, even the two opposite. We were the only ones here.

The only thing inside our cage was a small platform with five circles, glowing red.

"What the hell is this?" Lexi asked.

"Step on the circles," I replied.

Riya was already on the platform. She picked the center circle which glowed blue once she was standing on it. The gate began to rise. Lexi and I picked the circles on either end. I saw Lexi try to straddle the two circles, but the moment her second foot left her circle, it turned red again.

"One circle per person, I guess."

An automated voice spoke: "Please remain in place until the gate has fully opened."

The gate lifted very slowly. At this rate, I guessed several minutes until we'd be free. Two cages over, another team spilled into view—Juliet, Colleen, Micaela, and Harmony. Their fifth woman, Becca, must have been eliminated. They quickly figured out what to do, and I was confident their gate was rising faster than ours.

"Come on," Lexi grumbled through gritted teeth. "What gives?"

"I bet the more team members you have, the faster it goes," Riya said. I'd reached a similar conclusion.

"Then I guess we don't have to worry about Lily," Lexi muttered. In the cage right next to us, Lily was taking her spot in the center of the platform. Her gate was barely moving, but she didn't seem concerned.

Our gate was halfway up now, and Juliet's gate was swiftly catching up. If that voice hadn't warned us to stay in place, I would have suggested we run for it and hope we made it through the gate before it closed again. As the gates inched upward, a two-woman team and a three-woman team appeared in the other cages.

Even though I knew it was going to happen, my heart sank when Juliet's gate clicked into place. Micaela was the first out. Behind her came Colleen. Despite being a graceful dancer in the Aphrodite Trial, she stumbled, catching Juliet on her way down. The next moment our gate clicked into place.

"Come on!" I shouted to my friends, unsure of whether one or all team members had to reach the statue. If the latter, Colleen and Juliet's tumble might have saved this trial for us. I was barely out of our gate when Micaela pressed her hands against the statue's base.

The next moment, a loud boom reverberated through my chest, and an invisible hand pushed me to the ground. Rocks and pebbles showered the floor, and luckily the larger bits missed me. My vision flashed white, and my ears were ringing. Voices sounded far away. Micaela was on the floor, unconscious. She'd been the closest to the blast, but the base of the statue was still mostly intact. Harmony had pushed herself up on her hands and knees and was coughing. I rolled onto my back and looked up at the goddess, but the statue of Athena was gone from the chest up. I closed my eyes to keep out the dust, but I couldn't open them again when I tried. I heard my friends calling my name, and then I was floating.

TWENTY-EIGHT

I WOKE UP IN the hospital wing with a parched throat. Lee was there, working on his tablet.

"Water?" I croaked. My mouth felt as if all the dust from the explosion had settled on my tongue.

"You're awake," he said, sighing in relief. "Here." He handed me a cup.

"How are the others? How long was I out?"

"A few hours. Micaela needs another day or two here to recover, but Harmony is fine. Shaken, but physically fine. Everyone else was protected by the cages."

"And what's wrong with me?"

"Where to begin?" he teased. I glared at him. "Oh, you mean medically? A minor concussion and a small laceration on your head. We've fully healed both, and they'll be releasing you tomorrow. I also personally contacted your family to let them know you're all right."

"Can I talk to them?" I asked. A tightness in my throat caused me to swallow. Mom and Dad must have been worried if they were watching live.

"We're limiting contact between the contestants and those outside the competition while we investigate what happened during the Athena Trial."

"What *did* happen?" I asked.

Lee leaned back in his chair, frowning. "The Gaian rebels rigged the Nike statuette in Athena's hand to explode, and they sent a message: *There can be no victory.*"

"But you're safe. They didn't go after you."

"No, it's worse. They went after the participants of the games. If they can't get to me, they'll undermine the competition. I'm just glad no one got seriously hurt."

"Why do you think they were trying to hurt us?"

"I don't know. They certainly did a bad job if that was their goal. The explosion was relatively small, more for show than real destruction, because it could have been worse. My personal security has gotten tighter since the Aphrodite Trial, but whoever it is seems to know when our surveillance will be spotty. We think they tampered with the statue last night during a storm. Which brings me to some bad news." He fidgeted with his hands in his lap. "Your shifts in astrozalemetry have to pause for the foreseeable future."

"Oh," I replied. My shoulders sagged momentarily, but I straightened back up and nodded. "That makes sense. I'm a suspect again."

"I know it wasn't you. We've limited our own staff that will have access to that information, and the notice given to other departments about the storms will be much shorter."

"Is that safe?" I wondered.

"It's the only option we've got until we discover who the rebel is and how they're getting their information."

"It's one of the contestants," I blurted out, recalling the message from Mayor Russo.

He cocked his head to one side. "How do you know that?"

"It has to be," I said, recovering. "We have access. I don't think someone else could get to this part of the ship very easily, could they?"

He sighed and studied the floor. "Our security has reached a similar conclusion. They don't want me going on solo dates with anyone until they've figured it out. Or non-dates," he said, looking up to flash a mischievous grin. "The judges are still finalizing the results of the Athena Trial, but I'm pretty sure your team made the cut. The next trial is only a week away."

"And what is the trial?"

"It's a ball," he said, getting to his feet. "So we can finish that dance that was so rudely interrupted after the Aphrodite Trial."

"Let's hope there are no more assassination attempts then," I said grimly.

Lee laughed. "I meant you. You did push me, after all."

I rolled my eyes as Lee bent to gently kiss my hand, and the simple gesture sent a shiver of excitement through my body. He must have noticed because he spread another blanket over me before leaving.

"Thank you, Princely," I said softly.

He smiled. "Get some rest, Chloe."

The warmth from his touch and the blanket lulled me back to sleep.

⟫⟫⟩ ⟨⟪⟪

The next morning, Melissa woke me in my hospital room.

"You're cleared to go, but there's no class today. Instead, they're going to debrief all the contestants. I thought I'd come and get you ready here."

"You're getting me ready here? Why not my room? I could use a shower."

"There's one here you can use." She wouldn't meet my eyes, and her usual snark was absent.

"Melissa, are you okay?"

"Me? I'm fine. I—" She set down the clothes she had brought me and took a seat. "Chloe, I don't understand you Gaians. You destroy your own planet, and now your rebels are trying kill the prince and ruin the Goddess Games. I know it's a small minority, but I don't want those people on Atlantis. How can we ever hope to weed them out if there's one participating in the games?" She gulped, as if she'd given something away.

"I already figured there was a rebel among the contestants," I said. "And Lee confirmed as much yesterday."

"They're about to tell you in this meeting," she said.

"Aren't there dissidents on Atlantis, though? Doesn't anyone there dislike the monarchy?"

"Of course, but they're not—" She broke off again, struggling to find the words.

"They're not foreigners?" I offered.

She shook her head. "That's not exactly it. The critics on Atlantis usually draft petitions rather than plant bombs. I guess I'm also accustomed to those groups. I can't figure out why the Gaian rebels hate us so much when all we've done is try to help."

"They believe some ridiculous things," I replied. "But there are powerful Gaian groups that oppose them and want to do everything in their power to see this alliance succeed."

Where had that come from? And was I a part of those groups? Mayor Russo had been sparing with her contact so far, but my orders to keep an eye out for trouble were sincere and far more necessary than I'd anticipated.

"I hope you're right," she said. She may have come around to me, but the rest of Earth would be a harder sell. I couldn't blame her.

Melissa examined the skin beneath rue bandage on the side of my head. "Would you believe they didn't have to cut any of your hair to seal your wound?" she said. "Bless them. I'll leave your hair down, and the bandage can come off. I checked with the nurse."

A short while later, I was perfectly presentable and on my way to the meeting. Inside the lounge, the mood was somber. There was some whispering when I walked in, but Riya and Lexi waved me over.

"Thank god you're okay!" Riya said, squeezing me in a hug. "They wouldn't let us visit you. We were locked in our rooms again after the explosion."

"The prince sent us notes letting us know you were okay," Lexi said.

"I wanted to tell you how sorry I am for the way I acted yesterday," Riya said. "I knew I was being ridiculous, but—"

"There's nothing to apologize for. This competition is a minefield of secrets and feelings. We all misstep sometimes," I replied. "I never meant for you to think I was lying to you. I just don't like sharing that stuff, and I think we should agree not share details in the future. Okay?"

"Okay." Riya's shoulders relaxed.

"Well, I'm glad you guys patched that up," Lexi said. "Any idea what this is all about?"

"Some, but I think we should wait and listen," I said.

The meeting was brief. We were informed that Micaela had almost fully recovered, though they didn't say much else about rebels, explosions, or how we would be moving forward. Then, it was time for the trial results. Despite the Athena Trial not coming to its proper end, the judges had determined the fairest rankings possible. My team and Juliet's team had tied for first, as there was no way the judges could be certain which full team would have reached the statue first. Third and fourth place went to the other two teams I had seen enter the cages around the statue. Lily's team came in fifth. Sixth place went to a team that had been working on the third room's puzzle. The seventh- and eighth-place teams had made it to the final room, but not beyond. The team in last place had lost all its team members by the second room. At this point there were some tears and hugs as those women on the two lowest-placing teams were escorted from the room to pack their belongings.

Once the other women had left, Stefan cleared his throat to get our attention once again. "The Persephone Trial will occur in two weeks at the Persephone Ball, which marks the end of the Month of Persephone. The Persephone Ball also marks the change of seasons between winter and spring back on Atlantis. There is nothing you can do to prepare for the trial itself. Talia and I will conduct an interview with each of you in the days before the trial, and these interviews will be aired on Earth and Atlantis. The people of Earth and Atlantis will vote on their approval of each contestant, and the twenty-four with the highest approval ratings will remain in the games."

A popularity contest? I groaned. I was no good at those. These people would base their votes on the meager footage they'd seen of us. My dates with the prince had looked so... boring. Other women had been prominently showcased. Maybe the prince would invite me on another date in the coming weeks and make me look good. Improve my chances. After all, he seemed to like me enough to want me to stick around.

"I have two more bits of news. Bad news, I'm afraid," Stefan said. "In the intervening two weeks, the prince will be very busy with his duties and unable to take any of you on dates, even the winners. He offers his apologies."

I slumped in my seat. I'd forgotten Lee said no more solo dates. That plan was out the window.

"Finally," Stefan said, his voice grim, "it is my job to inform you that there is a distinct possibility a rebel has infiltrated the games. The attacks have coincided with the trials. We ask you to report any suspicious behavior so that we might investigate it. You have the morning to yourselves. In the afternoons, some of the choreographers from the Aphrodite Trial and other staff members will be offering various exercise classes from forms of dance and aerobics to martial arts and weightlifting. While optional, we suggest that you try a few out and learn more about Atlantis. After all, one of the thirty-five of you will become our next princess."

Thirty-five? We'd started with sixty. I had trouble believing so many women were gone. And the next trial would cull the contestant pool even further. Could I really make it to the top twenty-four? I'd qualified by a fluke.

With that, he dismissed us. I tried to follow my friends out of the room, but Talia caught me by the arm.

"Stefan needs to speak with you," she said.

Lexi turned and raised an inquisitive eyebrow. "I'll catch up," I said. She shrugged and kept going, so I turned and followed Talia to the front of the room where Stefan was standing.

"Ah, Ms. Woods. Thank you. Talia, you ought to go get some reactions from the women about the contestants who've been eliminated, as well as their thoughts on the Athena Trial. We didn't get to do a proper debrief after yesterday's attack."

"Gladly," she said, directing the camera drone to follow her. She practically skipped out of the room, thrilled with her task.

Stefan relaxed into a cushioned armchair. He motioned for me to take a seat across from him, but I hesitated. Something was wrong here. I was alone with Stefan, but there were no cameras.

"Ms. Woods, please have a seat. I can see you're uneasy. I'm supposed to take you straight to the prince, but I have a bit of advice for you first. Be sincere in your answers. There are times to tell lies with the truth, but not now."

My stomach did a flip. "What does that mean?"

"The prince cares about you. A lie of omission is still a deception, don't you agree?"

I furrowed my brow. "If that's the intention, I guess so. But what does this have to do with the prince wanting to see me?"

"I think you must have some idea," Stefan said, looking down his nose at me as he got back up and led me through a back door. "This way." He delivered me straight to the prince's quarters, where Lee stood gazing at one of those immersive screens like the one we had watched on our date. The room appeared to be a sitting room, and one of many rooms that made up his quarters. The view he was taking in was not a beach but a well-manicured garden. Stefan left, but Lee didn't turn around.

"Is this your view back on—"

"Chloe, stop." His voice was harsh, and my body stiffened. When he turned, he looked more like a troubled king than the playful prince I'd gotten to know. I wanted to rush to him, ask him what was wrong, but his command had stopped me in my tracks. "Are you a rebel?" The edge was gone from his voice, and he sounded defeated.

"What? No! Of course I'm not!"

"Then what is this?" He held something up between his finger and thumb. My blood went cold when I recognized it. Mayor Russo's commcard.

"You searched my room?" That was a violation. "Do I need to go count my underwear?"

"My father ordered the search. I wanted to oversee it and protect your privacy as much as possible."

"And make sure none of your notes got found?" I asked. "I have trouble believing this was to protect me."

"The question stands. What is this?"

My chest constricted. I fumbled for the words to explain it away, to give as little information as possible, but I remembered Stefan's advice. I had to tell him the truth, even if it meant confessing my real motives for joining the games. "It's a modified commcard, but I'm not a rebel. The opposite, really, and I have a lot to explain, if you'll listen."

I saw a flicker of the prince I knew in his eyes as he set the commcard down on the table. "I'm listening."

I explained that an elected official in my district had encouraged me to join the competition. "My mission was watch out for any rebels who may have made it into the games. To protect you in some small way. If the rebels succeed in killing you, the alliance between Earth and Atlantis is doomed. The games can't fail, but you know that already."

He bent his head and rubbed his temples.

"So far, they've told me to protect you and find the rebel, two things I'd do anyway. The morning of the Athena Trial I got another message, but I didn't open it. I knew what would be inside."

"You never read it? It contained solutions for the first and last puzzle in the Athena Trial. You were going to cheat." He shook his head. "You really didn't read it?"

"No, I knew it would have hints or tips about the trial. That's why I didn't open it. Plus, the messages are automatically deleted once I read them."

"So you never read the other message, after the trial hints?"

"No, why?"

"Read it for yourself." He nodded to a desk where his tablet lay.

I was glad to hear your injuries were mild. See if you can leverage your condition to spend more time with the prince. Men love a damsel in distress. I know you never wanted to outright win the games, but consider it. At least I know your loyalties lie with Earth.

My jaw was clenched tight by the time I got to the end of Russo's note.

"Why did you really join the games?" Lee demanded. "You can't expect me to believe that it was to protect me."

I closed my eyes, wishing he hadn't asked that question. I had to tell him the truth. That's what Stefan had said. "That was part of it, but if I'm being honest, I also hoped to advance far enough to become a noble. I thought if I did, I'd have some control over my life and career on Atlantis. I never expected to like you."

"So you wanted the perks of status with none of the responsibility." I flinched, and he turned away from me. Lee whirled back around, sounding angrier than before. "It also congratulated you on getting close to me. Allow me to offer my congratulations as well. You really had me fooled. Did you orchestrate meeting me to mention Flora? What's been real, and what's been a lie? Have you been using me the same way Brett used you?"

The accusation should have enraged me, but his words broke my heart. "Never, Lee. Whatever has been going on between us is real."

"Thank you," he said. "You can go now."

Lee looked at me, his chest heaving, but he didn't say another word. I left, somehow holding back my tears until I reached my room, where I sobbed into my pillow.

Lexi and Riya came for me after lunch, but I ignored them. I decided to read about the Olympian Athena to keep my mind occupied. The Athena Trial had sparked my curiosity about her. She'd gotten out of a few scrapes by less than virtuous means. I'd known that Athena was clever. I was proud that the prince had thought I'd do well in her trial, but now I wondered if he saw her negative traits in me as well, like her tendency to twist the truth and manipulate others. Was that really the person I wanted to be?

Around dinner, Melissa stopped by. I ignored her, too, but apparently our PAs could override our locks.

"I guess you know by now they searched your room," she said softly, putting a plate of food on my vanity table. "I don't know what they found, but they haven't asked me to pack your things. You're not leaving."

"I don't want to talk about it," I replied.

"Then eat. Get all your tears out today. Tomorrow you've got classes in the morning, and I signed you up for Atlantean pankration in the afternoon. There are a lot of different options, but this one is a lot like kickboxing and wrestling. Some exercise—and the opportunity to kick something—will do you good."

I didn't know if kicking something would do anything for the anger I felt at myself, but Melissa's tone made it clear that she was going to drag me out of my room tomorrow no matter what.

Twenty-Nine

Just two days after the trial, our schedules were back to normal. Well, somewhat normal. Our morning classes were the same, except my sessions in astrozalemetry had been canceled. Beyond that, I was worried that any minute, guards would come escort me out of the Palace Wing and I'd never see Lee again.

No one had thrown me out yet, so I went to breakfast. The food reminded me of another sore spot. I doubted the other refugees were eating quite as well as the contestants, but I would have happily eaten nutrient mush if it meant sharing breakfast with my parents again. All calls and messages with family had been put on hold until the rebel was caught. Lexi was halfway through a stack of pancakes. "You feeling better?" she asked between bites. "Your PA said you were sick."

I spooned some tart, yellow jam onto a thick slice of buttery bread. "I still don't feel great, but I was worse yesterday," I said, returning to my technically truthful ways. Not everything could or should be shared. I'd felt awful yesterday, but at the same time, I was free. There was nothing to hide anymore. Lee knew about my ulterior motives. I'd already told him about Brett. I told him that I hadn't lied about my feelings for him. He would have to decide if he believed me.

"Have you seen Riya?" she asked.

"No." I stopped chewing my muffin and glanced around. "Is she okay?"

"Maybe she got whatever you had?"

"I hope not," I muttered. "I don't think it's contagious."

A couple minutes later, Riya joined us, looking rather dressed up for a normal day of classes.

"Where have you been?" Lexi asked.

"My interview," she replied, piling her plate with scrambled eggs and biscuits.

"What did they ask?" Lexi said.

"Sworn to secrecy." Riya took a big bite of biscuit.

"Wonderful," Lexi said. "I was hoping to get the answers from you."

"You know that's not how interviews work, right?" I teased.

"I don't want to get caught off guard and say something stupid," Lexi replied. "Plus, I think Riya's got a pretty good chance of winning the Persephone Trial."

But I didn't. Not after what Lee had learned about me. I busied myself with spreading jam a little too evenly across my bread.

"Sorry, Chloe. I think you'll do great too. I definitely didn't mean it as a slight," Lexi said, her voice earnest.

I smiled back at her. "I know. It's not that. Just that bug from yesterday. Don't think I've fully recovered."

"You do look a little pale," Riya said, eyebrows knitted with concern.

I would miss them so much. I hadn't made real, new friends in a long time. "No matter what happens, when we get to Atlantis, let's hang out. Even if one of us is princess."

Riya nodded. "Promise."

"Deal," Lexi agreed. "And whichever of you wins, please set me up with one of the prince's hot friends."

I rolled my eyes. "Come on. We're going to be late for class."

The doctors had cleared me for physical activity, and thanks to Melissa, that meant pankration. Riya preferred some sort of Atlantean yoga, but to my relief, Lexi had chosen pankration too. Stupid Lily was also here, as were Juliet and Colleen.

The instructor hadn't shown up yet, but there were so many people here I was sure we had the right room. Finally a tall, muscular man dressed in athletic gear entered the room. He had black hair, and his piercing blue eyes darted from one woman to the next as he took stock of everyone in the room. He had been one of the judges from the Aphrodite Trial.

"What's that guy's name again?" Lexi whispered.

"Benton Elgos," I replied.

"He helped judge the dance contest."

"Yep. And he's the son of the queen's advisor, and a junior advisor himself." I hadn't paid him much attention at the dance competition, but he was handsome. A few years older than the prince, maybe twenty-five, but he lacked Lee's warmth. His serious expression made me think he probably made a good advisor too.

Benton led us all in some stretches and a warmup before pairing us off. He showed us some basic stances and moves that we practiced with our partners. Benton walked among the pairs, offering a mix of praise and criticism. Soon he reached Lexi and me.

"Good form with your arms, Lexi, but your balance is off. Shift more weight onto your back foot." Lexi adjusted her stance, and Benton dipped his head in approval.

"Chloe, almost the opposite." He reached out and adjusted my arms, then peered at me. "Are you sure you're feeling up to this so soon after the accident?"

"Yes, I'm fine," I replied. He was still holding my arms in position, and I just wanted him to let go.

He nodded and released me. "You know yourself the best. If you need a break, take it."

"Does it strike you as odd he's talking to us like he knows us?" I asked Lexi after he walked off. "Like asking me if I'm up to this?"

"He's a royal advisor. One of us is going to be princess. I'm sure he's made it his business to learn about us. Everyone has. That's been the point of airing the date episodes and the trials, right? Now with the Persephone Ball, we have to hope that those things were enough to make people like us."

"I guess so," I muttered, adjusting my stance as I saw Benton heading back our way.

"Look alive, Chloe," Lexi muttered. "Here he comes."

Benton made me a little nervous. He was serious, too, like he considered being our pankration instructor as important as being a royal advisor.

I spent that evening in the lounge, pretending to read as I eavesdropped on people's conversations. If I discovered the rebel's identity and reported it to Lee... It was a stupid fantasy. The rebel had eluded Atlantean security so far. My "insider" status had provided no insights. I slammed the book shut in frustration. If I was going to be kicked out of the contest soon, the least I could do was hand over the rebel to Lee as a parting gift.

⇝⇝ ⇜⇜

I hadn't expected to be around for the next day's pankration lesson, so when the prince hadn't booted me by the end of the week, I didn't know what to make of it.

About halfway through the lesson, we gathered in a circle to learn takedowns.

"When your opponent goes in for a kick, lock their knee in the crook of your elbow, then loop your other hand under and press their thigh. You are using the strength of your twisting body, not your arms, to rotate your opponent and force them off balance. Once they're on the ground, keep them there. Lily, will you come here and let me demonstrate?"

Lily didn't look pleased, but she stepped forward.

Benton walked us through the moves again slowly, stopping at the twist the first few times.

"I'm going to take you all the way down this time, Lily."

He did it so gently that it hardly seemed fair, so when he asked if anyone wanted to give it a try, I raised my hand.

"All right, Chloe." I was ready throw Lily to the ground when Benton switched it up. "Lily, since you've been part of the demonstration, why don't you try it on Chloe a couple of times first?"

Lily smirked. "Gladly."

Damn. I should have seen that coming, but it was too late to get out of it.

"Start off slow, just like I did. Practice the setup. Chloe, go ahead."

I tried to kick Lily, and she practiced the grab and twist, stopping short before actually completing the takedown.

"Once more," Benton instructed. We obliged, but this time Lily used enough force and speed in her counter to make me wince.

"All the way now."

The takedown happened quickly even though I was expecting it. Lily flipped me onto the mat hard enough to make me cry out. She smirked down at me, and I scrambled back to my feet, glaring at her.

"Okay, Chloe. Your turn. Same thing. Start slow and don't complete the takedown until I give you the go-ahead."

I grabbed her leg and twisted, stopping short as instructed. After I released her, Benton talked through the movements, explaining the mechanisms once more. Lily leaned in close. "Rumor is the prince is done with you. Must have gotten all he wanted." I clenched my hands into fists, but she continued. "Just like my brother. You'll never be more than a stupid pawn."

"Okay, Chloe," Benton said. "Full takedown this time. Focus on your form."

Screw that. When Lily attacked, I slammed her to the floor as hard as I could. She cried out and stayed down, coughing and gasping for air. I should have feigned remorse, but I couldn't. Lily was the absolute worst, and I enjoyed watching her gasp for breath.

Benton kneeled next to her. "You've had the wind knocked out of you. Sit up, stay calm, and try to breathe like normal." He turned to me and snapped, "Chloe! This is practice, not a place to take revenge for some petty slight. Colleen, take Lily to get checked out. Chloe, with me."

As he led me out of the room, I shrank under the stares and whispers of the other women. Once we were outside, he said, "I don't care what she said to you. You can't lose control like that. What would the prince think? Go cool off."

I obeyed. Now that the adrenaline was wearing off, the shame was sinking in. Benton was right. I may have knocked Lily down, but she was the one controlling me.

Pawn. That's what she had called me. I hated that word. I hated how true it was. Brett had used me. Russo had used me. I would never do that to someone else.

Except I had. I had planned to use the prince and the games to make a better life for myself and my family. It didn't matter that I had changed my mind. I was no better than the people who had used me. If the prince sent me packing tomorrow, I would deserve it.

THIRTY

The Persephone Ball was days away, and more and more contestants were called for their interviews, but not me. I tried not to read into it, but self-doubt was impossible to shake, especially after my conversation with the prince. What if it had been my last conversation with him?

"So, what are the odds of another rebel attack during the Persephone Ball?" Lexi asked at lunch. Her flippant tone couldn't disguise the worry in her eyes.

I grimaced. "Extrapolating from past experience, I'd say one hundred percent."

"Who do you think the rebel is?" Riya asked. We peered around the room at our fellow contestants.

"Micaela," Lexi offered.

"Really? You think she blew herself up?" Riya raised an eyebrow.

"It's perfect really. The explosion was small, and no one would expect she'd hurt herself," Lexi explained.

"Except you, brilliant detective that you are," I said, poking her in the arm.

"Oh, and you have a better guess?" Lexi crossed her arms.

"I really wish I did," I replied softly.

"I think it's Juliet," Riya said.

Lexi and I exchanged a look. Out of everyone else, Juliet was the person I least suspected.

"What?" Riya said. "She's too perfect. That's suspicious enough for me." Her lips twitched once before her serious expression broke into a grin.

"Promise me you both will be careful," I said. "At the ball especially, but for the rest of the competition too. The rebels will do whatever it takes to hurt the prince."

"Then you really need to watch out," Lexi said. "It's obvious he cares about you."

Riya got suspiciously interested in her soup.

"I may have royally screwed that up." I shook my head. "And no, I don't want to talk about it."

"Guess it's anyone's game, then," Lexi muttered. Riya did not look appeased.

I took a page out of Riya's book and focused on the hearty soup in front of me. *Anyone's but mine.*

⟫⟫⟫ ⟪⟪⟪

Melissa pulled me from pankration class two days before the ball and threw me in the shower like an angry cat.

"We were going to practice sparring!"

"You're up!"

"I don't want to be interviewed."

"Chloe, we've got a saying: You can wait for the wind or fashion oars. I don't know what happened after the Athena Trial, but if it wasn't enough to get you sent home immediately, then you can still do something about it."

"How? No one gets to see the prince until tomorrow."

"I'm pretty sure he'll be watching the interviews in advance. Whatever you have to say to him, you'll have to say to everyone."

My stomach lurched at the thought of confessing my feelings in an interview, especially if I got stuck with Talia, but I showered anyway. These interviews were mandatory, and I might as well not look like a mess on interplanetary television.

Melissa did my hair and makeup in silence. She offered me a savory pastry since I'd be missing dinner, but I refused.

"An empty stomach for this will be a blessing," I said.

"How about a cup of tea to soothe your nerves?"

"All right," I replied.

I expected her to dress me in green and gold, but she dressed me in a rich, dark yellow dress with a modest V-neck that was cinched at the waist. A matching set of amber earrings and a bracelet completed the look.

"You're certainly carrying your weight," I said, inspecting my reflection.

"I can see what the prince sees in you," she said.

"Saw."

"I won't be convinced of that until I'm packing your things." She smoothed down an errant curl, then sent me on my way.

When I opened the door to the lounge where my interview was to take place, fate had granted me at least one small mercy. Stefan, not Talia, greeted me.

"Ms. Woods," he said. "It's a pleasure. Please make yourself comfortable."

I could tell the cameras were already rolling as I situated myself in the high-backed chair opposite him. All thirty-five remaining contestants were being interviewed before the Persephone Ball so that Earth and Atlantis could get to know them. The interviews would air tomorrow and the day of the ball.

"Shall we get started?" he asked.

I nodded and gulped, trying not to fidget in my seat.

"Ms. Woods, why did you choose to enter the Goddess Games?" he asked.

I'd expected this question, but my tongue felt thick in my mouth as I prepared to answer. "I thought it would be a good opportunity to serve Earth, but I didn't expect the prince to be quite so charming."

"Do you think you would make a good princess?"

"Yes."

"Why? What makes you special?"

"Because I understand the fear on both sides. People from Earth are skeptical. Emotions range from terrified to grateful. People from Atlantis are skeptical. They've seen the damage to Earth and worry that we might bring that same destruction to Atlantis. Someone has to bridge the gap."

"And you think you're the best person for the job?"

I considered his question and shook my head. "No," I replied. "The prince is." A genuine smile crossed my face. "He truly cares about Earth and Atlantis, and about honoring xenia."

"It sounds like you admire the prince," Stefan said with approval.

"I do admire him. Very much."

"Some rumors suggest that you, well, *admire* him too much, to put it delicately. I thought you might like the opportunity to address these rumors."

"You mean the rumors that I'm sleeping with the prince?" I wasn't going to tiptoe around the lies anymore. "There's nothing to explain. The rumors are baseless. Rumor cares not for the truth; only for how far her wings can take her." It was an Atlantean aphorism.

Stefan clapped his hands together in delight. "I see you've been working hard in your Atlantean classes."

"Language is my favorite."

"Is there a least favorite?"

"Am I allowed to say etiquette?" I joked.

"The other thirty-four did, so I'll allow it."

We stayed on lighter topics for a bit. He asked me about my family, my opinion on Atlantean food, and my time in the games.

"You once described the prince in one word as 'princely.' If you had to do the same now, what word would you choose?"

I paused a long time, and the silence grew heavier and heavier. I knew a lot of words. Simple words, complicated words, flattering words. None of them could encompass all that I'd learned about Lee.

"I'm going to stick with princely. He'll know what it means."

"Oh, a secret meaning? Is there anything else you'd like to say to the prince?"

My heart pounded. This was my chance. Could I apologize here, like this? I certainly couldn't explain myself any more than I had already. I shifted my gaze from Stefan straight to the camera and gave my answer. "Yes."

He paused a few seconds before understanding dawned across his face. "Ah, but you won't say it here. Very well. I hope you get your chance at the Persephone Ball. Thank you, Chloe Woods, for your time, and best of luck to you!"

The camera stopped, and Stefan thanked me once again before dismissing me.

The prince would get my message. He had to.

Thirty-One

Despite the drama with Lily, I'd been enjoying the pankration classes more than I thought I would. I would miss them if I got eliminated at the ball tomorrow. After our warmup, Juliet tossed me a chest protector. She was my sparring partner today, and we were practicing using kicks to create space for running away.

"Do you think you'll come in first or second in the Persephone Trial?" I teased.

Juliet rolled her eyes, but color crept into her cheeks. "I'm not the one who's caught the prince's eye. I think he really likes you." She kicked me hard, and I stumbled backward.

I winced but shook it off. "Liked, maybe. Now I'm not so sure. But the trial isn't about him anyway. It's about Earth and Atlantis and who they want as princess."

Benton shouted from the front of the room: "Switch up offense and defense."

Now I was on the attack. "I think you'd make the best queen of us all."

"Maybe." Juliet grunted when I kicked her.

"I thought you liked him. You two seem to get along well."

"We do. He's a great person. And he's a great prince as far as I can tell."

"I'm sensing a but." Juliet opened her mouth to speak but took a deep breath and closed it instead. "I didn't mean to pry," I added. "This whole idea of competing to marry a stranger is a lot to handle."

"The idea of ruling a nation we just learned about is intimidating. What right does someone from Earth have to govern Atlantis?"

"My PA Melissa would probably agree with you." I recalled Juliet's date footage, where she'd been talking to the prince about Atlantean laws. "For what it's worth, I would trust you with that kind of power."

"Thanks," she replied, "but he needs a wife too."

I'd meant to compliment her, but my words only seemed to make her sad. Juliet was always so confident during the competition—poised and certain, a representation of the best Earth had to offer. For the first time, I got the feeling that, despite being the front-runner and Earth's sweetheart, Juliet might not want to win the competition.

⇒⇒⇒ ⇐⇐⇐

On the last night before the Persephone Trial, there was no fight left in me. After my interview the day before, I'd hoped Lee would reach out. How could I stay in the competition when I was so clearly no longer wanted there? It was past fifth watch, nearly one in the morning in Earth time, and I couldn't put my misery aside long enough to get some sleep.

I'd just turned my lights on low to read when my door notification chimed. In a heartbeat I was at the door. Lee stepped in. He was wearing casual clothes that made it hard to remember that he was Crown Prince Leonidas Agathon, not just Lee.

"Hi," I said. What else was I supposed to say? I glanced down at my own gray pajamas.

He crossed his arms. "You're probably wondering why I didn't kick you out of the trials," he said, bypassing the usual pleasantries. The dim light cast our conversation into a mood of unearned intimacy.

"Honestly? Yeah, I am. If for no other reason than you thought I was a rebel."

"The messages we recovered made it clear you were not the rebel. They supported your claim that you got close to me to try and protect me."

"Oh." I let the silence hang between us, but Lee was regarding me like he was waiting for something. What had I sent to Russo? I'd framed things in a way she'd want to hear, and now Lee thought that everything between us was a lie. Shame burned my cheeks.

Finally he spoke. "I watched your interview, so I know there was something you wanted to say to me."

"Oh, um..." I dared a glance into Lee's brown eyes. The anger was still there along with something else. Sadness?

"Or was that just for show?"

I shook my head. "I wanted to apologize."

"You already did that."

"I know, but I need you to understand that I wasn't using you. I know what it's like to wonder what was real and what was a lie. Even though it won't change how mad you are, I want you to know the truth so you won't wonder like I did after Brett. If I'd been pretending to like you, I never would have pushed you away. I never would have feared for my own heart.

"Do you remember in the hospital right after the Athena Trial, when you kissed my hand? It gave me goosebumps. You thought I was cold and put a blanket over me, but I wasn't cold. The opposite. Every kiss has filled me with fire. I can't fake that, but I can't prove it either. I'm sorry I didn't tell you everything sooner."

"So am I." He inspected the various brushes and cosmetics on my vanity, but he didn't say anything else, nothing about his feelings or whether he believed me. Why did I think my confession might make a difference? I'd made him question my motivations and feelings, just like Brett had done to me. I was no better than he was.

"I wasn't going to come hear you out, you know," Lee said, finally breaking the silence.

"What changed your mind?"

"Stefan. I learned something interesting from him. Of the forty-five women who qualified through the Artemis Trial but didn't make it to the games, do you know how many openly admitted to joining the competition so they and their families could get medical treatment or leave in the first wave?"

I shook my head, not trusting my voice.

"Thirteen. And I suspect that a lot of the initial sixty contestants also joined with ulterior motives, even if they didn't admit it." Lee shook his head. "I should have realized that marrying a stranger and ruling a new world wasn't as appealing as rescue or medical care. I thought about sending you home, but I couldn't. I decided to give you a chance to make it to the final twelve and earn that title you so desperately wanted. Even though you hurt me, I still care about you. I realize now how arrogant I was to think that all these women would be happy to marry me just because I'm the prince."

"They would be lucky to marry you because you're you," I said softly, "not because you're Prince Charming."

He studied me a moment, and then the corners of his mouth twitched up into a gentle smile. "Charming, eh?" Then, his smile grew serious, as if he was debating something. "I have to know, that fire you feel? Is it only when we kiss?"

"No, not just when we kiss," I replied. I forced myself to hold his gaze. "Every touch, too. Sometimes, all it takes is a look. A word. A memory."

"Like this?" He hesitated, then brushed his thumb gently over my cheek. Heat flooded my body, as if he'd brushed away a dam.

"Yes, Lee." I closed my eyes and took a deep breath, dizzy from anticipation. When I met his gaze once more, he'd pinned me with a predator's stare.

"Good," he said. "Me too."

He kissed me gently, as if asking a question, but there was hunger in his brown eyes. I locked my hands behind his neck in answer. The short distance between us disappeared, and I savored every scorching bit of contact. I kissed him hard, willing him to understand just how real my feelings were. His hands moved to my waist, and his fingers pressed into my lower back, like he was anchoring them there to keep from exploring my body. As we kissed, the heat of it melted away the barrier that had stood between us.

Lee broke the kiss, but I spoke first. "Everything since you found me at the ballroom window that first night has been real."

"I think I believe you," he said. The intense look in his eyes took my breath away.

"Are you sure you don't need more convincing?" I traced my fingers down his chest.

"I might want more, but I have to go, or my guard Luca will come barging in to rescue me." He kissed me again anyway until we were both breathless. "Save a dance for me tomorrow. I'd save them all for you if I could."

"I will. Good night, Princely," I said. I gave him a final, lingering kiss before he walked out the door.

My pulse was throbbing in my veins. I would still have a hard time sleeping tonight because those minutes we'd spent pressed together in the dark had kindled a flame within me. Something inside me was awake and more than ready to claim my spot in the next round of the games.

Thirty-Two

THANKFULLY, MELISSA LET ME spend the morning of the Persephone Trial sleeping in, but the afternoon was devoted to getting ready. She braided my hair and pinned it into an immaculate updo, adorning it with golden leaves. My makeup was heavier than usual: pink lips; shimmering peach eye shadow; and long, dark lashes.

"Do we have a specific uniform for the day?" I asked. Usually she showed me options before doing my hair and makeup so she could make minor adjustments to suit the clothing.

"Nope, but I did get you the perfect dress."

She pulled out a magnificent, emerald-green ball gown. The skirt was flowy with a generous slit down the side that would allow for movement. The top was ruffled along the neckline.

"It's a nod to your Artemis Trial outfit."

"My lucky green top," I muttered. That same trial outfit had delivered the mayor's commcard to Lee and revealed my secret reason for joining the games. I pushed that thought aside. This dress was too beautiful to jinx, and I reminded myself that the pants, not the top, had betrayed me.

"Almost there," she said, pulling out a pair of ornate, golden sandals.

"I'm ready," I said.

Miraculously, it was true. The prince had forgiven me. Melissa thought my interview had gone well enough that I'd pass the Persephone Trial, and after last night, I dared to be optimistic and walked down the steps into the ballroom with my head held high.

If I thought I looked good, Riya put me to shame. Dressed in bright layers of pinks and oranges, she was radiant. Her brown hair was up in an elegant bun, and a gold chandelier necklace fanned across her collarbone. Lexi was in a fitted, navy-blue gown, her red hair cascading around her shoulders in soft curls.

The ballroom, draped in green and gold banners embroidered with the Agathon double ax, was at capacity, and again I wondered where all these people had come from. Some were off-duty guards, personal assistants, and those who kept daily life running in the Palace Wing; others were the VIPs from the Feast of Aphrodite. The king was there, laughing and drinking with some Atlantean nobles. Lee was nowhere to be found, so the three of us snacked on hors d'oeuvres and sweet, fizzy drinks. I steered clear of anything that might make me embarrass myself, though Riya sipped from a glass of white wine.

"Our PAs look like they're having fun," Riya said, nodding toward a group of men and women laughing and dancing. An off-duty guard was twirling Melissa around on the dance floor.

"They certainly deserve the break. If they can make all of us look like this, they're miracle workers," Lexi said, gesturing toward the other contestants with a sweep of her arm. "Except maybe you, Riya. I think you'd outshine us all in a potato sack."

"Oh, stop. We all look great." Riya's eyes focused on something behind us. "Speaking of outshine..."

Lexi and I turned as a hush fell over the crowd. Prince Leonidas Agathon stood alone at the top of the steps to the ballroom. I'd expected him to wear Atlantean-style finery, perhaps an ornate tunic over loose pants. Instead, he wore an Earth-style suit jacket, but dressed down with no tie and his top button left undone.

"I still think he looked better on our pool date," Lexi said quietly. "Though it's a good thing he's dressed because you two are already on the verge of drooling."

I swallowed. Just looking at the man gave me butterflies, and I could not stop staring.

"Welcome to the Persephone Ball!" Lee proclaimed. He raised his hands in a triumphant gesture to receive cheers from the whole room. "Persephone was once a bridge between the Olympians and Atlanteans. In today's trial, we will find out who might be a suitable bridge between Atlanteans and Gaians. In honor of this sentiment, we've brought in the families of our contestants."

The cheering and clapping around me drowned out the prince's next words, but the influx of people from the vestibule was all the encouragement we needed.

"Mom!" Lexi cried, running off toward a tall, red-haired woman.

As I waited for my own parents to come into view, I stole a glance at the prince. Still at the top of the stairs, his eyes met mine. Even with such a distance between us, memories of last night sent warmth through me.

"Chloe!" Flora had found me, and my parents were right behind her. "Your interview was fantastic! You'll definitely do well in the voting. Oh, and we're all so glad you're okay! We tried to call after the Athena Trial explosion, but the prince personally called us and promised you were doing fine."

I hugged her, and she squeezed me back so hard I coughed. "I can't believe you're here! And that I get to hug you in person! Flora, where's your family?"

"They're back in our quarters. It was only supposed to be your parents, but the prince made sure I got an invitation too." Before letting go, she whispered, "He must really like you."

"Well, hopefully Earth and Atlantis do too," I said.

"Oh, lighten up. I think you'll do just fine. The Atlanteans probably like you because the prince does, and Earth likes you because you nearly died in the Athena Trial. Instant sympathy."

"You make it sound like I did it on purpose!"

By then my parents had found us, and I hugged them too.

"You look magnificent," Dad said.

"Well, there was a lot of work behind the scenes," I replied.

"Nonsense, honey. You've always been beautiful," Mom said.

"Yeah, you're glowing. I wonder why that could be," Flora said.

It was impossible to subtly elbow her in the ribs, so I settled for a brief glare. After the initial catching-up, my parents decided to try some of the food. They explained that their meals in the family quarters were filling and nutritious, but they lacked the variety that was being offered at tonight's celebration.

"So," Flora said, lowering her voice even though we were alone. "Is the prince a good kisser?"

"You've seen the date episodes."

"You're not going to tell me. That means you've got something to hide. Do you love him?

"I—" I broke off, confused. I'd meant to say no, but that didn't feel like the right answer. But yes was too big. Too uncertain. Before I could put the words together, Flora's gaze settled on someone behind me.

"Your Highness," she said, dipping into a curtsy.

"You must be the famous Flora." Lee's voice set my pulse pounding. I turned to see his dark eyes gleam with mischief. "I hear that belated birthday wishes are in order. I hope you got the gift?"

Flora blushed. "Yes, thank you, Your Highness."

"And are you enjoying *Her Alien Prince* as much as Chloe did?"

Now I was blushing too. Flora recovered herself and said, "I can't say, though I think Chloe prefers human princes."

"And what makes you say that?" Lee asked, his face lighting up as he flashed her a conspiratorial grin.

"Didn't you promise me a dance?" I asked, desperate to separate the two of them.

"So I did. But if you're volunteering for a dance, you must really want to keep us apart. Flora, we'll continue this conversation later, I hope?"

"Of course." Flora winked at me.

The prince took my hand and led me from the edge of the ballroom to the center. A few couples were already dancing, but more joined us on the dance floor. Several of the couples around us were guards out of uniform, and I wondered how off-duty they truly were.

"You look beautiful, Chloe," Lee said, leading me around the dance floor.

"I can't take my eyes off you," I replied.

"I like this Earth look," he said, glancing down at his suit jacket.

"Me, too, though Lexi thinks you look better in a swimsuit."

"If it's an opinion you share, then maybe swimming should be our next date."

I shook my head emphatically. "I can't swim."

"What? Then it's definitely our next date. I'll teach you. The future princess of Atlantis has to know how to swim." He avoided my eyes for a moment, as if he hadn't meant to say quite so much.

"Whoever she ends up being," I said, deflecting the awkwardness. "I mean, Lily can swim."

We laughed, and then a sudden panic hit me. "Our families are here. That means—"

"Yes," he said, pulling me in closer, steadying me, reassuring me with his solid presence. "Brett is here somewhere, but I have a trusted guard keeping an eye on him. Plus, I'll be around."

"Thank you."

We danced through that song and the next, but the prince had other suitors. He found Micaela next, and I was relieved to see her spin around the dance floor as if nothing had happened to her at the last trial.

I introduced Lexi and Riya to my parents and met their families. We spent the night eating, drinking, and laughing until it was finally time for the announcement of the rankings for the Persephone Trial.

There were twenty-four slots for thirty-five women, and after Flora's assurances and such a wonderful night, I was confident that I would make the cut. Maybe even close to the top. The contestants all lined up along the stairs. Lily slipped behind me and whispered, "Brett says hello."

I ignored her and listened to Stefan give the introduction. They would read the approval ratings from Atlantis first, then the ratings from Earth. The average score between the two would determine a contestant's rank.

"Our first-place contestant, with seventy-four and eighty-eight for a composite score of eighty-one, is Juliet Porter. Congratulations, Juliet. I don't think anyone is surprised," Stefan said. Riya and Colleen were both in the top five, with composite scores of seventy-eight and seventy-five. Lexi and Lily made the top ten, with scores in the low seventies. Micaela and Petra were in the top twenty with scores in the high sixties.

There were only four spots left, and my name had yet to be called. "Looks like Earth can see right through you," Lily whispered.

What did that even mean? Why would Earth hate me? In fact, for everyone except for Lexi and a woman I didn't know well named Natalie, all the Earth scores had been higher than the Atlantis scores. Twenty-one. Becca. Twenty-two. Harmony. Twenty-three. Yvonne.

What if I didn't make it? Would I have to leave and watch the prince fall in love with someone else, like Juliet or Riya?

"And our final contestant, with sixty and seventy-six for a composite score of sixty-eight is Trinity Duke. Congratulations, everyone. We invite all contestants to stay for the rest of the ball and say their goodbyes."

I could feel the camera drones trained on me. Talia was certainly hoping for a dramatic reaction, but I refused to give it to her. I didn't even look for my friends in case their reactions set me off. I wasn't going to collapse to the floor sobbing. Not here anyway. I blinked hard and hurried offstage so that I could process what had happened in peace.

I'd lost.

THIRTY-THREE

Fighting the words that kept echoing in my head, I headed straight to the refreshments and reached for a steaming cup of coffee.

I'd lost.

But what exactly had I lost? I'd lost the Goddess Games. I'd lost my chance to protect Lee and earn a noble rank. There was something else too. Something that I didn't want to admit, and that gaping hole in my heart stung the most. I went to stand by the window where I'd first met the prince.

"Chloe." He'd found me, just as I'd hoped. The vibrant Lee from our dance had been replaced with a somber prince. We both knew he had to honor the choices of both Atlantis and Earth.

"Lee," I said, putting on a fake smile to hide my misery. I would be a humble loser at least. "I'm glad I'll have the chance to say goodbye. I wanted to—"

He put his hands on my shoulders to stop me. "Something weird happened with the scores. Your composite score was a sixty-seven. You were in twenty-fifth place. Your Atlantis score was an eighty-eight."

"So my Earth score was..." I paused to do the math, but Lee saved me the trouble.

"In the forties."

"That's bad," I said. Why did Earth hate me? Could the rumors about Lee and me have caused that much damage? Lily had seen it coming, but I'd fooled myself again. I'd never expected to be especially popular on Earth, but forty-six percent was so low, I must have screwed up somewhere.

"And it was ten points lower than any other Earth score. An outlier. I'm going to review the polls myself and see if there's something I can do."

Hope fluttered in my chest, but then I blew out a breath and shook my head. "If the goal of the games is to unite Earth and Atlantis, what good is an Earth girl that no one from Earth likes?" I swallowed. "I'm not the right choice."

Though the prince kept his smile light, I could tell he shared my concerns. "Do you want to leave the games?"

I sensed the weight of his gaze and looked up to meet it. The right thing to do would have been to lie, say yes, and let him pick the right woman for the job.

"No, I don't want to leave."

"Why not?"

This was the part where I was supposed to lay my feelings bare, but I couldn't. "Please don't make me say it, Lee. It will only cause us both more pain."

Lee wrapped his arms around me, and I pressed myself against him, memorizing exactly how he felt, his warmth, the way his chin rested gently on the top of my head. "Then I'll figure something out. There has to be an error or a loophole we can use. I need to find Stefan." Prince Leonidas Agathon released me and disappeared into the crowd, so focused on his mission he didn't even say goodbye.

With the trial over, most of the contestants' families left. I said my own farewells to my parents with the promise that I'd see them again soon. Mercifully, they didn't comment on my loss.

Flora offered to stay, but she seemed ready to go back with my parents. "I'll be fine," I told her. "I want to say goodbye to some of the friends I made." It was true. No matter what Lee said, we both knew that bending or breaking the rules wouldn't help my case.

Soon, the ball took on a second nature, and I wondered if this was another nod to the dual nature of its namesake, Persephone. The lights dimmed, and neon colors swirled around the room. The classical and mellow songs of the evening transformed into the rhythmic bass of Atlantean pop and electronic music. I had never been to a club on Earth, but I'd seen them in movies. The whole experience was overwhelming yet exhilarating. I had one last evening with my friends, and maybe I'd get one last dance with Lee, though I hadn't seen him since our conversation. I was making my way to the dance floor when Lexi and Riya found me.

"Chloe, your dress!" Lexi exclaimed. "Did you know this would turn into a rave?"

The threads of my dress glowed blue-white, and there was a luminous Greek key pattern sewn along the hem that had been invisible until now. "No, but Melissa must have."

"I can't believe you're leaving," Riya whispered, barely audible over the music. She whirled on Lexi. "And I can't believe you're so flippant about it!"

"That's because I'm in denial. I don't think the prince will let her go," Lexi replied. "Wait here. I'm going to get us drinks. Then, we dance!"

I grinned. "Thank you."

While we waited, Benton Elgos asked Riya for a dance. She tried to protest, unwilling to leave me, but I nudged her toward Benton. Apparently there was more to our severe pankration instructor than met the eye, because I'd seen him dancing with several of the other contestants. "Go! Lexi and I will find you for the next song."

While I waited for Lexi, I bobbed my head to the music and enjoyed the general atmosphere. Most of the other women who'd been eliminated were still here having fun. Even Trinity had stayed despite her usual tendency to avoid the lounge, and I wondered if the loud music and terrible lighting made her feel more relaxed around all these people.

"Chloe," came a male voice from behind me. I stopped dancing and straightened, like an antelope separated from its herd. "That's a beautiful dress. Like I've said before, green suits you."

I whirled to see Brett Vasquez leering at me. His compliment was as unwelcome as his presence.

"*Agathon* green suits me. Now please go away." The last thing I needed was Brett reveling in my failure. Over his shoulder, I scanned the crowd for the guard Lee had assigned to keep an eye on him. Where was he?

"Too bad you didn't make the cut." Brett took a step forward, and I took one step back. I clenched my jaw and swallowed hard. The only thing worse than losing tonight would be letting Brett see me cry. He took my silence as an invitation. "Or maybe it's a good thing. After all, Earth clearly didn't want you as its princess."

He took another step forward, herding me away from the dance floor and toward the wings. If only he'd found me before the results had been announced. The Chloe from the start of the evening had been confident. Radiant, even. I'd had a plan. I'd had a future again. Why did Brett always show up to knock me down and take it away?

Better yet, why did I let him? Thanks to the games, I had connections. Brett had taken away my chance to make a difference back on Earth, but there would be plenty of opportunities on Atlantis. I had more than connections; I had friends: Melissa, the other contestants, and the prince. He gave me the chance to study astrozalemetry. Even if Lee couldn't find a way to keep me in the games, I would leave the contest with so much more than Brett could ever take away.

I drew myself up and spoke with calm authority. This was more my realm than his, even if only for a few more hours. "I asked you nicely before. Now I'm ordering you. Get away from me."

"But don't you want to know why your Earth score was so low?" I side-stepped and brushed past him, but Brett followed like a self-important gnat. "I figured you'd let it go, just like you let me cheat off of you on the weather analyst exam"

That was enough to stop me. I'd let his accusations go unchallenged once before. Never again. I turned to face him once more. "I didn't *let* you cheat."

"Sure you did. I bet you even blame me, but you knew what I was doing. You didn't say anything to the proctor, and I couldn't risk you turning me in later, so I had to act."

I bit back the argument brewing on my lips. He wasn't worth the energy. "You're a cheater, Brett, and none of that has anything to do with tonight's results."

Brett smirked. "Are you sure about that?"

Before I could press him for details, a tall guard with broad shoulders approached us and said, "Ms. Woods, the prince asked me to check on you. This way."

Now that he'd planted that seed, Brett was content to let me go. My mind raced with the implications. My Earth score. Cheating. If the vote had been tampered with, would it be enough for Lee to keep me in the games? Was there any proof?

Moreover, why would someone want me out of the competition, and why did Brett know about it? I might not have all the details, but I needed to find Lee and tell him. If it could keep me in the games, then it was worth a shot.

I set my hand on the guard's forearm, stopping him. "Where is Prince Agathon?"

"He's saying goodbye to one of the contestants in the Palace Wing. He'll be back soon."

"Thanks."

I left the guard and began to look for Riya and Lexi. Instead of my friends, I caught a glimpse of Lily leaving the ball. Was she looking for Lee? Waiting for his return was impossible after the news Brett had shared, but maybe Lily knew something about it.

This can't wait. Lee could be anywhere, but I doubted the prince would go all the way to the garden or the library. I hoped he was in one of the first- or second-floor rooms. I walked down the hall, listening and opening doors with no luck. Toward the end of the hallway, a shrill laugh came from behind a closed door. Lily. I could interrogate her first.

I checked each room as I tried to pinpoint the right one, until a cry of pain set me on the right course. Only that cry hadn't sounded like Lily. It belonged to a man.

I burst into the room and found Lee pulling a knife from his side. "Lee!" Lily's lips were pressed into a pleased smile as she moved to the door. I blocked her path.

"He looks about ready to pass out," she said. "Maybe you should go help him. Or you can try to stop me and let him die. Up to you."

I wanted to throttle her, but she was right. Lee looked out of it. We locked eyes for a moment, and then I rushed to the prince. Lily slipped away.

"Lee!"

I helped him onto the nearest couch. His eyes were wide and unfocused, and his speech slurred. He was bleeding a lot. I grabbed a blanket off a nearby chair and was pressing it against the wound when Juliet walked in.

Juliet looked from Lee's pale features to the bloody knife on the ground. "What happened?" she asked, kneeling across from me on his other side.

I grabbed her hands and placed them on the blanket. She instinctively applied pressure to the wound. "Lily stabbed him. She's the rebel. Stay with him while I get help."

I ran down the corridor to alert a guard. "Hey! The prince is down in one of the lounges. Juliet is with him. He needs medical attention. Lily stabbed him."

The guard ran down the hall, already calling for backup and medical. I was about to follow when I caught a glimpse of auburn hair in the distance. Lily. My body obeyed before my mind gave the order, and I sprinted down the corridor as fast as I could. She and Brett had gotten away with so much, and I wouldn't let her get away with this too. The guards were too occupied with saving the prince to hunt down his assailant.

She stepped into a transporter, but it revealed her destination. I stepped into the next transporter on the opposite side of the platform and crossed my fingers.

The doors opened, and my gamble worked. I stepped out in time to see the doors closing, Lily still inside. Her effort to send me running down the wrong corridor had failed. With a burst of speed, I reached out and stuck a hand in the door, triggering it open again. Lily tried to push me out, but I rolled my shoulder and put all my weight behind my charge. She was in heels, which made it harder for her to balance.

"Should've worn flats, bitch," I growled.

"I'll kill you, too, just like I killed the prince," she said.

"He's not dead."

"Yet."

We saved the rest of our breath for fighting. Lily was scrappy and all elbows, but I was a little stronger. She tried to kick me, but I dodged, grateful for the few pankration lessons I'd had. I didn't know anything about subduing someone, but if I could pin her down, eventually the doors would open, and I could shout for help. Try as I might, I couldn't get her on the ground. She avoided it at all costs. When the doors did open, instead of having her trapped beneath my body weight, I was doubled over in pain with blood pouring from my nose. Lily slid past me, and I almost gave up.

But spite is a powerful motivator. I wiped my bloody hand on my dress and resumed my pursuit. I couldn't tell if my nose was broken, but I breathed through my mouth as I struggled to keep up.

She paused at a fork, and I started to catch up. She was holding something close to her mouth. "I told you, I had an opportunity. I took it. Which way?" she asked. A communicator of some kind. Other rebels must be directing her escape. They had a plan. I had to catch her before she disappeared. She took a left, then ducked into the third room on the short hallway.

The door wouldn't open, so I looked in through the porthole. *Oh no.*

It wasn't a room. It was an airlock. Lily paced inside, though the room was only wide enough for her to take a few steps before she had to turn back and pace the other way. A small door mirrored the one I was peering in through, except that door would open into space. The realization of how close we were to the frigid void outside—how close *she* was—sent goosebumps up my arms. Was she somehow leaving through that door? She stopped pacing. I could still hear her muffled voice: "What do you mean no one's coming?" She let out a primal scream and slammed an open palm against the door before collecting herself again. "Yes. I remember. No price is too high. For Earth."

I swallowed. Lily's anticipated rescue was no longer coming. Good. The Atlanteans would arrest her, and she could waste away in prison.

Lily busied herself with something on the touch pad inside. Though I wondered what she was doing, I had a more pressing question.

"Why? Why hurt Lee?" I asked her.

"The royal family is guilty."

"Of what? Being an alien or cannibal or whatever psycho beliefs you rebels hold?"

"They've been lying to us. Things on Earth weren't great, but we were fine. You studied for the weather analyst exam. You know things weren't hopeless. There's another reason they wanted us to leave Earth. The planet wasn't going to become uninhabitable. Until the Atlanteans showed up, projections showed things improving on Earth. The Atlanteans have an ulterior motive. The real reason they're taking us from our home."

"And what's that?" I could hardly keep from rolling my eyes.

"Do you really think they'll find places for all four million of us? Because even Atlantis can't accommodate that many Gaian refugees. Not everyone will get their fairy-tale ending."

"It's not a fairy tale."

"The Goddess Games are a ruse. He'll never pick a Gaian bride."

"You're wrong."

Lily sneered. "You still think it could be you. That he loves you and he'll find a way. You have no idea what he's hiding."

"Then tell me." Once the guards showed up, I'd never have another chance to get answers. What was taking them so long? Was Lee okay?

"You'll find out. When the time is right."

Of course she wouldn't tell me.

She pressed something, and the light inside the airlock turned red. An alarm sounded. I struggled to read the Atlantean words on the outer screen, but I didn't need to. The tears on Lily's cheeks told me everything. She was opening the outer door.

I hated Lily more than I hated anyone, except maybe her brother, but I didn't want her to die. I wanted her to rot in prison on paradise, unable to enjoy the clean air and clear skies. The letters jumbled into one another, but I found the override. I pressed it, and nothing happened.

"You don't have to do this," I said.

"But I will anyway. Remember that I was willing to die for Earth. Are you?"

Lily was leaning against the outer door, struggling to breathe. All of the oxygen was being sucked out of the airlock. She would pass out soon. I jammed the override again and again, but the same error message appeared, and I couldn't read it.

She collapsed. I was watching her die in front of me when a team of four guards came running down the hallway. One restrained me, pinning my arms to my sides and pulling me away from the controls. Her grip relaxed a bit when I didn't struggle, and I could still see Lily, barely conscious, head lolling. One of the guards typed in a code, but it didn't work. He shouted to another guard, but hers didn't work either. Then, the outer door opened, and Lily's body spilled out into space as the artificial gravity lost its grasp. Her lilac dress clung to her body like a film, but her loose auburn hair streamed about her like Medusa's snakes.

My captor let go, and I fell to my knees, numb.

"She set the airlock," I said. "She was a rebel. I tried to stop it, but the override didn't work."

"She used a security lockout to block the override, but my security code didn't work either. Do you know which officer's code she was using?"

I shook my head. "Why would an officer give her their code?"

He exchanged a look with the guard who'd restrained me. "What are you doing here?"

"She attacked the prince. Tried to kill him. I wanted to catch her." The guard shook his head, as if the idea was too idiotic to believe. "Is the prince okay?"

"He's been badly wounded. Our best doctors are with him now. We've lost the opportunity to question a rebel spy, though, thanks to you."

"Don't put that on her. This was probably a suicide mission from the start," the female guard said. "If someone tried to kill the man I loved, I would have chased her down too."

My face covered in blood and tears, they escorted me to the nearest clinic. That's the moment I knew. The guard was right. I loved him. I was in love with Prince Leonidas Agathon.

THIRTY-FOUR

THE NEWS OF THE rebel attack had spread throughout the entire fleet by lunch the next day, and all the contestants were locked down once again. I hadn't been allowed to see Lee, no one had, but the prince released a video by dinner. Thanks to the ship's excellent medical staff, he was already on the mend. The quick actions of two of the contestants had made all the difference in his treatment. The rebel responsible was dead. The games would resume once he had recovered.

I struggled with the memories of my encounter with Lily. While I didn't mourn her, I regretted that she had died. In the end, she thought her death was meaningful, and that's the part that bothered me the most. These rebels were willing to sacrifice themselves for their cause, but their cause was built on lies.

At least that's what I had to believe. All their supposed evidence could be easily refuted. The true projections about Earth's future had been hidden from us to prevent panic until there'd been an alternate choice: Atlantis. And as for accommodating four million people, certainly that was within the Atlanteans' scope of power? That must have been where the cannibal rumor had come from. Some poor Gaian had doubted the Atlanteans could house us all, so the more logical explanation was that they would use us as a food source. I sighed and put my head in my hands. I'd given up trying to understand the rebels, much less why Lily had sacrificed herself.

Finally, two days after the attack, I was summoned to the same office as after the Aphrodite Trial. The king was there alone.

"How is he, Your Majesty?" I asked.

"It's lucky you and Juliet found him when you did. The rebel used a poison we were able to identify and treat. I doubt she meant to leave the knife behind, but you interrupted her."

"Poison?"

"Yes, Ms. Woods," King Darius began. "I find myself once again thanking you for saving my son's life. A smarter man than I would be suspicious; however, I am curious. Why did you leave the ball at that moment?"

"I needed to talk to the prince."

"Why did you chase down Ms. Vasquez rather than stay with Prince Leonidas?"

"Juliet was with the prince. The guards had been alerted. I saw her, and I ran. I didn't plan it."

"Did you really try to save her and override the airlock?"

"Of course I did!" I raised my eyebrows in understanding. "Even your own guards' override code didn't work."

"That's true. The evidence exonerates you, but you must understand how this looks, considering what you have to gain from her death."

"Gain? I won't pretend I liked her, but I don't gain anything from her death. In fact, one of your guards pointed out that they'd lost the chance to interrogate her."

"Ms. Woods, with Lily's death, there is an opening in the top twenty-four. You ranked twenty-fifth. If I choose, I can give her place to you."

I didn't speak. In my two days of near isolation, I'd been so worried about the prince that I hadn't been thinking about the contest. I'd already lost, and if Lee could just be okay, then I'd find a way to forget my feelings.

"Had this really not occurred to you?" the king asked.

I shook my head. "I thought I'd lost my chance."

"Your Earth score was very low, but at my son's request, we investigated the polling. We learned that Ms. Vasquez's brother had been spreading rumors about you in the hopes of swaying others and eliminating the greatest perceived threat to his sister's success in the contest."

That's why Brett had been so smug at the ball. He'd nearly managed to ruin my life again with his lies. "Does Prince Lee know?"

"Not yet. I wanted to speak with you first. The queen and I have our doubts about your suitability, but my son likes you, and you have a knack for saving him. Would you like to stay in the competition?"

"Yes," I replied with no hesitation.

"Very well. The games will decide. If you truly care about the prince, you may rejoin the games. Your success or failure, your standing with the people of Earth, and, unfortunately, my son's heart are all in your hands. Tread carefully, Ms. Woods."

***

The next day I was allowed to visit Lee in the hospital. Just over two weeks ago, our roles had been reversed.

"My father told me that you're staying," he said, propped up against some pillows in his hospital bed. "In the games, I mean."

"I am, though it wasn't the loophole I was hoping for."

"I know you tried to save her. I watched the footage from the security cameras. I have something for you, by the way." He leaned over and winced as he tried to open the top drawer of his bedside table.

"Relax, Princely," I said. "I'll get it. You did just get stabbed."

Inside was the tiny piece of technology that had nearly gotten me kicked out of the games: the commcard that Russo had given me.

"A warning about Lily came through on your device. They thought she might be the rebel and wanted you to investigate. The tip was too late. Lily had already stabbed me and left me for dead, but the next one might be useful."

"Next one? The rebel in the games is gone. And even if there was a use for this thing, I don't want it. Give it to your security team. That's what I should have done in the first place. Plus, I've got a better motivation to protect the Atlantean prince than some nebulous warnings from Russo." I grinned at him and reached down to adjust the corner of the bedsheet.

"What motivation might that be?" Lee asked, catching my hand and lacing his fingers through mine. His brown eyes pierced mine, and my pounding heart must have been audible over the low hum of medical machinery. I almost confessed, but the words caught in my throat.

"Ask me on another date once you're better, and maybe I'll tell you."

"Haven't you ever heard of 'show, don't tell'?" His eyes twinkled with mischief.

"No, but I look forward to finding out." I examined our interlocked fingers. "I don't know what trials the rest of the games will hold, but I won't fail again." I meant it. Before, any amount of success had been a victory. Now? I had to win. I had to pass every trial and beat every contestant in order to become a finalist. And then, I had to hope he'd pick me. "I'm in these games to win."

"You'd better be," he said, pressing my hand to his lips. Even that barest touch was electric, but Lee needed rest.

On the way back to my room, that buzz energized me. The king had given me a second chance in the games, and the prince had given me a second chance with his heart. I doubted fate had any more chances to give, and now that my heart was on the line, too, I had more to lose than I'd ever dreamed when I first stepped up to the line in the Artemis Trial. The Goddess Games were far from over, but I would overcome the challenges as they came. Because while spite had certainly been a powerful motivator in that first trial, love might turn out to be even stronger.

THANK YOU

Thank you for reading! Every review helps me immensely, so if you'd take a minute to review my book on Amazon, Goodreads, or wherever you leave reviews, I'd greatly appreciate it. If you want to receive monthly newsletters and updates about new releases and sales, join my newsletter at **www.ericarue.com**.

Also By Erica Rue

Kepos Chronicles

The Kepos Problem
The Ven Hypothesis
The Island Experiment
The Predator Analysis

The Atlantis Crown

The Goddess Games

Acknowledgments

First and foremost, I want to thank my husband Jacob. Without his support, I wouldn't be able to pursue this dream and bring my stories to life. I love you more than anything.

I'm grateful to my parents who continue to believe in me and encourage me, especially my mom Jane who lets me talk about my books and plans ad nauseum.

My wonderful beta readers' feedback helped shape the story into something better: Stephanie Mirro, Rachel Caudill, T.L. Swedensky, Janice Gross, Shelley Shearer, Jane Eickhoff, Margaret Burnside, and Martin Wilsey. I'd also like to thank Ian Leung for the quiet, consistent encouragement. You might not realize how much it meant. I also owe another huge thank you to Stephanie Mirro whose help with Kickstarter (among other things) was essential. You are an inspiration!

Then there's eternal gratitude for my wonderful editor, Jessica Hatch of Hatch Editorial Services for another amazing job. Any errors remaining are undoubtedly things that I reintroduced during my revisions. Andrea Fodor of Creya-tive Covers has been an absolute gem to work with as a cover designer, and I'm so glad for her patience waiting for the page count and back cover blurb as this book took far longer to publish than anticipated. I'd also like to thank Jacqui Naunton at White Deer Graphic Design for helping me tweak my imprint logo for Starwoven Books.

Acknowledgments

First and foremost, I want to thank my husband Jacob. Without his support, I wouldn't be able to pursue this dream and bring my stories to life. I love you more than anything.

I'm grateful to my parents who continue to believe in me and encourage me, especially my mom Jane who lets me talk about my books and plans ad nauseum.

My wonderful beta readers' feedback helped shape the story into something better: Stephanie Mirro, Rachel Caudill, T.L. Swedensky, Janice Gross, Shelley Shearer, Jane Eickhoff, Margaret Burnside, and Martin Wilsey. I'd also like to thank Ian Leung for the quiet, consistent encouragement. You might not realize how much it meant. I also owe another huge thank you to Stephanie Mirro whose help with Kickstarter (among other things) was essential. You are an inspiration!

Then there's eternal gratitude for my wonderful editor, Jessica Hatch of Hatch Editorial Services for another amazing job. Any errors remaining are undoubtedly things that I reintroduced during my revisions. Andrea Fodor of Creya-tive Covers has been an absolute gem to work with as a cover designer, and I'm so glad for her patience waiting for the page count and back cover blurb as this book took far longer to publish than anticipated. I'd also like to thank Jacqui Naunton at White Deer Graphic Design for helping me tweak my imprint logo for Starwoven Books.

www.ingramcontent.com/pod-product-compliance
Lightning Source LLC
Chambersburg PA
CBHW071250300726

48975CB00002B/622

LAST HUNT

BOOK **THREE** IN THE **HUNTER** SAGA

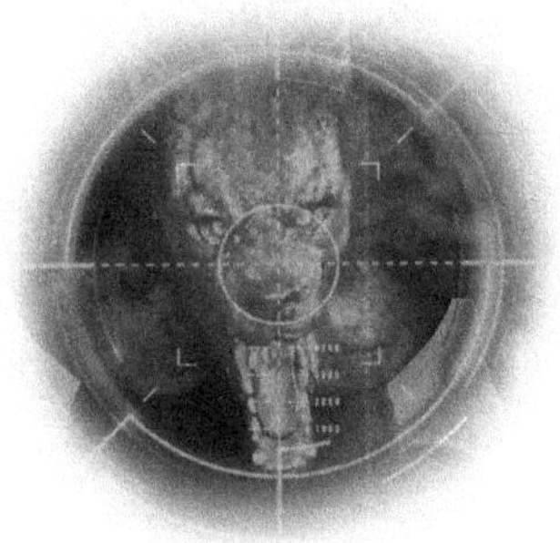

INTERNATIONAL BESTSELLING AUTHOR

JAMES BYRON HUGGINS

WILDBLUE PRESS

WILDBLUEPRESS.COM

LAST HUNT published by:
WILDBLUE PRESS
P.O. Box 102440
Denver, Colorado 80250

WILDBLUE PRESS is registered at the U.S. Patent and Trademark Offices.

ISBN 978-1-964730-87-5 Hardcover
ISBN 978-1-964730-88-2 Trade Paperback
ISBN 978-1-964730-86-8 eBook

Interior Formatting and Book Cover Design by Elijah Toten
www.totencreative.com